Noah was beginning to have suspicions about Celie Sherwood's origins.

He knew she wasn't what she seemed. He knew she was a supremely talented mimic with a command of languages and accents that was astonishing. But what if she were neither British nor French? What if not one but both nationalities were just part of her repertoire?

When she had regained consciousness she had been in no condition to assume an identity or accent other than her own. And as halting and whispered as her words had been, they had been flavored with the cadences of his own country. Southern-fried United States, to boot.

Who the hell was this woman?

Dear Reader,

Holiday greetings from all of us at Silhouette Books to all of you. And along with my best wishes, I wanted to give you a present, so I put together six of the best books ever as your holiday surprise. Emilie Richards starts things off with *Woman Without a Name*. I don't want to give away a single one of the fabulous twists and turns packed into this book, but I *can* say this: You've come to expect incredible emotion, riveting characters and compelling storytelling from this award-winning writer, and this book will not disappoint a single one of your high expectations.

And in keeping with the season, here's the next of our HOLIDAY HONEYMOONS, a miniseries shared with Desire and written by Carole Buck and Merline Lovelace. *A Bride for Saint Nick* is Carole's first Intimate Moments novel, but you'll join me in wishing for many more once you've read this tale of a man who thinks he has no hope of love, only to discover—just in time for Christmas—that a wife and a ready-made family are his for the asking.

As for the rest of the month, what could be better than new books from Sally Tyler Hayes and Anita Meyer, along with the contemporary debuts of historical authors Elizabeth Mayne and Cheryl St.John? So sit back, pick up a book and start to enjoy the holiday season. And don't forget to come back next month for some Happy New Year reading right here at Silhouette Intimate Moments, where the best is always waiting to be unwrapped.

Yours,

Leslie Wainger

Leslie Wainger
Senior Editor and Editorial Coordinator

Please address questions and book requests to:
Silhouette Reader Service
U.S.: 3010 Walden Ave., P.O. Box 1325, Buffalo, NY 14269
Canadian: P.O. Box 609, Fort Erie, Ont. L2A 5X3

Emilie Richards

Woman Without A Name

Published by Silhouette Books

America's Publisher of Contemporary Romance

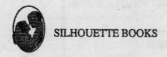 SILHOUETTE BOOKS

ISBN 0-373-07751-3

WOMAN WITHOUT A NAME

Books by Emilie Richards

Silhouette Intimate Moments

Lady of the Night #152
Bayou Midnight #188
*From Glowing Embers #249
*Smoke Screen #261
*Rainbow Fire #273
*Out of the Ashes #285
Runaway #337
The Way Back Home #341
Fugitive #357
Desert Shadows #401
Twilight Shadows #409
From a Distance #456
Somewhere Out There #498
Dragonslayer #511
†Duncan's Lady #625
†Iain Ross's Woman #644
†MacDougall's Darling #655
Woman Without a Name #751

Silhouette Books

Birds, Bees and Babies 1990
"Labor Dispute"
Silhouette Christmas Stories 1993
"Naughty or Nice"

Silhouette Special Edition

All the Right Reasons #433
A Classic Encounter #456
All Those Years Ago #684
One Perfect Rose #750
The Trouble with Joe #873

Silhouette Romance

Brendan's Song #372
Sweet Georgia Gal #393
Gilding the Lily #401
Sweet Sea Spirit #413
Angel and the Saint #429
Sweet Mockingbird's Call #441
Good Time Man #453
Sweet Mountain Magic #466
Sweet Homecoming #489
Aloha Always #520
Outback Nights #536
Island Glory #675

*Tales of the Pacific
†The Men of Midnight

EMILIE RICHARDS

Award-winning author Emilie Richards believes that opposites attract, and her marriage is vivid proof. "When we met," the author says, "the only thing my husband and I could agree on was that we were very much in love. Fortunately, we haven't changed our minds about that in all the years we've been together." The couple has lived in eight states—as well as a brief, beloved sojourn in Australia—and now resides in Ohio.

Though her first book was written in snatches with an infant on her lap, Emilie now writes full-time—unless the infant, now a teenager, reminds her that it's her turn to do car pool. She loves writing about complex characters who make significant, positive changes in their lives. And she's a sucker for happy endings.

For Brendan,
a superior son and storyteller

Prologue

Noah Colter wasn't in love with Paris. During his week in the City of Light he had walked the starlit Champs Élysées and gazed out at a sunshine-spangled Seine. He had eaten *coq au vin* and *haricot de mouton* in romantic sidewalk cafés and slept under crisp linen sheets in the finest Parisian hotels. And the magic of Paris hadn't touched him.

He had come to Paris on business, and he hadn't expected anything different. Noah collected cities with the same dispassionate interest that he collected High Renaissance art and sculpture. Every day of his stay he had taken some time to watch the world go by in a different language, but travel was only an academic exercise, something to occupy his hours and intellect.

At the moment a woman was occupying his intellect—as well as his gaze and the traitorous nether regions of his body. He had spent the past hour on a bench in the Jardin du Luxembourg, finishing up some notes. Surrounded by formal flower beds, potted palms and city dwellers enjoying the summer morning, he had glanced up now and then just to watch the show. It seemed as if most of Paris had found an

excuse to parade through the park. The woman was just one
of many who had strolled by his bench.

From the moment he had caught sight of her, Noah had
watched her weave gracefully in and out of groups of sun
worshipers and children preparing to sail toy boats on the
shallow concrete pond that dominated the center of the
park. She wore black, a simple knit dress that hugged her
hips and breasts and exposed a length of creamy thigh.
Whether the dress had come straight off Chanel's runway or
from a sales rack at Bon Marché, it looked as if it had been
designed for her.

She had an odd, noteworthy walk. She lifted herself high
with every step, as if she intended to stretch to the heavens,
and she tilted her hips forward and rolled them provocatively each time she moved. Noah's body, too long denied
sex and solace, was signaling its own response.

The woman was a creature of myth and magic, a Gallic
wood nymph with flowing red-brown hair and legs as long
as a Frenchman's imagination. Noah wasn't sure why she
had so swiftly affected his libido. He'd seen other more
beautiful women in Paris. He'd had dinner last night with
one of them, a business meeting that could have been more
if he had invited it. But he had sensed the trap in his dinner
partner's smile.

There was no trap in the wood nymph's smile. In fact,
since she'd first captured his attention, she hadn't smiled at
all. She surveyed the other occupants of the crowded park
as she hurried along, but she didn't meet eyes, and she didn't
nod. She scanned faces with a swift, covert calculation that
intrigued him. He didn't understand what she was looking
for, but he was sure that she was looking for something or
someone.

Normally he would have lost interest quickly and gone
back to work. Today, before he had time to think about
what he was doing, Noah stuffed the papers back in his
briefcase and got to his feet. He had a train to catch that
evening and an afternoon to kill. He was bored with art
museums and intrigued for the first time in days. Follow-

ing the woman to see where she went seemed perfectly forgivable in a city that prided itself on impulse and romance.

Once outside the park, he kept pace without getting too close. The decision to follow her was so whimsical and out of character for him that he was beginning to feel foolish. He almost hoped he would lose her, but the crowd thinned when she turned down a narrow street lined with shops. He could see her clearly until the moment she turned into one of them.

He didn't know what he had expected to discover. An assignation with a lover, perhaps, an amorous greeting by a young Frenchman with soulful dark eyes and a three-day growth of beard. Or lunch with her girlfriends at one of the bistros near the Sorbonne. But he hadn't expected to see the young woman take a white apron from the hands of a scowling old woman, tie it around her narrow waist and step behind the counter of a second-rate Latin Quarter café. She had elegant cheekbones and the posture of a princess. He would not have been surprised to see her on either side of the desks at the university, but he was surprised to see her serving coffee and brioche.

Surprised enough to stay and watch her some more.

There was a newsstand on the corner, and he bought the most recent *USA Today*. Then he strolled into the café and up to the counter. The old woman was gone now, and the wood nymph was alone. His French was serviceable, but his accent was pure generic United States. He smiled in apology before he spoke.

"*Café au lait, s'il vous plaît.*"

She gazed at him for a moment before she moved away to get the coffee. Her face was as intriguing as her walk. She had a long thin nose and lips that were neither narrow nor full. Her thick eyebrows were a darker hue than her hair, shading eyes of a clear, bright turquoise. Those bright, clear eyes seemed to cloud over subtly as she realized he was examining her.

She presented the coffee with warm milk frothing over the top and into the saucer.

"Do you have any recommendations for what I should have with it?" he continued in French.

"Everything is good." She spoke with the alluring accent of a native. Her voice was soft and lower than he had expected.

"A croissant, then."

She didn't comment. She merely served it and told him how many francs he owed.

The café was dingy, with only four tables inside. He chose an empty one in the corner, where he could spread out his newspaper and still see the counter. He had no agenda except to pass time pleasantly. He had enjoyed the casual cat-and-mouse challenge of following a lovely stranger through the Paris streets, and now he intended to enjoy his paper.

Through the years Noah had become a student of psychology and an astute judge of people, and both had served him well in business. He had personally chosen or sanctioned every management level employee at Tri-C International, the corporation founded by his great-grandfather nearly a century ago. Noah had never had cause to regret a single decision. He enjoyed imagining the lives of others, their hopes and fears, their daily existence. But his observations always ended the same way. He learned what he could, then he moved on alone. No ties, no complications, no heartbreak.

He found the sports section and automatically scanned for the baseball scores. Once he glanced up and saw, in the split second before she averted her eyes, that the young woman had been taking his measure.

Some time later he folded his paper and finished his last sip of coffee—now cold. His sojourn at the café had come to its natural end. Now he had only an afternoon to fill before catching his train. He folded his paper and looked for the young woman one more time.

The area behind the counter was empty, and he was alone in the café.

Intrigued, he stayed to see if she would return, but the only person to join him was a dark-haired man who wandered in from the street. When no one came to serve him, the man peered over the counter, as if to see if anyone was hiding. Then, mumbling to himself, he left the café, too.

Ten minutes later the counter was still unmanned when the old woman returned. As she charged to the rear her scowl deepened into rage. She rounded the counter, cursing softly. Then she pushed open the dark curtain that separated the counter from a small back room. Noah could see that the room was empty, but a door leading into the alley was wide open. A white apron hung from the doorknob.

The young woman was gone. And Noah had gotten more entertainment than he had bargained for when he first caught sight of an auburn-haired wood nymph in the Jardin du Luxembourg.

Chapter 1

Celestine St. Gervais examined herself in the mirror. Her hair was neatly sectioned and clipped in fat pin curls. Her hands were still unsteady after her escape from the café, but that didn't stop her from picking up the scissors. Long strands of cinnamon-colored hair fell to the floor at her feet. She worked quickly and carefully, unpinning a section, pulling it taut with a comb and shearing off a lock of hair. Then another section and more hair.

When she was finished she stared at her handiwork. The style was shorter than she'd planned, but she had been forced to even out the final product after she'd surveyed the back with the help of a hand mirror. Now the bob neatly grazed her collar. With a sigh she sectioned the hair in front once again and gave herself long wispy bangs.

It was a very English style, simple and serviceable. It was not particularly well wrought, but that could be remedied when she got to London and went to a hairdresser. The main point was that she looked very different.

But not different enough.

One hour later she hardly resembled the same woman at all. She had washed out the auburn rinse she'd used since coming to Paris and returned her hair to its natural color, a pale ash brown so neutral that changing it was usually simple. Today had been no exception.

Her face was neutral, as well. She had no features that were remarkable, which had been her greatest sadness as an adolescent. But now she was glad for the blank canvas. She had gamely tweezed her eyebrows into thin, tidy arches and washed away any traces of cosmetics. She had exchanged her turquoise-tinted contacts for those that made her blue eyes a smoky gray.

And now she didn't look the same at all.

She tested her new image. "Yes, thank you," she said in an upper-class English accent. "I would like to apply for the position you have advertised in your window. My name is..." She hesitated. "Tina," she said. "Tina St. James."

She wasn't sure that the new name was correct. She crossed the narrow room to the bed and slid her hand under the mattress to retrieve a clear packet of documents. She riffled through the ones on the top until she found what she was looking for. "Tina St. James. Just great," she said sarcastically. "American."

The picture on the passport of Tina St. James showed a very different looking Celestine. The only time she had used this passport her hair had been long and curly. In that incarnation she had also been a brunette who wore royal blue eye shadow and spoke with a Brooklyn twang. She riffled through the documents again and pulled out more passports, selecting the one that she now most resembled.

It was an English passport, which was exactly what she had hoped for. "Lesley McBain." Born north of London in Stevenage, raised by an older sister who moved from place to place after the death of their parents. Lesley McBain, who was poor but proud and willing to do almost any job as long as it was decent.

Yes, that would be her cover story. Surely she should be able to find something to do in London until she had enough money to escape into the country somewhere. She would need a job immediately, because she had very little in the way of savings. Paris was an expensive city, and the only job that she had been able to find hadn't paid well.

Now, of course, she couldn't even go back and get the wages Madame Duchampier still owed her.

She sank to the bed and held the passport against her chest. Was she making a mistake? Dear God, was this a textbook example of paranoia, or had the man in the dark suit really come to Paris to kill her? He was the general age of the others and clearly an American. And he had followed her from the park, through narrow streets crowded with tourists and students. He had followed her to the shop; then he had waited a little before coming inside. Once there, he had sat at one of the few indoor tables and watched her.

And watched.

Her eyelids drifted shut. She could still see him. He was striking, with conservatively cut brown hair brushed back from his face, a strong square jaw and hazel eyes that gave nothing away. His eyes were shadowed by a jutting brow and his face defined by a straight, ski slope nose—beginner's hill. His suit was an expensive one, silk and wool tailored in England or Hong Kong. His shoulders were broad, and she was certain they demanded expert tailoring.

There had been something ruthless about his face that had nothing to do with individual features. Something aggressive about the way he held himself that hadn't eased as he'd sipped his coffee and pretended to read his paper.

She rested her head against the wall. She was exhausted, and she had only a short time to pack and get to the Gare du Nord. As always, she wouldn't take much with her. She had few clothes that suited her new image, anyway. A long flowered skirt, a lavender knit top, a navy jacket with cheap brass buttons, tailored gray trousers. Marie St. Germaine, with her auburn hair and stylishly thin body, had nearly worn out a good pair of jeans, a narrow skirt with buttons unfastened halfway up her thigh, and a tight saffron-colored sweater that had hugged her small breasts provocatively.

Now "Lesley" would stuff those clothes and the black dress she had worn today into a paper sack and leave them for the concierge to distribute or throw away.

She ran her fingers through her hair, and for just a moment she mourned her shorn locks. She had little vanity left, but she had enjoyed the way long hair had felt trailing over her shoulders. She had enjoyed the way men had looked at her, too, even if she couldn't safely look back.

She doubted that anyone would look twice at Lesley McBain, and that was, of course, the way it would have to be. The new haircut was no-nonsense, and the clothes she would take to London were at least a size too large. She would slouch a bit, and her smile would be tentative. When she wasn't smiling, she would set her lips in a prim line, like a woman determined to make the best of bad luck. She might try glasses again, as she had once before. Pale blue frames, in a style that was several years out-of-date.

Celestine had learned not to cry about hairstyles and clothes. Hair grew back eventually, and clothing could be purchased. But she had never learned to be philosophical about a life on the run. She had been so many people in the past four years that sometimes she wasn't sure who she was.

Or if she really had to run at all.

She thought again of the man in the dark suit. Was he waiting for her somewhere just beyond the walls of this attic room? Would he find her again before she fled Paris? Or was the man with the wide shoulders and the expressionless eyes just a tourist who had chosen to pass an afternoon in a quaint French café?

She didn't know. She might never know. But she did know this. She was still alive.

And that was the way she intended to keep it.

"So, Noah, will you come back to Paris and see us again?" Jeanette Girbaud handed Noah a folder of facts and figures that had been her excuse for coming to the train station to see him off.

"If it's necessary." Noah smiled to soften his words.
Jeanette was every bit as attractive in the harsh lighting of
the cavernous Gare du Nord as she had been by candlelight
last night. She was a petite brunette several years older than
his thirty, with an exquisitely proportioned body and an ex-
pressive face. As the French operations director of Tri-C
International, she had proved to be every bit as crafty as he
had hoped, and she would soon be moving up in the company's chain of command.

"It won't be necessary . . . just pleasant," she said with a
small smile. "Surely you fell in love with my beautiful
city?"

"It's a city to be proud of."

"Then I may look forward to your return?"

He toyed with ignoring the real message behind her question. Then he shook his head. "Jeanette, I would never get
involved with a Tri-C employee. It's impossible."

She lifted a brow. "No?"

"No."

"Tell me this then, Noah. Do you get . . . involved with
anyone? Because you seem to me to be so..." She shrugged.
"Alone."

He was surprised at her frankness, and more surprised at
the concern that was obviously behind it. "I'm not an unhappy man."

"Not unhappy. Perhaps my English isn't perfect enough
to comprehend that. But 'not unhappy' does not sound like
a state one would recommend."

"My life suits me."

"Yes, well, it does not suit me to see you living it this way.
But it seems I have little choice in the matter." She smiled
warmly. "Have a safe trip to London."

He reached for her hand and squeezed it. "Thank you for
showing me Paris."

"If I could not show you more, at least I could show you
that."

He watched her walk away. He was a student of walks, as
well as of many things. Jeanette's stride was purposeful. She

moved quickly for a small woman, but with infinite femininity.

He thought of the young woman whose walk he had admired earlier that afternoon. The scene at the café had intrigued him, and since then he had pondered reasons for her disappearance. The older woman, who must have been the shop's owner, had been furious. Noah's French was good enough to know that the woman had a sailor's vocabulary, but not good enough to understand the finer points of her oratory. He just knew that the lovely auburn-haired woman had vanished, and that even if she returned, her job would not be waiting.

He made his way through customs and boarded the train. At the entrance he stored his garment bag; then he found his seat. He had bought a ticket for the seat beside his own to avoid conversation, and he stowed his briefcase on it. He had elected to take the new Eurostar to London instead of a ferry or an airplane. The high-speed train traveled under the English Channel, and he had followed the construction of the "Chunnel" with interest. He wasn't in any hurry to get to London. He had been there many times and always enjoyed it, but there was no one waiting for him at the other end. He would be on his own until he decided to return to Colorado, where Tri-C International had its corporate offices.

The decor of the car was soothing, and the dove gray seats were comfortable. They were out of the station before he was even aware they were moving, and out of Paris before he opened his book. One paragraph into it he looked up as a young woman brushed his arm on her way to another car. She mumbled an apology in proper British English. He had enough time to see that she was attractive in a demure, inhibited sort of way, with sleet gray eyes, the fresh-scrubbed cheeks of a milkmaid and clothing preferences better suited to a larger woman. Then she turned away and continued down the aisle.

He gazed back at his book, a mystery he had already solved, and started the same paragraph again. But he couldn't concentrate.

The young woman was already out of sight, but she stayed in his mind. For some reason he was reminded again of the woman he had observed at the café in Paris. He didn't know why. The first young woman had been auburn-haired and sensuous, with showgirl legs and a tiny waist. This one, with her utilitarian hair, cheap navy blazer and prim, resigned expression, had looked as if she would close her eyes and think of England if a man ever tried to make love to her.

They were nothing alike.

They walked alike.

He snapped his book shut and tried to remember. Over the years he had become so good at watching people that the tiniest details were fixed in his mind. The first woman had lifted herself high on the ball of each foot, gently swiveling her hips as she moved.

And so had the second.

It seemed an odd coincidence. He had never seen anyone move quite that way before. And now, just hours apart, two women with identical walks had captured his imagination.

The French countryside sped past him at 186 miles per hour. He set his book on the next seat and closed his eyes. The slow-motion glide of two different women moved across the dark canvas of his mind.

Damn fate to hell! The man from the café was on board. She was on an express train hurtling like a lightning bolt toward a tunnel residing inconveniently under the English Channel, and there was a murderer on the train with her!

A murderer who had already stalked her once today.

Celestine sank into an empty seat that faced the automatic doors leading in the direction of the man's car. She had touched him. She had accidentally brushed her hand against his shoulder. If she hadn't, he might never have looked up and met her eyes.

Maybe he didn't know who she was. Maybe he hadn't recognized her.

Celestine was afraid to blink, afraid that in that infinitesimal crack in time the man would step through the doors, pull a gun and make quick work of Lesley McBain, alias Marie St. Germaine, Elena Kovacs, Tina St. James and others too numerous to mention.

A small sound escaped her clamped lips, but no one turned to look at her. She was one of hundreds of passengers, a colorless, insignificant presence. No one here knew that a man had come on board to kill her. No one knew that he wasn't the first to try and might not even be the last— unless he succeeded, of course. Then the competition would certainly be out of a job.

She tried to think. There was no way off the train. That fact could work for or against her. At this speed, she couldn't take a dive out an exit, even if she knew how to open one without alerting everyone on board. If she did jump she would save the man the trouble of murdering her, and he could probably claim his reward. On the other hand, the man couldn't shoot her, then escape. This was not a steam locomotive plowing new trails through the Wild, Wild West, and the man was not Jesse James. There was security on board, and highly sophisticated communications equipment. He would not get away with her murder.

Not here.

She swallowed another moan. Even if the man didn't attempt to kill her while they were on board, Waterloo Station was only two hours away. She might meet her own personal Waterloo there, between newsstands and rental car offices. Or he could track and kill her when she left the station. She was a master of evasion, but he was a professional. He stalked the helpless for a living. If he had a business card, it probably read Assassins-R-Us.

Anger began to bubble up through the fear that at first had nearly paralyzed her. She could not let fear overtake her now. She had lived this long because of her intelligence and creativity. Courage hadn't hurt, either. She had stood up to situations that would have defeated a coward. She was brave, resourceful.

She might be crazy.

Perspiration beaded her forehead, despite the pleasant temperature in the compartment. She tried to push away her last thought, but it was almost as frightening as the man's presence on the train. God help her, she might be imagining all of this. She might really be as unbalanced as she had been raised to believe. The man might be a stranger with no interest in one Celestine St. Gervais. The man on this train might not even be the same man who had stared at her in the café. Perhaps neither of them existed. Perhaps all of this, everything that had happened in the past four years, was a crippling delusion.

She had brushed her hand against his shoulder. A shoulder clad in a dark wool blend. A shoulder that was too wide for conventional tailoring.

It was the same man, and she couldn't give in to panic or a crisis of self-esteem. Maybe she *was* crazy. But she was living, breathing crazy, which was preferable to sanely dead.

The compartment doors slid wide, and her heart beat double time. As if on cue, as if in her wildest imaginings she had somehow called out his name, the man in the dark suit entered, and the doors closed behind him.

She turned her entire body toward the window, although she knew it wasn't going to do any good. The man was not stretching his legs. He was not on his way to buy a sandwich. He had come to find her.

"Do you mind if I sit here a moment?"

She would have known the man's voice in a room without windows or lamps. He spoke English with the same baritone resonance with which he had spoken French this morning. She had to force herself to turn and answer. She frowned, as if she were slightly annoyed. It gave her a much-needed moment to get the words out. "I'm sorry, but my husband will be back momentarily."

He smiled. The smile wasn't menacing. He simply looked like a man who always got what he wanted and enjoyed the challenge. Ice formed inside her. She had to remind herself not to blink, not to shrink back in her seat.

"I think I know you," he said. "Your face is...familiar."

"I'm afraid you have me confused with someone else. I've never seen you before in my life." Her voice emerged as calmly as any well-bred English lady's. The ice that was now a solid, choking mass inside her frosted it perfectly.

Despite her response, he took the seat across from her and leaned forward. "You don't remember me from the café this morning? Café au lait and a croissant?" He searched her face as he spoke, as if he were a detective looking for clues.

"I assure you, I don't remember you," she said regally. "And I don't drink café au lait or frequent cafés."

He nodded, but clearly he didn't believe her. "Paris is a lovely city, isn't it?"

"My husband certainly thinks so." She saw his gaze flick to her hand, then back to her face. Too late, she realized she wasn't wearing a wedding ring, although she had been known to on occasion. He lifted a brow.

"We were there proselytizing for our church." She made up a story as she went along. "I find it a very wicked city. Much too absorbed in things of the flesh. Drinking and dancing and personal adornment." She pursed her lips in distaste. "I'm a simple God-fearing woman."

He didn't seem offended by her lecture. If anything, he seemed more intrigued. "The woman that you...remind me of would find none of those things offensive."

"There are far too few women with my values."

"And yet at the core..." He smiled again, as if he were sharing a secret with her. "I believe that you and that woman are very much the same."

"This is all quite interesting, I'm sure, but I really must ask you to leave now. My husband will wonder why I'm talking to you. We have a very old-fashioned marriage."

He didn't stand. "If you hadn't bumped into me earlier, I wouldn't even have...confused you with that other woman."

She attempted surprise. "Did I bump into you? I'm sorry, of course."

He leaned toward her and lowered his voice. "You know, you really are a tremendous actress. I'm in awe of your talents, but I really have to warn you. You have the most distinctive walk I've ever seen. The next time you pretend to be someone else, you'd better change the walk, too." He straightened. "And just for the record, I liked your hair long and your morals a little looser." He stood and touched his hand to his brow in mock salute. Then he turned and started back the way he had come.

The doors closed behind him as Celestine sat frozen in her seat. Terror eclipsed all reason, and for a moment she considered leaping off the train no matter what the consequence.

He knew who she was. She hadn't even begun to fool him. And now he was playing with her.

There had to be a way to escape. There had to be a way to get off of the train and out of the station before he caught up with her. But even as wild, impossible schemes flew through her head, the doors slid open again.

Something as pitiful as a whimper formed in her throat, then died when she saw who had entered the compartment. A man in uniform had stepped through the opening, a man with an Inspector Clouseau mustache and chapped red cheeks. She couldn't tell what his role was, exactly. He might be a conductor or a security guard. But in the moments before he started down the aisle in her direction, she made her decision. She beckoned to him.

He stopped, frowning as if to let her know that he had better things to do than converse about the Eurostar's financial prognosis or find her a blanket.

"Sir," she said with Lesley's prim and proper accent, "I have a terrible problem." She managed Lesley's most pathetic smile.

"Yes?"

His English was pleasantly accented. He was obviously French, but she decided not to switch languages. At the moment she was not up to the challenge of speaking French with a British flavor. "There is a man on board," she said softly. She looked away, gave a panicked glance at the door, then turned her eyes back to him. She paused and raised a trembling hand to her lips. "He was just here with me. Oh, I'm so frightened."

"Frightened? Of what are you frightened, mademoiselle?"

"It's a long story. This man…he's dangerous." That part, at least, was not a lie. "You see, we used to be lovers…" Her voice dropped, and the man leaned closer. "I've left him, and he threatened to kill me if I ever did…. He followed me…."

"I am truly sorry, but what has this to do with your travels to London?"

She lowered her voice and watched as he was forced to move closer to hear her. "He's insane with jealousy." She wrung her hands. "He could try to kill me. Right here. He's enraged."

"Here?" He shook his head. "On a high-speed train? He would have to be a sick man indeed to try such a thing."

"He is. Oh, he is." Celestine could see that she was losing him. The story sounded preposterous, even to her ears. "I'm afraid there's more." She leaned toward him. "I left him because he makes his living smuggling—" she took a deep breath and looked away "—drugs."

"You can prove this?"

"What kind of proof could I have? I lived with him! I know what he does, but I'd hardly bring samples with me to show the authorities."

"Then what is it you expect me to do?"

"Detain him."

"I don't have that authority, mademoiselle."

"I know. Oh please, I know. But if he's detained in London, if customs detains him and does a thorough search, they'll find all the evidence they need in his luggage and on his person."

"He has drugs with him now? You're certain of this?"

"I wish to God it weren't true. But he's part of a highly sophisticated drug cartel. And he never crosses a border without samples of what they have to offer."

"You would make a statement to this effect?"

She shook her head and wrung her hands. "No! I couldn't! Don't you see? Even if he's put in prison, someone else would come after me. I'll deny everything if I'm questioned. The only answer is to have him detained, as if it's a routine customs check. Then search him and everything he has with him. Everything. He's terribly clever."

"And while we are searching, you will disappear, of course?"

"Yes. Please. It's my only chance. Don't you see?"

He considered, but his decision wasn't apparent from his expression. "Where is this man?"

She recited the car's number, the general location of the man's seat, and a detailed description of his clothing and features.

"And his name?"

She shook her head. "His name is—" she didn't even hesitate as she invented one "—John Albert. But he won't be traveling by that name. He has a dozen aliases and passports. He may even be traveling as an American or a Canadian."

"I see. And what will you do until we arrive?"

"Is there a safe place on the train where I can go? A place where he won't be able to find me again? Please?" Tears filled her eyes. "I must have your help."

"I can't make this decision alone, but perhaps we can arrange something that will ease your mind. Get your things and follow me. If you wish, I'll have your luggage transferred."

"Oh, thank you." The tears spilled to her cheeks, and they, unlike her story, were entirely genuine.

He clicked his heels in old-world fashion and gave a brief, stiff bow. She told him where to find her only suitcase and took her overnight case and a Marks and Spencer shopping bag from the overhead compartment.

"This way," he said, motioning for her to precede him.

She left the compartment with one swift backward glance. No one was watching. For all her fellow passengers knew, she and the uniformed official had been having a friendly chat. She hurried through the next set of sliding doors. Each step she put between herself and the man in the dark suit was one step toward survival.

Noah was tired. He would be staying at a town house near Kensington Palace, and he was looking forward to a hot shower and a late dinner. The train ride had been pleasant but less than spectacular. Even the twenty-odd minutes under the English Channel had seemed like nothing more than a brief subway ride.

After his chat with the mystery woman, nothing eventful had happened to break up the monotony of the trip. By the time the train reached England it had slowed considerably, and he had been reduced to counting stations and inventing stories about why the young woman had fled Paris and changed her identity.

He hadn't been so intrigued by anything or anyone in a long time. He was certain he was right. Despite the drastic changes in her appearance, despite the faultless British accent, he knew this was the same woman he'd seen in Paris. The silky grain of her skin was the same, the shape of her eyes, the delicate heart shape of her face. Her cheekbones were elegant enough to be memorable. And he was a connoisseur of faces.

What had led her to make such a drastic change? And why was she so frightened? It was the terror that had convinced him to abandon questioning her. Despite her remarkable dramatic abilities, she hadn't masked her fear of him. And he'd had no right to satisfy his curiosity at her expense.

But he hadn't extinguished his curiosity completely. At one point he had gotten up to stretch his legs and look for her again. He hadn't intended to speak to her, just to look and see if she really was traveling with a man. But even though he had covered most of the train, he had not been able to spot her.

Now he stood in the customs line, waiting for permission to set foot on English soil. He had his passport ready and his garment bag slung over his shoulder. The line was long and moving as slowly as an American driver in a British roundabout.

"I've never seen it this way," said the man just ahead of him, who was weighted down with cameras and suitcases. He was wearing surfer shorts and a Hawaiian aloha shirt, as if he had wanted to be sure no one mistook him for a European. "They seem to be questioning everyone."

"Maybe they're looking for someone or something."

"I s'pose. I hope they find whatever they're looking for soon and let the rest of us through."

The line inched forward. Noah passed the time scanning the crowds for the young woman, but she was nowhere in sight. Apparently she had outwitted him. Or perhaps her line had moved at a normal speed and she was in a taxi right now, planning where she would eat supper.

He finally reached the desk and watched as the man in the mismatched Hawaiian prints sailed through customs with no problems. Noah set down his garment bag and produced his passport. The woman behind the desk gazed at him for a moment without speaking. Just as he was about to ask if he could proceed, two men in uniform strode from the sidelines and flanked him.

"Is there a problem?" Noah asked. "My papers are in order. Take a look at them."

"We'll need you to come with us," the older of the two men said.

"Is there a problem? I have identification."

"Of course you do, sir. Now, will you please follow us?" The man moved closer, making it clear that if Noah didn't follow, he would be detained by force.

"Certainly."

Noah stooped to lift his bag off the floor, but the man's arm barred his progress. "Don't touch that!"

Anger began to seep through Noah's innate caution. "Look, that's mine. It belongs to me. I can carry it just fine."

"I said, don't touch it." The older man jerked his head toward his companion, and the second man tugged the garment bag from Noah's hands.

"I demand to know what this is about."

"It's about coming with us, sir." The older man put a hand on Noah's arm.

It was almost humorous. The man was fifty pounds lighter and four inches shorter than Noah's six-one. Noah could have shaken him off with a snap of his wrist. He almost did, but his good sense surfaced just in time.

"Fine. Let's get this over with."

"That's the right attitude, sir."

"Just do me one favor, okay?"

The man waited.

"Don't call me sir again."

"Just follow me."

With a growl low in his throat, Noah did as he was told.

Chapter 2

Celestine had grown accustomed to attics. In her years away from home she had seldom been able to afford better accommodations, and she had decided that someday, when she was no longer on the run, she would produce a coffee-table book entitled *The Garrets of Europe*. No one could do it better.

Her London attic was actually a flat. She had two rooms on the fourth floor with a toilet and sink in what had once been a closet, and a hot plate and electric kettle in the corner of the living room. The shared bath was down the hall, with a narrow antique tub that was nearly as long as the walk to reach it. The ceilings in the flat sloped sharply, but they bottomed out at windows that overlooked New Row, a charming brick lane near Covent Garden. She had been supremely lucky to find such picturesque and affordable accommodations in a section of London that was high-rent. In the month since her escape from Paris she had been happy here. If all went well she would live out the days until she turned twenty-five in this flat, in this city, with no threats to her security.

Then, at last, maybe she could go home.

She had found a job at an appliance repair shop almost immediately after her arrival. She had abandoned the dumpy persona of Lesley, who had traveled on the Eurostar, and adopted a crisp professional look and a new name to go with it. As Celie Sherwood she'd had her hair cut professionally and streaked with blond highlights. The style was tapered around her face and longer in back, and both style and color suited her well. Her eyes were their natural blue again, and she wore flirty round glasses with navy blue wire rims. Her clothing style was classic, her makeup subdued. On arrival in London she'd fibbed her way through three job interviews, and she'd been offered two of the positions the next day.

Now she was on her way to the job she had chosen. But not before she made a phone call.

She was sure her telephone had been installed during the War of the Roses. She had to dial each number the old-fashioned way, and the dial was so stiff and heavy that by the time she was finished with the long series of numbers, her index finger ached. She tapped it against the wooden crate she used as a telephone table and prayed that Allison would wake up and answer.

"For pity's sake, who is this!"

Celestine smiled and gripped the receiver. "Allie, it's me...."

There was a short, grumpy silence. "Celestine?"

"Look, I know what time it is there, but I can never reach you during normal hours. You're always out whooping it up."

"Are you all right?"

"I am. Fine, in fact. I have a job and an apartment. But I'm not where I was."

"Where the hell are you?"

"The less you know, the better. I don't want anyone to come after you. I just had to hear your voice."

"My voice at..." There was a pause, as if Allie were looking for a clock. "Three-thirty in the morning t'ain't so grand."

"Have you spoken to Whit?"

"Not recently."

"I'm thinking about coming back."

"Gawd, sweetcakes, that might not be smart...."

"I know. But it's almost time for a showdown."

There was a crash in the hallway outside. "Celie?" Her name sounded between fierce taps on the door. "Celie, are you up?"

"I've got to go, Allie. Check on Grandpa Sutter for me, will you? Whit says he's fine, but I need to be sure. I haven't been able to get him by telephone."

The pounding started again.

"Don't worry," Allison said. "And take care of yourself. Please."

"I will." Celestine hung up.

"Celie, are you up?" the man in the hallway repeated.

"Of course I am." There was no peephole on the centuries-old door. Celestine opened it because she knew that Marshall Winston was standing on the other side. He shared the fourth floor and the bath with her, and over the past weeks they had become friends.

Marshall eyed her gray striped suit with a wry twist of his narrow lips. "Oh, my dear, I do wish I could get you into bright red, or maybe some of that yummy coral we're showing this year."

"In my next life, Marsh." She stepped aside and gave him room to come in.

"We have the sweetest little white chiffon number in our window. It was made for you."

"That's at least *two* lifetimes away. Would you care for some tea? It's still warm."

"Probably not." He strolled to the window and peered out over New Row. Fog filled doorways and crawled sluggishly along the street like the special effects in a poorly made Sherlock Holmes movie. "Lovely day. Brilliant."

"Why aren't you at work?"

"I thought I'd toddle in about noon." Marshall owned an exclusive dress shop several blocks away. His eye was better than his business sense, and he was always one step from going under. Luckily women loved him and his unerring sense of style, even if he couldn't add two and two. Marshall loved them, too, but his heart was newly pledged to a handsome young weight lifter named Bobby who juggled bowling pins and swallowed fire in front of the nearby market pavilion.

"Well, I'm on my way out," Celie said. "I'm a working girl, you know."

Marshall made a tsking sound. "Celie, why don't you look for something better? Something that suits you more? You obviously have an education."

"But not enough. And no references to speak of. Besides, I'm happy. And I only have to walk about ten yards to work." The appliance repair shop was just across the street, and Celestine's boss Harry, an old curmudgeon who was better with his hands than with people, had been the one to point her toward this flat. The job demanded little thought, but the shop had one profound attraction.

No American tourists ever wandered through its doors.

Marshall wagged his finger in her general direction. "You will absolutely not let me mold you into someone else, will you? Oh, I understand you perfectly. You will never change a hair on your head or a thought inside it. You were born into the world just the way you are, and you'll go out exactly the same."

Her gaze didn't flicker. "You definitely have my number. That's me. Celie Sherwood, eternal stick-in-the-mud."

There was a shrill whistle from the street. Celie peered out the window and saw the object of Marshall's affection waiting below. "Bobby's here." She waved, and Bobby, a big, blond man in tight black leather, waved back.

"Well, I'm meeting Bobby for breakfast," Marshall said. "Toodle-oo."

She leaned over to kiss his cheek. "Toodles, darling. And give Bobby my love."

He sauntered out the door and toward the stairwell. After he'd gone, she grabbed her raincoat and took one look around the apartment before she locked the door behind her. The brief examination was an old habit. There were secrets hidden in odd places. A thorough search would disclose them all, but a casual search would turn up nothing. Satisfied that things were exactly as they were supposed to be, she started down the stairs.

At first Noah wasn't certain that the woman in gray who stepped out of the front entrance of the narrow town house was the woman from the train. But moments ago he had seen the lights go off in the front attic apartment, and he had been assured by a private investigator that the woman living there was Celie Sherwood. He had also been assured that Celie Sherwood was really Lesley McBain, the woman who'd had him detained at Waterloo Station.

And detained. And detained.

Even now, a month later, anger bubbled up inside him at the memory. The investigator had run into one dead end after another in his search for little Miss Sherwood. It was only a chance remark by one of the customs agents that had alerted Noah to the reason for the humiliating detention in the first place. There had been little to go on after that, but Noah had hired the right man and paid him well.

And now the search had led him here.

From his seat he had a fog-besmirched view of the appliance repair shop. As he watched, Celie Sherwood took a few steps toward the curb. She stopped to rifle through her purse, as if she had misplaced something; then, apparently successful, she closed her purse and started across the street. From this distance, and through the fog, she looked nothing at all like what he remembered of the woman on the train. But the moment she crossed the street he knew. Her walk was as familiar as two vivid memories.

He pulled the collar of his all-weather coat higher around his neck and paid cash for his overpriced muffin to the Indian woman in a shimmering blue sari who had come outside to see if he needed anything else. A month had passed, and Noah had waited patiently for this moment. He could wait a little longer. He would confront the woman in gray right before the shop closed its doors for the lunch hour. Then he and Miss Celie Sherwood would have one informative hour to chat.

"I'll post the invoices on the way to lunch if you'd like, Harry," Celestine said. "They'll go out quicker that way."

Harry grunted from the back room. Then he appeared, umbrella in hand. He was a grizzled old man with youthful, supple fingers that could repair nearly anything. "I'll do it. Going by there."

"You're sure?"

He grunted in answer and scooped the envelopes off the front counter. Harry was a good man and an undemanding boss. He just wasn't much for conversation.

"I'll lock up when I leave," she said.

He took his hat from a rack by the door and grunted once more. The bell attached to the door caroled merrily when he slammed the door behind him.

Celestine busied herself straightening the counter. Then she carried a pre-WWII toaster back to Harry's workbench and penned a note to attach to it. "Owner says...the morning's toast tasted...like a relic from...the Great London Fire."

With one ear cocked for the bell, she dusted the bench and threw away the remains of Harry's breakfast. Satisfied that she'd done what she could, she went back up to the front.

The man from the café was leaning against the counter watching her. She took one step backward before he raised his hand to stop her.

"I wouldn't go anywhere if I were you, Celie. Because if I don't catch you—which is unlikely—I'll just find you again, and then I'll really be angry."

She didn't even swallow. She lifted her chin. "I don't know what you mean."

"Don't you?" He smiled, but his face was still carved from stone.

He wasn't dressed in a dark suit, or any suit, today. He was wearing faded jeans, an ivory shirt unbuttoned at the neck and a hunter green corduroy sport jacket under a brown trench coat. The jacket and coat were unbuttoned, and her gaze dropped momentarily to search for the telltale outline of a gun.

Unsuccessful, she looked him straight in the eye. "I don't know what you mean, and I don't know you. I think you have me confused with someone else."

"Do I?"

"You'll have to pardon me, but I don't have time for this. I'm about to go to lunch. You'll have to come back in an hour."

"Why? To find you gone? Because I think you'd desert Mr. Harry Atkins exactly the way you deserted Madame Duchampier in Paris. Without a backward glance."

She frowned. "I really don't know what you mean, and I don't have time for guessing games."

"Let me refresh your memory. You used to work in a café on the Left Bank. Your hair was long and a different color. You didn't wear glasses, and your French was as impeccable as your English. You called yourself Marie St. Germaine. That part was easy to discover. I had my man bribe your former employer, who does not, by the way, hold you in high esteem."

"You've confused me with someone else. My name is Celie Sherwood, and I have never worked in Paris."

"Have you ever been searched by a customs agent, Celie? Or is the name Lesley?"

She didn't answer. She didn't even blink.

He continued with a shrug. "Customs can be very thorough. Humiliatingly thorough. You might be surprised at the numerous inventive ways that drug smugglers have found to get their product from one market to another. And the agents know them all. Every single body fold and crevice. Then there are X rays...."

"I'm leaving now."

"I don't think so." He rounded the counter. He moved like a jungle soldier. Had there been twigs under his feet, not a one would have cracked.

"I'll scream," she warned.

"Will you? In French? English? How many other languages do you know?" He moved steadily closer. Not a bird would have flown away at his approach.

"You're unbalanced, and if you don't leave immediately, I'll call for help."

He was standing just in front of her now. There was a door in the back of the shop, but Celestine had realized immediately that she wouldn't be able to reach it before he overtook her. Unless someone else came into the shop and distracted him, she was doomed. Her gaze flicked past him to the door.

"It's locked," he said in a neutral tone. "Now, tell me who you are and why you had me detained."

"I don't know what you're talking about! Who are you? What gives you the right to interrogate me this way? I'm a British citizen, and you're standing on British soil."

"Let's start there, shall we? A Celie Sherwood *was* born on British soil—in Bourton-on-the-Water, in fact—about twenty-four years ago. But the real Celie entered a cloistered convent in Wales when she turned eighteen. Now she has no need for any legal documents. So I suppose she might not even object to you borrowing her name and identity. But *I* object. Strongly."

"I don't know who's been filling your head with lies, but I *am* Celie Sherwood. It's true I was born in Bourton-on-the-Water, but none of the rest of your story makes any sense."

"Why? Just tell me that. I'm a stranger to you. I've never done a thing except while away some small part of a Paris afternoon in the café where you worked. I was bored, and you were easy on the eye. But I never approached you. I didn't even stare. I'm not a stalker. I'm not part of some crime ring that wanted to kidnap you and sell you into white slavery. I was just a businessman in Paris with too much time to kill.''

She shuddered at the last word. He frowned, as if even that nearly imperceptible shudder had registered. The steel in his voice bent a little. ''I'm no threat to you. I don't know who you think I am, and I don't know who *you* are, but I can assure you, I'm not here to hurt you.''

''Then leave me alone! Go! You want to prove that you're as meek as a lamb? Then turn around and walk out that door and out of my life.''

''There's the small matter of a strip search that I didn't exactly enjoy.''

''I never worked in Paris. I never turned you over to a customs agent. I've never even ridden the Eurostar!''

There was a long silence. His hazel eyes searched hers. They communicated nothing, but she knew what he was thinking.

''Did I mention the Eurostar?'' he asked at last.

''I just assumed that's what you were talking about. It comes into Waterloo Station, and you were in Paris.''

''Did I mention Waterloo?''

She was panicking. He was so close. No matter what he'd said, it would be a small matter now for him to pull out a gun or a knife and kill her with professional efficiency. Harry would come back and find her bleeding on the saw-dust-littered floor. Harry would hate answering the inevitable questions that would come with her death.

''I—''

A scuffle at the front door wiped another desperate lie from her lips. She heard a key turning in the lock and one mumbled curse. The bell tinkled, and the door flew open. Harry stood in the doorway. ''Forgot my wallet—''

Celestine didn't wait for the man in front of her to respond. The distraction was all she needed. She turned and fled through the back of the shop, around Harry's work-table and straight for the door. It opened, as she had prayed it would, with one thrust of her hip. In a moment she was outside in a thick London fog, running for her life.

Noah hesitated for a split second. He wondered if he really had enough reason to follow Celie Sherwood—or whoever she was. She was terrified of him. She was a superb actress, but the terror had peered back at him from robin's-egg blue eyes. If he followed her, she would be even more terrified. He might prompt her to do something both of them would regret. He could and should let this go and get on with his life.

Swearing under his breath, he took off after her anyway. He was too involved to quit now. Celie obviously believed he was going to harm, even murder, her. Maybe he had a look-alike who really did mean her harm. Or maybe he fit a description that someone had given her. He wondered why a woman who looked as demure as Celie was so frightened for her life.

He wanted to tell her that she had nothing to fear. He had moved beyond his own anger to concern for her safety. He had become involved, something he knew better than to allow. Now he was paying the price, and quite possibly she was, too.

The alley behind the shop was a dead end, and he took off toward the right, in the direction he was sure she must have gone. He reached the end just in time to see a flash of gray duck through a shop door. He wished she had worn red or orange, something that would signal her every move in the midday fog. A light rain began to fall as he ran toward the shop and pushed open the door.

A butcher stood with both hands on his hips, cursing loudly. Noah pushed past him, past sides of lamb swinging from ceiling hooks, and ran through the open back door. This alley was open at both ends, leading to different lanes. He heard a screech of brakes to the right and followed the sound just in time to see Celie dashing across the lane as a motorist lectured her through his window.

She turned and saw Noah, then took off running again. He held up his hand to the motorist and ran after her. She had a good start on him, and both the streets and walkways were too narrow for speed. She knew where she was going, and he didn't. She was smaller, and she maneuvered her graceful body with the finesse of someone who had been chased often.

The closer they got to the steel-and-glass market buildings, the more crowded the streets became. They were in the hub of London entertainment, surrounded by restaurants and shops, all of which were booming with business. Noah knew they were attracting attention, and soon someone else would start after them. The heavens chose that moment to open, and rain doused the startled onlookers, who promptly forgot the peculiar sight of a man and woman racing through the streets of London and scurried for cover.

The rain obscured what little vision the fog had left him. Noah shaded his eyes and kept moving, but he wasn't so certain now that he was on the right track. He thought he saw a woman dart diagonally toward a church on the cobblestone square near the market pavilions. He followed her, but when he reached the spot where he had seen her, she was no longer there.

He tried a different direction, then the welcome shelter of the market itself. But Celie Sherwood—who was supposed to be steadily praying away her days in a Welsh convent— had disappeared once again.

"Bobby! Oh, Lord, Bobby! You've got to hide me. Please. Now!" Celestine collapsed against the massive chest of the blond weight lifter who had stolen Marsh's heart. She had prayed that he would be here in his usual spot on the square, performing.

Bobby wrapped his strong arms around her. "Celie? For pity's sake, what's wrong? What are you doing here?"

"There's a crazy man after me! He came to the shop and started threatening me. Then he chased me through the streets. I don't know if I've lost him or not!"

Bobby held her at arm's length. He had green eyes and hair down to his shoulders. He wore skintight black leather pants and an open leopard print vest over his massive bare chest. In the few short weeks that he'd been busking in the streets of Covent Gardens, he had become a crowd favorite. He'd even made enough money to share some of it with Marshall, which was the quickest shortcut to Marshall's heart.

Bobby rubbed his palms up and down her arms. His green eyes were troubled. "Hey, you're safe. I won't let anybody hurt you."

"You've got to hide me!"

He frowned. "My place is pretty far away."

"I know. Too far." Celestine peered through the pouring rain. They were standing in the entrance to a shop that sold kites and model airplanes. It was deeply recessed, and they couldn't be seen from a distance. But if the man happened to come this way...

Bobby shrugged into a leather jacket that matched his pants. "We'll go to Marsh's shop. I'll take you the back way. It's a labyrinth, but I've done it before. Anyone who tries to follow us will get lost immediately."

"I thought about going to Marsh's. But anyone who knows me, who's been watching me—" She shuddered. "That's the first place they'd check, isn't it?"

"I'll be with you, and so will Marsh. If someone comes looking for you, we'll take care of him."

"Yes. Okay. But please, we've got to hurry."

Bobby grabbed her hands reassuringly. Then he stepped out to the sidewalk and looked both ways. "I don't see anybody. Come on. And stay close."

The September rain was cold. Celestine was already soaked to the skin, but the rain was still an assault. She followed Bobby along a snaking route that would have confused any pursuer. She was quickly lost herself, and she concentrated on the sight of Bobby's muscular body just ahead of her.

She was growing exhausted. Just as she was about to ask Bobby to rest a moment, he stopped and motioned for her to join him under an overhang between two buildings.

She reached down and removed a shoe so that she could massage her foot. She was glad she'd worn practical heels. Anything higher would have finished her off right at the beginning. "Where are we?"

"Not far from Marsh's."

She was trying not to cry, but the tears were in her voice. "You really meant it when you said the back way. I'm so lost."

"And scared, poor thing."

"I can't thank you enough. I didn't know who to turn to." She tried to smile. "I'm so glad you were there."

"What did that man want, Celie?"

She wished she could tell him, but that was impossible. "I don't know. Nothing. He was crazy. Unhinged. He thought I was somebody else, and he was making threats."

"Somebody else?"

"Yes—no. I don't know. He frightened me, and I ran."

"You're rather good at that, I think."

She peered between the buildings. No one was out in the lane in front of them. The buildings around them appeared to be deserted, and the rain had chased everyone else inside. "I did run at school, and I'm still in good shape."

"That's not quite what I meant."

She looked back at him. "Do you think we'd better move on?"

"I don't think you've quite got the picture, Celie girl."

His smile seemed inappropriate under the circumstances. She felt her first flicker of fear. "Pardon?"

"Celie. A nice name, though a bit unusual, wouldn't you say? It calls attention to itself. I should think that was something you wouldn't want to do."

"I don't know what you mean."

"I think you do."

She backed away, but she quickly came to a halt against a brick wall. She tried not to sound frightened. "You know,

I can find the shop from here by myself. Marsh and I will figure out what to do. Thank you for getting me this far." She turned to bolt, and his hand clamped down on her arm.

"I don't think so, Celestine."

His words were obscured by a clap of thunder. But she knew what he'd said. She knew. "Let go! You're hurting me."

"That's really a pity. As is the fact that I have to hurt you more...."

"Who in the hell are you?"

"Don't you know? I'm not your worst nightmare. I'm your *every* nightmare, darling."

She struggled to free herself. He was holding her with his left hand, but he was as strong as he pretended to be for the tourists. He tugged her closer, and helplessly she gave ground inch by inch, kicking and flailing. As she watched in terror, his right hand slid inside his jacket.

He pulled out a knife with a six-inch blade and flourished it dramatically, as if this were part of his act. "Just so you know, darling, it's women I like, not men, no matter what poor old Marshall thinks. And I'd intended to have my fill of you some night next week before I did this. But you've made it all so simple today. So very simple."

She screamed as he raised the knife. He smiled as if he were genuinely looking forward to what was coming. "There's no one nearby to hear you, darling," he said with his mouth against her ear. "Make it easy on yourself and let me do this right."

Chapter 3

Noah heard the scream at the same moment he'd decided to give up the chase. Despite his raincoat, he was soaked to the skin. Common sense told him that he would not find Celie, that he had lost his chance to discover why she was afraid of him or why she'd had him detained at customs. Celie Sherwood was a mystery and would remain one forever.

The scream made confetti out of his decision to forget her. He was running toward the sound before he'd made a conscious decision to investigate.

The rain was coming down in sheets now, and lightning crackled all around him. Everyone with a choice had taken cover. Except for a woman with something to scream about, he had the streets to himself.

He'd run past half a dozen buildings before he realized he could be going in the wrong direction entirely. Everything always seemed louder in London. The houses and streets were brick or stone; there were high walls everywhere for sound to bounce off. The scream might have come from far away, and as yet it hadn't been repeated. He slowed his pace and tried to think. But before he could change his course, another scream sounded. Closer this time.

He rounded the next corner. The street he had come to was really nothing more than a lane behind what looked like a row of deserted buildings. Renovations were in progress, and a jackhammer and forklift were chained in place under makeshift canvas shelters. Because of the rain or the lunch hour, no workers were in sight.

Most of the buildings were connected, Georgian row houses defined by different styles of trim. But there was a narrow covered walkway between two of the buildings. Noah headed for the walkway, which appeared to lead to the next street. Two figures materialized as he stepped inside. One was a giant in black leather. The other was a woman.

He recognized the scream and the woman at the same moment. Celie looked terrified, but she was fighting like a demon for her life. Boxed in by brick walls, her scream was almost as much of a weapon as the knife glinting in the giant's hand. But one was annoying and the other was deadly.

"Leave her alone!" Noah started toward the giant's upraised arm. Celie was already bleeding, and her glasses were in pieces at her feet. Noah could see that much and little more, but he could see that the giant was trying to strike her again. She twisted and turned against him, struggling to break free, but he held her fast.

"You want trouble?" The giant turned on Noah and grinned. Noah was a large man, a fact that had often deterred smaller men spoiling for a fight. But this man was huge, and obviously thrilled to have yet another potential victim. Noah held up his hands in surrender and began to back away. The giant slashed his knife through the air twice and laughed. The moment he turned back to Celie, Noah sprang.

He had calculated the distance exactly, and he landed where he'd hoped, against the shoulder of the arm holding the knife. Noah grabbed the giant's wrist with one hand and gave a swift chop to his forearm with the other. With a howl of pain the giant released Celie, but not the knife. He swung around to grab Noah, but expecting that, Noah had already danced away.

Celie stumbled toward the opposite end of the walkway, bent over as if she couldn't straighten. Noah saw only that much before the giant sprang at him again. Noah sidestepped neatly. The giant was strong, but not swift. The muscles he had so lovingly developed hindered him now. Noah kicked him in the thigh, then in the back of the knee. The giant sagged, and this time Noah landed a kick against his elbow. The knife went flying across the walkway toward Noah.

"You're going to die," the giant said.

Noah dove for the knife, then tossed it from hand to hand with the finesse of a street fighter. "Think so?" He gripped the knife in his palm and slashed the air as the giant had done. He was breathing heavily. "I'm an angry man. And I don't like...men who hurt women."

The giant hurtled toward him with his head tucked like a battering ram. There was no room to move away. Noah could only brace himself and turn so that he wouldn't go down. Time stopped momentarily. He waited, and as he did, he could see that the fight would be decided here. If he went down under the giant's massive body, he would not come back up alive.

His head slammed into the wall, and his feet slid forward as the giant tackled him. But he didn't drop the knife, and he didn't fall. Not completely. He grabbed the giant's hair and jerked his head backward, then as the man's eyes widened he held the knife against his throat. "What's it going to be, Goliath? Do I get to see you bleed, or are you going to leave while you still can?"

"Why...give him a choice?"

Noah's gaze flicked to Celie. He hadn't tried to keep track of her. He had halfway expected her to escape again. But now she stood just in front of him holding a stone that looked as if it had once graced the wall of a row house. She brought it down hard against the back of the giant's head.

Then, as the giant collapsed in a boneless heap, she collapsed on top of him.

Celestine didn't know where she was. Her body felt as light as a feather. And wet. Water sluiced against her face, and as desperately as she wanted to sink back into oblivion, the water made that impossible. She tried to speak, but the only sound to emerge was a moan.

"Hold on, Celie. I'll get you to a hospital."

"No..." She began to struggle. Someone was holding her, carrying her. She opened her eyes, and rain washed them until she squeezed them shut again. "No... Leave me..."

"Not on your life."

"They'll find me.... Can't go... No hospital... Kill me..." Her tongue refused to work properly. Her brain was slowing to a standstill. But the fear was as vivid as always.

"You're bleeding! I can't get it to stop completely. You have to go to a hospital."

"They'll kill me. You'll kill...me." She thought perhaps he'd already tried. But that didn't seem right. She couldn't remember exactly what had happened or why. She only knew she was terrified. She tried to struggle, but her limbs were weightless. Then *she* was weightless, soaring somewhere far away from the rain and the man carrying her.

The next time she regained consciousness she was still in the man's arms, but the rain no longer pelted her.

"Can't you go any faster?" the man holding her asked someone.

Another man answered. "Sorry, guv, but the rain's made a snarl of things. It'll just take a bit longer. Is she any better?"

"She'll be fine."

"And you're certain she doesn't need to be in hospital?"

"No. She's fainted, that's all. She hasn't had a thing to eat today. She just needs her own bed and a good hot meal...."

"Oxtail soup. And hot tea with plenty of sugar."

"Just the thing." The man's arms tightened around her. He sounded as if he were talking through clenched teeth.

"That's your street up ahead."

"Good."

"Will you need help getting her inside?"

"We'll be fine."

She liked the sound of that, although she knew what a terrible lie it was. She wasn't going to be fine. She would never be fine again, never live like a normal woman. Never live...

She tried to speak, to tell him she knew it was a lie, but she couldn't even moan. Then it didn't matter anymore, because she was soaring again.

Noah was glad he was staying in the town house that Tri-C International kept for executives traveling through London on business. He normally found the town house unsettling, too Victorian and homey for his taste. Betty Prynne, the housekeeper, loved gardens, and she'd painstakingly filled the yard with flowers and shrubs for every season. The interior, with its high ceilings and dark, ornate woodwork, was softened by pastels and interesting pieces of antique furniture, as if it had been lovingly decorated by somebody's wife. Today, the comfort and relative privacy were pluses.

It was still raining hard when the taxi pulled up in front. The sky was as dark as night, and he was glad that none of his Kensington neighbors would be able to see clearly that the newest resident of the house was carrying a woman wrapped in his brown trench coat.

Noah knew why he'd brought Celie here; he just wasn't certain he had made the right decision. Just before she'd blacked out for the last time, she had stared at him. The terror in her eyes had turned to something more chilling. He could see that she knew she was going to die, and she had already begun to mourn the inevitable.

In that instant he had realized that he could not fail her. He didn't know how, and he didn't know when, but someone, somewhere, had failed this woman terribly. She had been brought to this place because of forces he knew nothing about. And now, if he betrayed her, too, she would be doomed.

The taxi driver, a young man with a Vandyke beard and sad brown eyes, sheltered Noah with a large umbrella, and together they scurried to the front door. Celie was surprisingly light in Noah's arms. Until that moment he hadn't realized just how thin she was.

He handed the young man his key, and he unlocked the door and opened it a crack. Noah took the key and pressed a bill into his hand. "What's your name?"

"Nigel. Nigel Clark."

"Look, Nigel. My wife would be mortified if anyone ever found out that she'd fainted this way. Please don't say anything about this. Even if you're asked."

"Why would I be asked?"

Noah lowered his voice. "She's a celebrity in America. She's on television, a new show, nothing you get here. But she's very protective of her privacy."

"I see." Nigel looked down at the folded bill in his hand. His eyes widened.

"And if no one turns up to interview her in the next few weeks, I'll know you've kept this little episode to yourself. And there'll be another hundred pounds delivered to your workplace."

"Very good, guv."

"Thanks for your help."

Nigel nodded, pulled the umbrella over his head and started back into the rain. Noah entered the town house and closed the door behind him. "Betty? Betty, are you here?"

There was no answer. Betty had probably stepped out to do the day's shopping. He had told her that morning that he would be dining in tonight, and now he cursed that decision. Betty knew something about everything, and she could be trusted to help with his injured "guest."

He still wasn't sure he had made the right decision by bringing Celie here. He had managed to treat the knife wound to her shoulder with a makeshift compress of a handkerchief and the trench coat belt before bundling her up, but he hadn't been able to investigate her injuries any further in the taxi for fear of alerting the driver. Now he didn't know what he would find when he examined her again.

He carried her up the stairs to the first bedroom on the second floor and shoved the door wide with his knee. A mahogany four-poster bed draped in lace stood in the middle of the room, and he reached it in four strides. He managed to throw back the lace coverlet before he laid Celie, coat and all, on the white linen sheets.

She was the color of the linen, and she didn't even stir as he unwrapped the coat and stared at her jacket. It was in shreds—courtesy of the giant—and bloodstained, but it still hid the worst of the evidence. He removed the blood-soaked compress and looked around for something he could use to cut the jacket free. There was nothing in sight. He didn't want to leave her, not even for a moment, but he had to get the jacket off. At the doorway he turned to be sure she was still unconscious; then he strode down the hall to his suite to get the mending kit from his bathroom.

Celie was lying in exactly the same position when he returned. She was paler, if possible, and absolutely still. He lowered himself to the bed beside her and contemplated the best way to remove the jacket; then he began to snip at the fabric and the blouse beneath it.

The job was painstaking. The scissors were meant for clipping threads, and his patience was short. But he worked as quickly and carefully as he could until he had freed the bulk of the sleeve. He tugged it down at the wrist, then cut away everything else that blocked his view.

The wound was worse than he'd imagined, a deep, jagged slash that looked as if it had nearly reached the bone. He wondered how she had been able to lift the rock, much less bring it crashing down on the giant's head. Celie was a woman of mystery, but one thing was apparent. She was as courageous as anyone he had ever known.

The wound was bleeding, and would continue to bleed until it was stitched. And despite the superior quality of the mending kit, there was nothing in it that would suffice for this job. She needed a professional's skill, anesthetic, antibiotics. He shook his head even as he prepared a new compress from freshly ironed tea towels he'd snatched from the linen closet in the hallway. He folded two towels and pressed them against the wound. He was going to have to call for an ambulance, and he was going to have to tell the authorities what he knew of the truth and caution them to protect her.

"Mr. Colter?"

He jumped at the sound of Betty's voice on the stairwell. He hadn't heard her arrive. "I'm in here. And I need you."

She entered the room, hands on ample hips. "I'm sorry to disturb you, but I wondered when..." She stared at Celie, then at him. "Good Lord."

"It's all right, Betty." Of course, nothing was further from the truth. He grimaced. "It's not all right, as a matter of fact. A man tried to kill her. I rescued her, and before she fainted, she begged me not to take her to the hospital. I think she's afraid for her life."

"Oh, Mr. Colter."

"I think we're going to have to call an ambulance."

"But if she's afraid..." Betty stepped closer. She was nearing sixty, with the round body and salt-and-pepper hair of a woman who was comfortable growing older. "Poor dear. What exactly happened to her?"

"A man took a knife to her." He lifted the compress momentarily. Betty stepped closer and squinted at the wound. The bleeding had slowed a little. "I've seen worse, and I've seen better. Any other injuries?"

"You've seen worse?"

"Aye, I was a surgical nurse in Glasgow before coming to London. Then I came into a bit of money, and I took this position. Far easier on the feet."

"I haven't examined her. We just got here. I think this is the only wound, but I'm not sure."

"Let's get to it, then."

"Get to it?"

"Aye. You check her over quickly while I ring a friend. Don't take too long, as she needs pressure against that wound until it can be stitched. I think we can take care of this. If that's what you want."

What Noah wanted was to start the day over, without confronting Celie Sherwood. He wanted to relive a certain day in Paris when he should have headed as far away from the city as possible the moment he saw a red-haired wood nymph. Whoever Celie Sherwood was, she was a stranger to him. He did not need this complication, and he did not need this burden.

"I don't know what to do." He stared at Celie's pale face. "I'm not responsible for her."

"Of course you're not."

He heard the censure in Betty's soft voice. "I'm not. And if we take care of her here, we become involved. Don't you realize that?"

"Aye. And I can see that you believe involvement is not a thing to wish for."

He looked up. Betty stared straight into his eyes. He couldn't criticize her. All Tri-C's employees knew that they were free to speak their minds. Open communication was one of the things Noah had insisted on since the day he had taken over the company. "It's *not* a thing I wish for."

"Then shall I call for someone to take her away or for assistance to treat her here?"

"You think you can do this?"

"Not alone, surely. But I've a friend, a man. He was a surgeon for years, then he took to the bottle." She shrugged. "His right to practice medicine was taken from him. But he doesn't drink anymore, and his hands are steady again."

"You think he'd come?"

"Aye. He lives not far away. He would do anything I asked."

He hesitated, but his decision was already made. "Then call him."

"Aye." She started toward the door. "If you find anything else, call me."

Noah was left alone with Celie, still unconscious and lying as still as if she had died.

Noah had undressed women before. He was familiar with the female form and all its variations. But he couldn't remember undressing one who lay as still as death....

Except once.

He closed his eyes against that memory, still as painful, as fresh, as the moment when it had occurred. The room was cool, but he felt his hands begin to sweat, and for long seconds he couldn't catch his breath. Then he opened his eyes and stared at Celie, and he knew he had to help her. The choice had been taken from him the moment she had stared at him and the acceptance of certain death had clouded her eyes.

God help him, no matter how much he wanted to, he could not abandon the woman who called herself Celie Sherwood.

He reached for the buttons of her blouse. They slid through the buttonholes easily, and in a moment he could spread the blouse wide. Celie had no tan at all, and her thin blue veins stood out like flaws in an otherwise perfect pearl. There was blood caked on her shoulder and chest, but no additional wounds that he could see. Her bra, covering small, firm breasts, was soaked with blood, and he eased his hand beneath her to unsnap the clasp. He couldn't remove it without removing her blouse completely, and he would need help for that. He was forced to continue his investigation using his hands instead of his eyes.

Her skin was smooth, but not nearly as warm as it should have been. It seemed to contract under his hands, and once she moaned. He was struck by the oddity of this. He had responded to her at first sight in Paris, even subdued tantalizing fantasies about making her moan when he stroked her naked body. Now he was getting his wish, but not in quite the way he had imagined.

"You're going to be all right, Celie," he murmured. "We're going to take care of you."

His examination was cursory, but he could detect no other wounds. He unzipped her skirt and pulled it low on her hips. There were no wounds here, either. The man with the knife had been aiming high. Noah was beginning to believe that the wound in Celie's shoulder was the extent of it.

He placed another tea towel against her shoulder and held it there. She moaned again, and her eyelids fluttered open. She stared into his eyes, but he doubted that she saw him. "You're going to be all right," he repeated.

"Don't..."

"You have a cut on your shoulder. I'm trying to stop it from bleeding."

She began to thrash from side to side, and he placed his free hand against her opposite shoulder and pressed. "Don't, Celie. You'll make the bleeding worse. No one's going to hurt you. We're trying to help you."

"Don't... I don't..." Her eyes closed, and she went limp.

Betty strode back into the room. "Jerry's on his way. How is she?"

"She regained consciousness for just a moment."

"Poor lamb."

"This seems to be the only injury."

"Let's get her undressed."

He almost protested. He was already more intimately involved than he had ever planned to be. But Betty couldn't do this alone. He sighed harshly. "Just tell me what to do."

"First let me finish cutting away this part of the jacket. There. Now lift her. Carefully. I'll slide the rest of it off, then we'll start on her blouse and underthings."

"Great."

"Have you never seen a naked woman, Mr. Colter?"

He looked away. "Let's just get this over with, shall we?"

"It's glad I am that you became a rich man and not a doctor, although they're often one and the same, aren't they?"

"Betty, what are you doing?"

Betty was blithely snipping away Celie's bra. "Cutting away what's left of her clothes. She's thin, but shapely all the same, isn't she?"

Noah glanced down at Celie and saw that Betty's assessment was completely accurate, but his hands had told him that much already. He looked away again. "Is this first aid or a beauty pageant?"

"I could stitch this wound myself, I think. If it weren't so uneven..." She shook her head. "Aye, it's better that Jerry do it. She's a bonny wee thing. We don't want to leave a nasty scar."

"How long will it take her to recover?"

"That will depend, of course, on how willing she is to take things slowly. If she has help?" Betty shrugged. "In a week or two she should be able to do for herself. Of course, if she doesn't take care of it..." She shrugged again. "I've seen infections set in, despite the most reasonable precautions."

"A week or two?"

"Does she have a safe place to go?" Betty asked.

"I told you, she's a stranger to me."

"I'm going to get soap and water to clean her up a bit. You stay here and hold the compress in place. Jerry should be arriving momentarily."

Noah was left alone with Celie again. He wondered what she would say if she regained consciousness once more and found him sitting beside her staring down at her naked torso. She was terrified of him. What had she thought when he appeared from nowhere to rescue her? Had her opinion changed, or had she fantasized yet another preposterous story that implicated him in some crime against her?

And who was the giant in black leather? Someone she had just happened upon who had taken that opportunity to attempt a robbery or, worse, a rape at knifepoint? That seemed unlikely, but the entire scenario from beginning to end seemed worse than unlikely. Yet he was living it, and so was she.

His gaze drifted to Celie's breasts, despite his best efforts to control it. He imagined, just for a moment, what she would look like under different, better, circumstances. She wasn't model thin or centerfold voluptuous. She had the body of a real woman, delicate and altogether feminine. Now that body was caked with blood, and bruises were already beginning to appear on her pearl white skin. He felt such a surge of fury that for a moment he almost didn't recognize the feeling. A man had done this to her. A man had intentionally inflicted these injuries and tried to inflict more. She had screamed for help, but he was almost sure that she hadn't expected any.

She had expected to die.

He forced his gaze back to her face and saw that she was watching him.

"Why don't you just... get it over with?" Her voice sounded as if it came from far away. Her eyes were bleak.

"We have a doctor coming to stitch your shoulder. No! Don't try to move. The bleeding's slowed." He held her in place as she tried to sit up. "Look, we're going to get you cleaned up and dressed again, then you can sleep. You're safe here. I don't know what you think is going to happen, but you're safe. The man in the black leather jacket is probably still lying where we left him. I brought you here instead of a hospital so he couldn't find you if he ever wakes up."

She struggled against his hands. "Let me go."

"No. And if you keep this up, I'm going to call an ambulance and have them take you to a hospital anyway. Do you understand? I can't be responsible for you bleeding to death."

"Why not?"

The lack of hope in her voice was so moving that for a moment he couldn't answer. "I don't know who you think I am. Or what you think I want with you. But I probably just saved your life. Does that ring a bell?"

"What do you want... with me?"

"Right now I'd like you well and out of this house. But barring that, I'll settle for you being a good girl while we get you stitched up. Then we'll figure out where to go from there."

There was noise from the hallway; then Betty bustled in. "Jerry's here. Is our patient awake?"

Noah realized that he was still pinning Celie down to the bed, and that she was half-naked. Suddenly he didn't want another man looking at her the way he had.

The way he hadn't been able to stop himself from looking at her.

He released her, reached down and pulled up the lace coverlet so that it covered her breasts. He realized that it was a useless gesture. Betty would uncover her again to wash her.

But he couldn't just leave Celie that way, exposed and helpless.

She was still watching him warily. "I can leave, or I can stay," he said. "You could pass the time insulting my integrity while they work on your shoulder."

"Who are . . . you?"

He considered that. He didn't want to tell her who he was. Not really. His name was too well-known, along with a number of events that were connected to it. The thought of destroying what little privacy he had and opening up his past for examination by this woman was distasteful. "Noah," he said. "Noah James." And it was true, to a point.

He stood up and turned his gaze to Betty. She didn't seem surprised at the lie. If anything, she seemed to understand. "Now out of here, Mr. James," she said. "We'll take care of her. We'll call you when we've finished."

A haggard, balding man Betty's age and relative size came into the room. He was carrying an old-fashioned medical bag, and he looked pathetically eager to begin work.

Noah nodded. He took one last look at Celie. She closed her eyes. He wondered what she thought. Did she believe they were trying to help her? Or, in her mind, was this just an extension of what had happened earlier?

What was she running from? And why?

He understood about people who ran away. He wished there was some way to tell her there was no place on earth so remote that she could hide forever. He had found that no matter where he ran, when he looked in the mirror he was still Noah James Colter.

"Be brave," he said. "But you already are, aren't you?"

She didn't answer, and she didn't open her eyes. She lay very still and waited for whatever was going to happen next.

Chapter 4

"She came through it fine. She's asleep. Jerry gave her something for the pain. Thought I'd have to stroke her throat like a wee puppy to make her take it, but at least now she'll sleep a bit." Betty shook her head as she plugged in the teakettle. She had found Noah in the kitchen searching for something to eat and shooed him to a table at the window. "She didn't even whimper, poor lamb. And we must have hurt her."

"She's not one to whimper," Noah said. "That's about the only thing I know for certain."

"Well, I know *you* lied about who you are."

Noah closed his eyes. He was exhausted and just beginning to realize that Celie wasn't the only one who'd been battered by a giant. "This is already too complicated. I didn't want to make it more so. And I thought if she knew my real identity she might use it against me some way. I don't know . . ."

"I suspect it's not easy being Noah Colter."

For just an instant Noah thought about the young boy who would have given anything to have a genuinely warm woman like Betty listen to him this way. As a child he had yearned for affection and attention with a hunger that had nearly devoured him. Now he wanted neither. "It's very easy to be Noah Colter. My life is every teenage male's fantasy."

"And we know just what part of his body a growing lad thinks with."

"How long will she sleep?"

"An hour, perhaps. Two, if we're fortunate."

"I wonder how long it'll be before Scotland Yard comes knocking at the door."

"And why should they do that?" Betty was just reaching for a silver tea canister. Her hand stopped in midair. "Well, of course I know. What am I thinking?"

"I bribed the taxi driver not to say anything. But when the man who attacked Celie is found, there'll be questions asked. And it will only be a matter of time before someone tells the police something that will lead them to the driver and eventually to this house."

"Perhaps that would be for the best. You said yourself that she needs protection."

"But if I thought she needed their kind of protection, I would have called the police immediately, wouldn't I?"

"You've no faith in the authorities, and it's no wonder."

He didn't comment. Betty was determined to be warm and understanding, and he was determined to ignore it. "Either I let them take her, or I take her somewhere myself."

"And where would you be taking her? Back to America? You'd smuggle her out of the country some way?"

The idea was intriguing, but not for the reasons Betty might be thinking. Noah was beginning to be suspicious about Celie Sherwood's origins. He knew she wasn't what she seemed. He knew she was a supremely talented mimic with a command of languages and accents that was astonishing. But what if she was neither British nor French? What if not one but both nationalities were just part of her repertoire?

When she had regained consciousness she had been in no condition to assume an identity or accent other than her own. And as halting and whispered as her words had been, they had been flavored with the cadences of his own country. Southern-fried United States, to boot.

Who the hell was this woman?

"Are you truly considering kidnapping the poor girl?" Betty asked when he didn't answer.

"This isn't a crime novel, Betty," he said with irritation. "I'm just trying to think of a way to keep her safe until I know more about her."

"I know a place," Betty said, not at all taken aback by his tone. "Of course, if you don't want my help..."

He was only half listening. "Where?"

"My sister Joan has a cottage in Kent. It's nothing fancy, you understand, just a place we sometimes go to escape from the city. It's surrounded by farmland. There's nothing to it but fields and more of the same. There's hardly a soul goes near it. I've been there for weeks and never seen a human face. But there's a village not far away, with a store and a church if you've need of supplies or prayer."

"And you think she'd let me use it?"

"I'll tell her I'm wanting it for myself for a bit. She won't question. She's going on holiday to Madrid and won't be needing it. It's rarely used these days."

"That might do."

"Until you think of something better."

"How far from here, would you say?"

"That's the beauty of it. More than one hour, but less than two. It depends on whether you spot it the first time you pass by."

Noah considered the offer. His first impulse was to send Betty there with Celie. Celie was more apt to stay at the cottage and recover if he wasn't with her. But he rejected that solution. He didn't know anything about Celie except that someone was obviously pursuing her. He couldn't put Betty in danger because it was more convenient for him.

He considered accompanying Celie to the cottage and taking Betty with them. But in what capacity? He didn't need a housekeeper, and Celie probably didn't need a nurse. If anything went wrong, Betty could get there quickly enough. And, as before, he hated to subject Betty to unnecessary danger. Even if he was right there, there was no guarantee that everyone could be kept safe.

The last time a woman had been under his protection, she hadn't survived.

"If the cottage isn't often used, won't it seem odd to whatever neighbors there are to have us move in?" he asked.

"I'll ring the closest family and tell them you'll be there on holiday. I'll say you're husband and wife. Having a bit of a honeymoon and wanting to be alone."

Betty's story, as distasteful as it was, would probably work well enough to keep the locals away. And if anyone traced Celie to the cottage, no story would be elaborate enough to protect them, anyway. He made up his mind. "All right. I'll take her there, if she's willing to go. But she may have a better idea. In fact, I hope she does, and that it doesn't include me."

"Is that so? I rather thought you were enjoying this."

He looked up sharply. Betty's smile was nearly as wide as her hips. "I value honesty but not interference in my life," he warned.

"No? That's what's wrong with you, you know. You let no one interfere. It's a pity for you I'm so old and secure here that I do whatever I please."

"You're not that secure."

"Just try and sack me. My shortbread and scones have more friends among Tri-C International's executives than you do, Noah Colter."

He tried not to smile, but he ended up giving in reluctantly.

Noah had eaten, showered and changed before Celie awoke again in the early evening. Betty had hovered over her all afternoon, waiting for her to stir. At the first signs of life she came to fetch him in the library, where he was going over a stack of faxes that had arrived during the day.

Celie's room was dimly lit when he entered. He half expected to find her gone. After all, he knew that she was capable of staging amazing disappearances. But she was still there, propped up on two pillows, her arm resting in a sling close to her body. And she was as pale as a proper English ghost.

He stood at the foot of her bed and crossed his arms over his chest. "How do you feel?"

"Like I've been sliced to pieces."

The words were slow and sleepy, but he noted that the accent was British again. "How well do you see without your glasses? Because Goliath ground them to splinters under his feet."

"Well enough."

"Then can you see that I'm waiting for some answers?"

Her shoulders drooped, but her chin lifted. All in all, it was a tie between courage and defeat. "I don't know who you are or what you want from me."

"Why did you take off running, then?" He hesitated. "Maybe I ought to be clearer. Why did you take off running today? From the repair shop? Let's start there and work backward."

"You frightened me. I thought you were going to hurt me."

"Come off it. I didn't threaten you. I told you I just wanted some answers."

"I didn't have any. I didn't know what you were talking about. I still don't."

He waited a moment until he was sure he was in control of himself. "You came very close to dying today. Do you know that?"

"It would be difficult to forget."

"Do you mind telling me why?"

"Why?" She seemed perplexed, although she didn't quite meet his eyes.

"Right. Why someone tried to kill you? This may seem like a small thing to you, but it's fairly significant to me, since he tried to kill me, too."

"I don't *know* why. I don't even know if he was trying to kill me. I think ... I think he had something else in mind. And when I struggled ..."

Noah shook his head. "You told me he was trying to kill you."

"What?"

"That's right. You begged me not to take you to the hospital. You said that if I did, they would find you and kill you. Who are 'they,' Celie? And how does this guy fit in? You've got to tell me or I can't help you."

"Help me?" For once her reaction seemed absolutely genuine. She seemed astounded. "Help me?"

"I fail to see why that's so surprising. I brought you here, didn't I?"

"*You* were the reason I was running away in the first place. You and your ridiculous story about trains and cafés."

"Look, if I wanted you hurt or dead, I would have left you and Goliath alone to slug it out."

She stared straight back at him without blinking. He could see that his logic had made no impression on her. "Don't you think you owe me some sort of explanation?" he continued.

"Why did you bring me here?"

"Apparently my judgment is as poor as your disguises."

"What do you want from me?"

"Just the truth."

She still spoke slowly, as if he were a child or she was still drugged. "My name is Celie Sherwood. I was born in Bourton-on-the-Water. I'm not a nun, and I haven't been to Paris since I was a child. You frightened me with all your questions, and I ran away. I don't know who the man with the knife was."

"All right. Then I can call the police and report this incident? They can take you to the hospital, where you belong, and I can forget the entire episode?"

She swung her legs over the bed. He saw that she was wearing a voluminous flowered nightgown that probably belonged to Betty. Before he could stop her, she slid to her feet.

And swayed.

He skirted the bed just in time to catch her. She sagged in his arms, a tattered, dispirited rag doll. He clasped her against his chest, and for a moment he didn't want to let her go. "I can help you," he murmured against her hair. "Celie, I can help if you'll just tell me what's going on...."

"I have to... get out of here."

"You're too weak to go anywhere by yourself." He sighed. "Look, I'm not trying to keep you here against your will. You can go, if you want. But let me call somebody to come and get you. You lost a fair amount of blood, and you have to keep your arm immobilized while your shoulder heals. You're going to need help for a week or two while you recover."

She didn't answer. Frustration filled him. He wanted to push her away, to forget that she existed, but instead his arms tightened around her. She was trembling from shock, from fear. And then she was sobbing.

"Celie..." He stroked her hair. "Damn it, Celie, who are you, and what the hell is this all about?"

She didn't answer, but the force of her sobs increased. He could feel her fighting them, then feel her efforts fail. She cried silently, as if she had learned a long time ago that tears were something to be ashamed of. That touched him more than he wanted it to.

"Let's get you back to bed." His hand stilled against her hair. "Rest some more, then we'll talk again."

"There's no one to call...." The words were wrung from somewhere deep inside her.

"How about your boss?"

"No! I can't go back there..."

"Okay. Okay. You don't have to." Hands at her waist, he held her away from him. "But you have to tell me what's going on. I can't help if I don't know."

Her face was contorted with pain, and she seemed to grow paler. "I'm afraid...."

"Why?"

"I can't tell you. It would put you in danger, too."

"I'll take my chances."

"Please..."

He shook his head, but he could see that he wasn't going to get any further right now. She was on the brink of collapsing. Before she could, he lifted her off her feet and set her on the bed. "Rest a little while. Then I'm going to get you out of here."

Despite her distress, she hadn't taken her eyes off his face. Now her eyes widened. "Where?"

"Betty, the housekeeper, has a sister who owns a holiday cottage in Kent. We can go there."

"Why?"

"I brought you here by taxi. I'm afraid the police are going to trace us to this house after they find your attacker. He was still breathing when we left him, but he wasn't in good shape. You pack a real wallop with a rock." He folded his arms again, to keep from touching her. She needed comfort, but he wasn't the man to give it to her or any woman. "They're going to come looking, and if they do, the questions I've been asking will seem like child's play. Do you want to stay and answer them, or do you want to go where they won't find you?"

"You said 'we.'"

He frowned, not certain what she meant.

"You said 'we' can go there. You're coming, too?"

"What, do you think I should just turn over the keys to you? House keys, car keys? I'm sorry, but I hardly think I can trust you any more than you trust me."

"Why would you do this for me...?"

He heard the unspoken remainder of the question. *Unless there's something in it for you.* He had asked himself the same thing. What was in this for him? He didn't like the answer, but it was the only answer he could give her. "I'm intrigued," he said. "By you, by the situation." He shrugged. "I don't intrigue easily."

"And you'd put yourself in danger... because you're intrigued?"

He stared at her. She was visibly trembling. She could not do this alone. He was caught in the web she had woven. He turned away. "I have nothing to lose by helping you."

"I can't believe that."

"Believe it." At the door, he paused. "If you want to leave here without me, feel free. If you're still here in an hour when it's fully dark outside, we'll head for Kent."

Her shoulder ached, and the room pivoted on some unseen axis. The man who had sewed up her shoulder had insisted she take pills afterward, and she had been too weak to resist. Now she couldn't think clearly. Was that a result of shock? Blood loss? Or had she been drugged to comply with their wishes? Was this all part of a plan to render her helpless?

But what could they gain that way that they couldn't gain by just killing her?

Celestine bit her lip to keep from moaning. Her mind was still fuzzy, but her shoulder felt as if it were on fire. Her arm was immobilized in a sling against her body, useless. Even if she could remove the sling, she knew the arm wouldn't function. She would faint from the pain if she tried to use it. It was her right arm, too, and she was right-handed.

She rested her head against the pillow and tried to think. What had the man called himself? Noah? Noah wanted her to trust him. He wanted her to tell him the truth. But Noah had been watching her since Paris. He had traced her to the repair shop; then he had mysteriously found her again, just in time to stop Bobby from killing her.

She had been the one to introduce Bobby to the rock. Noah had threatened Bobby, but Noah had been willing to let him go.

This time the moan escaped.

The bedroom door swung open, and the plump woman with the kind eyes came into the room. Betty, Noah had called her. The housekeeper. Or so he had said.

Betty strode toward the bed. "Oh, dearie, the painkiller's wearing off, isn't it? You're going to be uncomfortable for a good long time, I'm afraid."

"Where...where are my clothes?"

"In tatters, I'm sorry to say. But I sent Jerry off to buy you some others."

"I have to go."

"Aye, I expect you do. But you'll like the cottage. A wee one, it is. Stones as old as kingdom come and a pitched roof the birds will roost under if they have their way. There's a loft... But never mind that, you'll see it all soon enough."

"I'm not going...."

Betty frowned. "You've a better place to go?"

Celestine thought that any place had to be better. She had to leave immediately, change her identity again, lose herself in another country, another life.

Except that she had no money with her. None. And all her papers, the passports and birth certificates that she had painstakingly accumulated and paid so dearly for, were back in the attic apartment on New Row. And she couldn't go back there. If Bobby knew, who else knew, as well? Who else had traced her to the apartment and her job? Who might be waiting?

"Miss Sherwood?" Betty perched on the edge of the bed. "You're in some sort of terrible trouble, aren't you?"

Celestine wondered what it would be like to confide in this woman. Her life had been significantly short on people to whom she could talk about anything that really mattered. She had told so many lies that she wasn't even certain she knew how to tell the truth anymore.

Betty shook her head. "If you keep it all bottled up inside, it will take its toll. You understand that, don't you? And if you can't tell us what the problem is, then we can't help you find a solution."

"There is no solution."

"You think not? Well, the swiftest way to find one is by taking the first step. But you must take it soon. Mr....James is certain the police will be here sometime before midnight. That doesn't give you much time to decide where you should go." Betty leaned forward earnestly. "You can trust Mr. James. If he says that he'll help you, he will."

"Who is he?"

Betty smiled a little. "I'm sure he'd rather be the one to tell you about himself. But I can tell you this. He's a good man. And if you don't tell him I said so, I'll tell you this, as well. He's a man who has suffered, and he recognizes it in others."

Celestine sensed that she wasn't going to get anything else out of Betty about Noah James. "Tell me about Kent."

Betty stood. "I should think you could hide there until eternity ends and no one would be the wiser. If you need a place to recover, it will do as well as any."

Celestine realized that she was faced with an impossible choice. Either she had to go back to the apartment on New Row, retrieve her papers and the little money she had stashed away, or she had to trust Noah James and Betty. At least for a little while. There were no other choices. She could not wander injured and penniless until she could arrange to have money wired to her. And she could not leave London without money and papers. She was caught between one alternative that was almost certainly deadly and another that was only a little more promising.

"I'll go to Kent," she said at last.

"All right. Just as soon as Jerry arrives with new clothing, we'll pack you off. Would you like more pills for the pain?" Betty reached into her pocket and held out a plastic container.

"No. I won't be taking any more."

"I'll give them to Mr. James, then, just in case you change your mind. There's no value in misery."

At the doorway, Betty turned. "You've made a good decision. Mr. James will be certain that nothing happens to you. I only hope you'll let him help you put things to rights. It would be the best thing possible for both of you."

Chapter 5

Celie dozed on the way to the cottage. She pulled herself awake frequently, jerking upright as if she were ready to spring from the car. Noah wished she would just relax and give in to her exhaustion, but he supposed he was asking for the impossible. She was always on guard, even when she was white-faced with pain.

He didn't enjoy the drive. He had to concentrate to stay on the correct side of the road, particularly after he left the motorway. He was sure that the country through which they were driving was scenic in the sunshine, but at night it was only a dark haze of rolling hills. He followed Betty's directions carefully, but he still got lost once and had to retrace his route. "Take the first road at the top of the second hill" had not meant the winding driveway leading to a sheep farm buried at the bottom of a low knoll beside a moon-dappled pond.

By the time he pulled up to what he hoped was the right cottage, he was sure that Betty had been correct. This was a nearly perfect place for Celie to hide. If he'd had trouble finding it with detailed directions and an ordnance map, then Celie's pursuers—if there were pursuers—would probably wander through the Kent countryside until they were so thoroughly lost they would never be heard from again.

Celie had not awakened when he turned off the engine, which was a measure of how done in she really was. He sat with his hands on the steering wheel, gazing out at the cottage and wondering what he had gotten himself into.

The cottage was stone, something Betty had called Kentish rag, and about the size of the toolshed on his estate in the Rockies. It stood beside a narrow stream that glistened like a length of silver ribbon in the moonlight. The roof was sharply peaked, as Betty had said, with gables looking over the patch of gravel where he had parked his rental car. There were tall shrubs that bordered a front yard of sorts and a magnificent willow tree that shaded the side of the house closest to the stream. It was picturesque, to be sure, and private. It was also completely unlikely that he and Celie would be able to hide anything from each other here. They would be living in each other's back pockets.

"We're there?"

Noah wasn't surprised Celie had finally opened her eyes. He turned to look at her. "It looks like it. But I won't be completely sure until my key unlocks the front door."

"It's so . . ."

"The word that comes to mind is *small*." Noah opened his door. At the last minute before getting out he turned and pulled the key from the ignition. Celie might be temporarily one-armed, but with her tenacity, she was still capable of stealing the car and driving off into the night. And by the time he found a neighbor who could tell him where to report the theft, she might be a curly-haired brunette serving Wiener schnitzel in Frankfurt or Vienna.

He was halfway to the door when he heard the car door slam. She was following him, which didn't surprise him at all.

The walkway was stone, bordered with knee-high lavender that had dried into spiky gray plumes. Absentmindedly he plucked a shriveled blossom and crumbled it in his hand as he walked. He lifted it to his nose...and he was instantly transported back to a tiny concrete block house in Tarpon Springs, Florida.

For a moment he couldn't take the next step. He couldn't breathe. Lynn was with him as surely as she had been in the days of their marriage. Lynn, who had died because he had not known how to protect her.

"Why did you stop?"

He heard Celie's voice as if from a great distance. His head roared, and despite the chill in the air, he began to sweat. He didn't, couldn't, answer her. He made himself take a step instead. One, then another, until he was standing under the deep overhang at the front door.

The door was painted a brilliant blue. He saw that much and little more. He slid one sweaty hand into his pants pocket and pulled out the ancient key that Betty had given him. He wasn't quite steady, but he managed to insert it into the keyhole and push.

The door swung open.

"There's a light here somewhere." His voice sounded normal. Only he knew how much effort it had suddenly taken to control it.

He found the light switch and flipped it. Two lamps came on, one a floor lamp beside the door, the other a table lamp across the room beside a wide stone fireplace.

The room was, at best, cozy. The walls looked as if they had been plastered by a medieval craftsman with poor eyesight. Massive exposed beams garlanded with dried flowers and vines held up the roof. The farthest end of the downstairs had been partitioned into smaller rooms. A bathroom door was ajar, revealing a room smaller than a walk-in closet. The room beside it, which was only slightly larger, looked as if it contained a double bed and a dresser. There was a narrow hallway beside that room leading to what looked to be a generous kitchen that had been added on some centuries after the bulk of the house had been built.

Celie was still standing outside, or rather, she was leaning on the door frame, as if the walk up the path had sapped
all her strength.

"Come on in and sit," he ordered. "There's a rocking
chair in the corner over there."

She didn't move. He turned and watched her. She was
scanning the room with narrowed eyes, as if her life depended on seeing into every corner and crevice.

"No ghosts or goblins or men in black leather," he said.
"But I wouldn't be surprised if we see a mouse or two. At
least until they've figured out they have company."

She still didn't move. Her eyes had turned to the wooden
steps leading to a narrow loft that ran the length of the
downstairs. The steps were not quite a ladder, not quite
stairs, but something in between. The loft had a low wall
along its edge, but he supposed it was possible for someone
to be crouching there, waiting for the best moment to strike.

"I'll check upstairs, if you'd like," he said.

Her expression didn't change. She clearly thought that his
reassurance would be only slightly better than nothing.

"Celie, you're going to have to trust me if this is going to
work out," he said.

She turned her eyes to him. In the lamplight they were the
soft, innocent blue of a baby's. His son Josh's eyes had been
that same color. But Josh's eyes had never held such suspicion.

He tried for patience. "In your situation I might feel exactly the way you do. Although that's hard to say, since I
don't know what your situation is. But under most circumstances, it's hard to trust a stranger."

"I'm not here because I trust you. I'm here because I have
absolutely no choice."

"Flattery's not your strong suit, is it?" He smiled a little
to let her know he understood at least some of what she was
feeling.

Her gaze wandered his face. She seemed surprised at the
smile, and he supposed she should be. He didn't smile of-

ten. As a boy he had learned that a smile was a breach in the strongest defense.

"Will you check upstairs?" she asked at last.

"Will you still be here when I come back down?"

She nodded. "I'm hardly in condition for a ramble through the weald."

"Weald?"

"That's what we call this part of Kent."

"And you'd know that from all your years of study in English schools?"

She raised a brow. "The upstairs?"

He climbed the steps and scanned the loft. There were several beds there, as if it had once been a communal sleeping area. He could glimpse his car through one of the small windows.

"No one home," he said when he'd returned to the first floor. "I'll just check the back."

"Thank you."

The bedroom and kitchen were much as he had thought they would be at first glimpse. The kitchen was a welcome addition, spacious and airy, with windows looking out on fields and what looked like a thick stand of trees just beyond the cottage. There was a fireplace in the corner, appliances just new enough to qualify as modern and a big scrubbed pine table in the center of the room. He could visualize children around this table and a woman stirring a kettle of bubbling soup at the stove. He could almost hear laughter and the playful teasing of people who loved each other.

But perhaps it had never been that way.

He escaped back through the hall. "We're alone," he told Celie, who was still standing in the doorway. "Let's get you into bed. You look like you're about to collapse."

"Where are you going to sleep?"

"I'll give you first choice. There are beds upstairs and one over there." He pointed to the small bedroom. "Where will you feel safest?"

"In the Alps somewhere. With a vicious St. Bernard for company."

"I wasn't sure you had a sense of humor."

"There has been surprisingly little today to laugh about."

Compassion filled him. He really didn't want to feel anything for Celie Sherwood except curiosity. And he wouldn't have felt compassion if she had been pitiful or helpless. But her strength, her determination, made him think of an Olympic marathon he had once witnessed. One of the runners, a woman, had nearly collapsed at the race's end. But despite obvious distress, despite the fact that she had already lost all chance of a medal, she had finished one wobbling, heart-wrenching step at a time while the crowd cheered her on.

No one seemed to be cheering for Celie. Except, possibly, him.

"I don't like the idea of you on those steps," he said. "You're too weak to negotiate them safely. But if I'm down here, intruders would have to get past me to get to you. So it's your choice."

"Is there a lock on the bedroom door?"

He strode across the room to check. "No. But you could wedge a chair under the knob."

"I'll climb."

"Have it your way. Do you want me to help?"

"No."

"Somehow I didn't think so. Better use the bathroom, get a drink or do whatever it is you have to do now. Because once you've climbed those stairs, you're going to be up there a while. I'll take your bag up while you get ready."

Jerry had shopped and returned with underthings, a sweater and skirt, which Celie was wearing now, a change of clothes and a light raincoat. Betty had added some toiletries, but Celie had little to show for her twenty-some years. She was, in practical terms, the poorest woman he had ever known.

He readied the loft while she was in the bathroom, taking Betty's old nightgown out of the plastic bag containing

Celie's new clothes and laying it across the biggest bed, which he'd made up with fresh linen from a cabinet in the corner. He opened one of the windows and propped it with a stick to start some fresh air circulating; then, when he was sure he had done what he could, he descended and waited for her to emerge.

"I think you should take something to help with the pain," he said when she came out. "Or it's going to be a very long night for you."

"I don't think so."

"Celie, do you really think you could fight me off if I wanted to hurt you? You'd be dead and buried now if that's the way I wanted it. So wise up and take something to help you sleep. Because you're not going to get better if you use up all your resources." He reached in his pocket and held up the pills Betty had provided him with. "You don't even have to let me know what you decide." He held them out to her.

She eyed them carefully; then she held out her hand. Betty had warned him not to give her the entire supply, but this was not a woman who would use them to end the mess she'd made of her life. Celie would go to her reward kicking and screaming.

"There's one more thing." He reached in his pocket and held out his hand again. Lying across his palm was a plain gold ring. "Betty's idea. In case anyone stops by, we'll need to look married. That was one of the ways I knew that Lesley McBain was a fraud, by the way."

She ignored that. "Whose is it? Where did she get it?"

He saw the distaste in her expression, but he held out the ring resolutely. "She said it belonged to someone in her family, but it's not valuable. You're going to have to wear it, Celie. I can get away without one."

She took the ring and slipped it on.

"Does it fit?"

"Well enough."

He nodded. "I'll be right here in the morning. And then we're going to talk."

She turned away. He watched her climb the steps. She wobbled once, and for a heart-stopping moment he thought he was going to have to rescue her. But she finished the climb without his help.

He left his door open, in case she called for him during the night. It was a long time before he was able to fall asleep.

The sunshine woke her, but the noise, or rather the absence of it, was the first thing she really noticed. Since leaving home she had chosen to live in large cities where it was easiest to remain alone and to disappear, if necessary, without causing too large a stir. Small towns, with their universal preoccupation with strangers and gossip, had been off-limits. So it had been a long time since she had heard silence punctuated only by the calling of birds and the rustling of leaves.

Haven House.

For a moment she could almost imagine she was back in North Carolina, lying in the room that had been hers as a child. Mockingbirds sang in a grove of pines, and the air was scented with ocean breezes. Haven House, where she had been safe and protected.

But this wasn't Haven House. And no one had protected her in many years, no one except Stephen, who had died for his efforts.

Celestine heard a new rustling, then the sound of footsteps. She listened warily. Noah James was a stranger to her, a stranger who had followed her through the streets of Paris, a *determined* stranger who had traced her to New Row and beyond. Noah had wrestled Bobby to the ground before Bobby could finish her off, but he had not struck the final blow. She had done that.

Noah had been prepared to let Bobby escape.

She considered that moment again, as she had done repeatedly yesterday. She was convinced that Noah was somehow involved with Bobby and with everyone else who wanted her dead. He claimed to be a stranger who'd just had too much time on his hands in Paris. But she didn't believe him. She just didn't know what he wanted with her.

She had no idea what he *could* want with her. Except her life.

The footsteps sounded as if they were dying away. She tried to remember what the cottage looked like. There had been a short hallway to a room in the back. A kitchen, most likely. Perhaps Noah was going there.

She slowly edged herself upright. Her shoulder throbbed as if Bobby's knife were still embedded in it. She had slept only fitfully. She had been in too much pain to sleep well, and she had refused to take the pain medication. She had only taken the pills from Noah because she had been afraid he might use them in her food. Funny the way she had learned to think in the past four years. If she wasn't truly paranoid, she could do an excellent imitation.

Maybe no one else was trying to kill her at all. Maybe Bobby was just a maniac with a knife, a modern day Jack the Ripper who chose his victims at random. Maybe he looked for blondes, or women in suits.

Maybe everything that had happened to her in the past four years was a coincidence, an accident, or simply a product of her fevered imagination.

Sure.

She pushed away her doubts. She knew they assailed her at moments like these because they had been planted deep inside her from the moment that Haven House had become a battleground and not a haven at all. But she didn't have to listen, and she didn't have to heed them.

She dressed with considerable difficulty. The clothes that had been bought for her were roomy and shapeless. She carefully slid her arm from the sling and threaded it through the sleeve of the cardigan she had worn yesterday.

She nearly blacked out with the pain, just as she had last night when she had taken off the sweater.

Helpless tears filled her eyes. What would she do if Noah stopped playing whatever game this was and came after her today? She had the scissors from the mending kit she'd

taken off the nightstand at his house in Kensington, but they
were a poor weapon. If Noah tried to kill her, all the odds
were on his side. And he had certainly come far enough
from civilization to keep anyone from finding her body.

But what benefit would her death be to anyone unless her
body was found and identified?

She heard the footsteps again below her. Then a creaking
noise. At first she thought Noah was coming up the stairs,
and she felt for the scissors, which she'd placed under her
pillow last night. But the noise continued and continued,
and Noah didn't appear. She managed to get her arm back
in the sling and tuck the scissors in the bottom fold; then she
got to her feet and edged over to the side, placing her feet
with care so that he didn't hear her. She stayed as low as she
could without crawling until she reached the wall that
looked over the room below.

Noah was sitting in a rocking chair in the corner by the
fireplace with a large black cat curled up on his lap.

For a moment she almost couldn't believe it. She had en-
visioned a murderer stalking her one furtive step at a time.
The man in the rocking chair looked like anything but an
assassin. As he rocked slowly back and forth he stared at the
cat with something akin to fascination. But he made no attempt to push it away.

He was dressed in jeans—good ones, judging from the
cut—and a partially buttoned forest green shirt that was
tucked haphazardly into them. His hair was rumpled, and
his feet were bare. He looked sleepy, slightly grumpy, perhaps, and surprisingly—considering her fears—attractive.

It had been a long time since Celestine had seen a man in
the early morning. She had forgotten how appealing a day's
growth of beard could be, how provocative the glimpse of
a man's chest. She'd only had one lover, and over the years
she had forced herself not to think of him. They had been
young and breathless with the excitement of their liaison.
And now, of course, he was dead because of her.

She wondered exactly who this man was. Really was.

"Do you know anything about these creatures?"

Celestine wondered how long Noah had known she was watching him. She straightened so that she could look over the wall with more ease. "Black cats are bad luck."

"Then I imagine one crossed my path the day I saw you in Paris."

"I haven't been to Paris—"

"Since you were a child. And you've never ridden the Eurostar or pretended you were a dumpy moral crusader. I remember all that."

"Really? I rather thought you didn't remember. You keep trying to trip me up."

"I opened the back door to look outside and this—" he pointed to the cat "—came waltzing in. What do you suppose it wants?"

"Mice?"

"It seems a bit too contented for a mouser. They're lean and hungry, aren't they? Not that I know anything about cats."

"I always had cats as a child." She wondered why she had blurted that out. Not that it was much in the way of an admission of any sort, but she was going to have to be more careful.

"I never had a pet."

"You seem to be taking to it quite nicely."

"How did you sleep?"

"Quite well, thank you."

"You're an amazing liar. One of the best I've ever encountered."

"What makes you think I'm lying about that?"

"Because in the wee hours, when you finally did sleep a little, you moaned. You're in a lot of pain, and you probably haven't taken a single pill to combat it." He looked up from the cat. "Are you coming down?"

She navigated the steps with considerable care. When she was safely down, he shooed the cat from his lap and stood. "I made coffee. Would you like some?"

"Please."

He started for the kitchen, and she followed after a stop in the little bathroom. The cat, bushy tail held high, waited for her, then followed, too.

The kitchen was a nice surprise, sunshine-flooded and spacious. Noah waved her to the table in the middle of the room, and she sat where she could see him best. The cat jumped up on a chair in the corner and curled up for a nap.

"We drink a lot of coffee in the States," he said as he poured her a cup from an old-fashioned percolator. "I live out West. We drink it strong and black. That's a Southern tradition, too, I think." He looked up. "Isn't it?"

For a moment she forgot to breathe. He seemed to be waiting for something.

He knew.

She kept her voice calm and her accent carefully English. "I wouldn't know. I've never been to your country."

"Haven't you? You've never been to Georgia or the Carolinas? Then how did you learn the accent?"

"I don't know what you mean." She reached for the cup, and he handed it to her.

"I could swear, Celie, that right after you were injured and before you could remember who you were pretending to be, you spoke with an American accent, Southern-style."

"You have a truly splendid imagination."

"Maybe I do. Let me see if I can use it to make up a story."

"Oh do, this should be good."

He leaned against the counter, arms folded across his chest. "Once there was a young woman on the run. I don't know what she was running from, exactly, but she was terrified. So she crossed an ocean to put distance between herself and whatever she feared, and she took on new identities and accents. She was very good at hiding, as it turns out, but she made one serious mistake. She didn't realize that her walk was unusual, unusual enough to be notable. And because she didn't, a man who likes to study people noticed her. And strangely enough, he noticed her again when she was trying to become somebody else. And he knew she was the same person, despite the many changes she had made.''

The wedding ring on her left hand glinted in the sunlight as Celie swirled her coffee and thought about what he'd said. It was absolutely true, at least the part about her, and the longer she tried to deny this much of the story, the harder he would dig for the rest of it.

If he didn't already know the rest of it.

''Why are you trying to help me?'' she asked at last.

''Damned if I know.''

She nodded.

He opened a cabinet and reached for bowls. ''Would you like cereal? Betty sent some along. We have enough supplies to keep us a day or two before we have to find a store.''

''Yes. Thanks.''

He placed a carton of milk on the table, and she put down her cup so that she could add some to her coffee. It was a frustrating experience. Two arms had not been a whimsical heavenly decision.

''Are you right-handed?'' he asked after he set a blue crockery bowl filled with muesli and milk in front of her.

There was nothing to be gained from lying about that. The answer would be apparent soon enough. ''Yes.''

''Let me know if you need help.''

It would be a cold day in hell before she asked, and she suspected he knew it. She lifted the spoon in her left hand and began to teach herself to eat with it.

''So, are you going to tell me the truth?'' he asked, when he was settled across from her. ''Because I've taken about all the chances I intend to take with you. For all I know you're on the run from the police, and I'm aiding and abetting a criminal.''

''You're not.''

''Why should I believe you?''

It was a fair question—if he was truly the innocent man he claimed to be.

She was halfway through her cereal before she answered. She wished he wouldn't watch her eat. She was at a decided disadvantage, and the table around her bowl was quickly covered with milk splatters and cereal crumbs. Her shoulder ached, and she had never felt so exhausted. She wanted to put her head on the table and sob, but there was no way she could do that. She put down her spoon and looked up at him. His face was a blank mask. He was waiting for her explanation.

"You first," she said. "How can I trust you with the story of my life if you haven't told me anything about yourself?"

He refolded his arms and slid to a more comfortable position against the counter as if he intended to stay there a long, long time. "This is a delaying tactic."

"Who are you? Something besides a name, please. And why does anything about me matter to you?"

He appeared to be considering whether he would answer or not. "I'm a consultant. I work with large corporations on ways to include safety features in their products. I travel extensively, which is why I happened to be in Paris the first time I saw you."

"What kind of corporations?"

"The ones that hire me." He shrugged. "I head a team of experts in a variety of fields. I'm the front man, more or less."

To her ears it was all very vague and impossible to check out. "The house where you took me. Is it yours?"

"No. I'm doing some consulting for a company that keeps it for the use of their executives. I was invited to stay there."

"Does that company have a name?"

"Tri-C International."

The name meant nothing to her. "For someone who was just passing through, you seemed on fairly intimate terms with the housekeeper."

"I've worked for Tri-C before, lived there before. Betty and I are old friends."

"Why do you study people?"

He didn't answer for a moment, as if he were weighing alternatives. "I found out a long time ago that watching people was a lot smarter than becoming intimate with them. In my job, I need to understand what makes people tick. Being able to tell the truth from a lie is absolutely vital in what I do. But personal involvement can cloud judgment. So I watch, I stay objective, and I learn."

"And as a side benefit, nobody can hurt you. Interesting." She sipped her coffee. Some of what Noah said had made sense with the little she did know about him. He definitely traveled. If he was successful enough to work with large corporations, he was probably wealthy enough to afford tailored suits and expensive ties. And maybe he really had gathered a lot of useful information by paying attention to the people around him. Maybe he'd even paid enough attention to notice when something was out of the ordinary.

"Are we done?" he asked.

"If you're a consultant, shouldn't you be consulting? Can you afford to just take time off this way? Don't you have deadlines to meet? And what about a family who expect you to come home?"

"No family. And my schedule is flexible as long as I can send and receive faxes."

"We're in the middle of nowhere."

"I have a portable computer with fax capability. And there's a phone in my bedroom."

That was welcome news. Now she wished she hadn't chosen the loft.

"It's your turn...." Noah picked up his cup from the counter and made a mock toast with it. "Don't let anything stop you. I have all day."

She shook her head. "You know, you've just described a life with no ties to speak of. No family, a job as flexible as any I've ever heard of, a life on the road. You could almost be describing the life of a professional hit man. And the only thing you would need besides a computer with fax capability would be a gun."

"I'm fresh out of bullets at the moment."

"If I call Tri-C International, will anyone there have heard of you?"

"If you reach the right people, certainly. But I'm not an employee, and I'm not on the company roster."

"How utterly convenient."

"Why would I want to kill you, Celie?"

She was saved from having to answer by a crash at the back door. She ducked, automatically shielding herself behind the table. Noah leaped forward, but not in time to prevent the door from flying open.

"There she is, the wicked darling!" A tall woman in burlap-sack brown strode into the kitchen, straight to the corner and grabbed the sleeping cat from its chair. "She will not stay home, will you, Snow White? She simply will not cooperate with any plans I have for her. And how clever of you to keep her here until I could find her."

The woman held the now protesting Snow White high above her head and swung her back and forth. Then she clutched the cat to her ample bosom. "Now, good morning to you both. How long have you been married, if you don't mind me asking, and what exactly can I do for you while you're in Trillingden?"

Chapter 6

The woman looked so expectant that Noah couldn't follow his first inclination and shoo her out the door. She wasn't old so much as ageless. Her hair was the color of her sweater and tweed skirt, but heavily threaded with gray. Her skin was a healthy pink, webbed with a hundred fine lines. She was a large woman, big-boned and vigorous, and her smile made it clear that she expected immediate answers to her queries.

"My name is Marian Farnsworth," she said, as if that set everything straight immediately. She stuck out her hand.

"Mrs. Farnsworth." Noah took her hand. "I'm Noah James."

"Knew some Jameses over Charing way. A rather paltry lot they were. I hope you're not related to them?" She turned to Celie. "If you are, you will need to think carefully about having children, my dear."

Noah harvested a smile before it could bloom out of control. Celie looked as if someone had just lobbed a grenade in the kitchen and she had forgotten to duck.

"I'll remember that." Celie nodded.

Noah rested his hand on Celie's left shoulder, like a new husband might. "You don't have to worry. I don't have any family here that I know of. And if I do, they're a hundred times removed."

"Can't be too careful, I always say." Marian squinted at him carefully. "Blood will tell. I breed sheep, of course, and I understand these things. There's a lot to be learned from sheep."

"This is my...wife, Celie," Noah said. He turned toward Celie and lifted one brow, silently daring her to correct him.

"Newlyweds, or fairly so. Yes, I know. I'm surprised to find you out of bed at this hour." Marian extended her hand to Celie, whose skin color had gone from ghost-pale to a healthier pink. "I'll take your left hand, dear, since your right seems occupied in that absurd contraption."

Celie shook, then took her left hand back quickly. She glanced down, as if to be certain she still had fingers.

Noah answered Marian's initial question. "We've been married just two weeks, but we've hardly had a chance to be alone since."

"Well, I won't bother you. Not often, anyway. But we will be having a tea in your honor tomorrow afternoon, of course. My place, the next farm east. And all the neighbors will be there to look you over, so you'll certainly want to attend. We think quite highly of Joan and Betty, and if they've sent you here, then we shall approve of you, as well. Just as soon as we've had the opportunity."

Celie was the first to speak. "I don't think—"

Marian waved her free hand in the air. "Absolutely do not thank me. We're a tightly knit community. And we tolerate no strangers in our midst. So you shall be our friends, instead." She stopped waving her hand long enough to glance at a man-size watch adorning her wrist. "And now I must go. Three o'clock tomorrow afternoon, and don't be late. And if Snow White comes to visit again, don't concern yourselves. I'll just come back and collect her. She's a wicked, wicked cat, our Snow White."

She was gone as quickly as she had appeared. Noah watched her march away, the immobile cat locked under her arm as if it always rode there.

"What was that?" Celie asked at last.

"A product of the pastoral Kent countryside."

"Wildwoman of the weald."

"I suppose that if you live here, you learn to get straight to the point on those rare occasions when there's someone new to talk to." Noah tightened his grip on Celie's good shoulder before she could turn away. "Don't go anywhere, Celie. We may have suffered an extraordinary interruption in the conversation, but we're not finished here. Not even close."

She shrugged off his hand. "I'm finished for now, even if you're not. I'm not feeling well at all."

Noah knew a stall when he heard one, but he knew that at the same time she was telling the truth. The color had gone from her cheeks again, and she swayed visibly, although her chin was still stubbornly lofted in the air.

He had to force himself not to steady her. Yesterday he had learned the slender perimeter of her waist, the womanly swell of her hips. He had been too preoccupied to think much about how good she felt, how wonderfully soft and female. But those impressions had lingered. As he had fallen asleep last night he had thought about the way her flesh had felt against his as he'd carried her up to the bedroom and about the silky length of her hair brushing his hands and arm. Even as she lay in the loft above him and moaned in pain.

He'd also thought about how absurdly sexual attraction would complicate this arrangement.

He reminded himself of that once more and let her sway. But he stayed close, in case he had to catch her. "Will you at least take aspirin? It won't affect the clarity of your thoughts. And you'll still be able to stab me with those ridiculous scissors if I try to wring your neck or shoot you with my nonexistent gun."

"Scissors?"

"The outline is obvious from this angle. Are they the ones I used to cut off your clothes yesterday?"

"You cut off my clothes?"

"Yes. And if I'd wanted you dead, that would have been a wonderful time to kill you. You were lying on the bed half-naked and unconscious. I could have done whatever I wanted with you."

She pondered that, but she didn't meet his eyes, as if the vision of that kind of intimacy was disturbing. "I'd like aspirin."

"Sit." He pointed to the chair.

She was sitting when he turned back from the sink with a glass of cold well water and two tablets from a bottle Betty had sent along. "Here." He put them in front of her. "I should have given you these last night, but I really thought you'd be smart enough to take the others."

She swallowed the pills as if she were already willing them to take effect.

"You'll feel better soon."

"I'm sure you're right."

"And in the meantime, you can answer some more questions."

"I would really like to rest."

She did look as if she couldn't endure an interrogation at the moment. Frustrated, he nearly said he would wait. Then he remembered the willow-shaded stream he had seen last night. "Fine. I know just the place."

She drew her shoulder blades together stubbornly. "The loft will be fine."

"I've got a better idea." Noah opened the back door and peered outside. "We've got to be careful not to let that cat in again, or Marian will be living in our kitchen."

"Betty said we would be isolated."

"Betty has a few things to answer for." Noah stepped outside; then he jerked his head toward the woods just beyond them. "It's a short walk. Think you can make it?"

"All right."

He was surprised. He had fully expected that he would need to persuade her, but perhaps she thought it was better to be outside than alone inside with him.

It was a clear morning, with no sign of the rain clouds that had helped hide their escape both from Bobby and London. The air was warming already, and it promised to be one of those beautiful days of late summer when every gardener in England yearned to be outdoors. He followed a stone path bordered by bushes with graceful conical blooms. A cloud of small white butterflies lifted as he approached but didn't fly far, as if they expected to settle back to collecting nectar as soon as he'd passed.

"Butterfly bushes," Celie said.

He turned and saw her reaching for a deep purple blossom. "That's really what they're called?"

"For obvious reasons. Officially, buddleia. This one is probably Black Knight."

"So you're a gardener?"

"Not really." She hesitated, then shrugged. "I worked at a plant nursery for a while."

He couldn't let the opportunity go by. "As Celie Sherwood? Or Marie St. Germaine?"

She ignored the question. "Smell them. It's a subtle fragrance, but lovely, I think."

He remembered his encounter with the lavender last night and declined. "It's not much farther."

"Don't worry about me."

It was excellent advice. He didn't want to worry about anyone. He had lived his life that way for years, and he had no intention of changing. But since the day he had first seen this woman, she had engaged his emotions. And one of those emotions was concern. He was wary of her and whatever demons pursued her, but, despite everything, he wanted to protect her.

They turned at the edge of the woods and started down toward the stream.

"How pretty." Celie stopped and gazed at the water just below them. It was lined on both sides with rocks, some large and flat enough for good sunbathing.

"Even prettier than I expected. And there's a good place to sit." He pointed to a rock with another behind it to lean against. "Can you make it down?"

"Yes."

He really didn't want to touch her again. But he didn't want to pick her up off the path, either. The climb down wasn't steep, but she was barely on the road to recovery. He held out his hand. "Come on. I'll help you."

"I'll be fine."

"No, you won't." He took a step back toward her and took her hand. "Come on."

She didn't try to pull away, but she didn't move.

"Look, Celie, I'm not much fonder of this arrangement than you are. But I'm not going to let you stumble and hurt yourself. I'll help you now, but the moment you don't need my assistance I'll stop. Fair enough?"

He didn't wait for an answer. He started down, and after a moment of resistance she sighed and followed, allowing him to keep her hand in his.

She was safely settled before he released her. He chose a spot several feet from where she was stretched out against the rock, so that she wouldn't feel crowded. He settled himself in a comfortable position and waited for her to speak.

The only sounds he heard for minutes were the songs of birds and the ripple of water swirling gently around rocks. The sun was warm against his face, and he rolled up the sleeves of his shirt while he waited. A car passed the cottage, and somewhere not too far away a dog barked in response.

"What do you want to know?" she asked at last.

"Start at the beginning. Finish with the ending."

"You're right. I'm running away."

He turned a little so that he could see her face. She wasn't looking at him. He suspected she was looking into her past, twisting it, editing it, choosing splinters of it to share with him. But even that was an improvement.

"That's not exactly the beginning," he said. "Why don't we start with your name?"

"Call me Celie Sherwood."

"But you're *not* Celie Sherwood."

"No. You're right about that."

He felt the smallest thrill of victory. "Wouldn't you enjoy hearing the sound of your real name?"

"The last time I heard my real name, a man was trying to kill me."

"Bobby?"

"Yes."

"Then you don't really think he was just some Jack the Ripper wanna-be. You think it was up close and personal?"

"Most of the time that's what I think."

"Most of the time?"

"When you're running, you don't have much perspective. I thought Bobby said my name, but I'm not sure. You develop instincts, but sometimes they fail you."

"Yours failed that day in Paris."

"I don't want to talk about Paris anymore."

"Does that mean you're admitting you were also Marie St. Germaine?"

"No, it doesn't."

He bit off an angry response. He was pushing too hard. And if she was going to share anything with him, it was going to have to be at her own speed and in her own way. "I'm sorry. Go on. Tell me what you can."

She faced him, and she searched his face. He saw her questions. What could she say? And how far could she trust him? On a journey of one hundred miles she had taken only the first baby step.

"I witnessed a murder." She waited for his reaction. He was careful not to have one. "The man who was killed was . . ." She took a deep breath. ". . . my lover."

"Are you afraid that whoever killed him wants to kill you, too?"

"I know they do."

"They?"

She turned away. "That was a figure of speech."

"Then you don't know who the murderer was?"

"No."

"I see." Of course, he didn't really see. There was obviously much more to the story than this.

"The murderer thinks I know his identity. He wants me dead, too," she said.

Now she was using "he." He wondered if she was trying to purposely mislead him. "Wouldn't it have been a lot simpler just to go to the police and ask for protection?"

"Do you really think they would have the resources to help?"

"No," he admitted. "Probably not."

"That's what I thought, too. So I ran away—"

"From where?"

She immediately fell silent.

"Celie, I have good reason to suspect you're an American like me. Can't you at least tell me that much? It's a big country, with millions of people. That's not asking much in the way of information."

"The less you know, the better for us both."

"Why? Because you want to protect me? Or because you still don't trust me?"

"You're in good company. I can't trust anybody."

"So what is your plan? To change identities, move from country to country for the rest of your life? How do you pull that off? Faked passports? The birth certificates of dead people or people who've dropped out of normal society?"

"I'm not going to tell you anything else."

He wondered if the little she had told him was true. If it was, there was one more question she had to answer. "Did you have anything to do with this murder? Is it the law you're running from?"

"No!"

Her answer was so immediate and forceful that he believed her. He might be wrong. She was a stunningly accomplished liar, but this once, he thought she was telling the truth.

"Okay."

She was silent for a while. She had said she was finished, but then she spoke. "Why were you going to let Bobby go?"

"Let him go?"

"Yes, after the worst of the fight. You were going to let him go until I hit him with the stone."

"What should I have done? Slit his throat right then and there? I doubted somehow that I could trust you to go for the police. And there was no one around to help me keep him there. I either had to kill Bobby or release him. And I don't see myself as a casual executioner."

"Maybe you knew him."

"Maybe we were in it together? Maybe I knew he was taking you to that spot?"

She shrugged.

"You're not thinking straight. How could I possibly have known you'd go running to Bobby after you left the repair shop? Even if he and I are in league, how would we have known what you'd do?"

She didn't answer.

He continued. "You say that someone wants you dead. I've had a dozen easy chances to kill you since I found you in that alley. I haven't harmed a hair on your head. In fact, I brought you here to protect you. Doesn't that say something to you?"

"This has gone beyond easy explanations. The moment I trust someone, the moment I let down my guard..."

"Bobby wasn't the first to come after you, was he?"

"No." She met his eyes. "No, he wasn't the first. Why do you think I'm running?"

"How many times? How many close calls?"

"Enough."

There was something about the way she said the word that told him volumes. She had moved beyond fear for her life.

She was resigned to death, expected it at any moment. She had been so threatened, so haunted, that she had learned to accept the reality of her situation, even as she fought against it with every breath.

"Celie." He shook his head. "I can't imagine what it's like to be you."

"I tell myself it's like having a terminal disease. I don't have symptoms, but death is always waiting just ahead. Only in my case, the old grim reaper is going to jump out from behind a bush someday. I'll never know what hit me. Or who."

"Do you really believe that?"

"Most of me believes it. There's just the tiniest part of me that believes I'll come through this alive, that I'll defeat whoever is after me and someday I won't have to run at all."

"How can you defeat someone whose identity you don't know?"

"One small defeat at a time. Like getting away from Bobby. Like surviving this." She pointed to her shoulder.

"Like changing your identity again and disappearing to Fiji or the Australian outback?"

A flash of humor sparkled in her eyes. "The outback, mate? What's there for a sheila like me? Think I'd make a dinkum jilleroo?"

He marveled at the way she'd switched on the thick Aussie accent and slang. "Sounds like you've already been there."

"When I was a little girl I used to wish I could see the world. My friends wanted to be ballerinas or pediatricians. I wanted to wade in the Antarctic and climb Mount Everest." She actually smiled. "Not necessarily at the same time."

"I think you've gotten some of what you wished for."

"Perhaps."

"But not the way you wanted." He leaned toward her. Her smile changed to something more suspicious the closer he moved. "Let me help you."

"What could you do?"

"I have connections. I can make sure you're safe. I can help you find out who's doing this to you."

"I travel alone."

"If you'd been traveling alone in that alley you'd be six feet under about now."

"Who's to say I won't be six feet under soon enough?"

"No one. But your chances are a damn sight better if you have some help." He straightened. "It's your life, Celie. And I'm a stranger. I don't really blame you for not trusting me. Your situation has made you paranoid—"

"I'm not paranoid! I haven't imagined any of this. It's real. I'm in constant danger, and it's real!"

He stared at her. One word had been important enough to make her abandon all pretense of reserve. "I meant your experiences have made you extremely cautious," he said. "And that's all I meant. I was in that alley, remember? I know you're not imagining the danger."

"I'd like to go back up to the house."

"All right." He stood and held out a hand. "But think about what I've said. I can help you. I'd like to, if you'll give me a chance. But I have to know the truth. All of it. And that means you're going to have to trust me."

She didn't answer, and she didn't take his hand. She used her good arm to push herself upright. They walked back to the cottage in silence.

By late afternoon Celestine was still waiting for Noah to go out so that she could use the telephone. They had hardly spoken since their encounter at the stream. She had rested; he had fixed lunch, which she had eaten alone in the loft; she had rested again.

She didn't know much about Noah James, but she did know he wasn't a man who liked enforced leisure. Early in the afternoon she'd heard the soft hum of his portable computer, and she'd wondered exactly what he was doing. Was he transacting business with Tri-C International or one of the other companies he purported to consult with?

Or was he contacting Millie or Roger? Was he telling them, via computer, that she was firmly in his grasp and it was only a matter of time until the problem of Celestine St. Gervais no longer existed?

She listened for footsteps. He walked back and forth between his room and the kitchen, but he never approached the loft. She wouldn't allow herself to sleep, which she badly needed, but she closed her eyes and drifted for part of the afternoon. When she finally heard the click of the front door, she got up and peered over the edge of the loft. She could just see Noah walking to his car. She edged her way down the steps until she had a better view. He opened the car door and reached inside for something—sunglasses, she thought. Then he closed the door and started toward the road on foot.

She didn't know where he was going or why, but her chance had arrived. She headed for the little room where he was sleeping, to search for the telephone.

She was pleased to see that he had already turned off his computer and disconnected it from the outlet. Moments later, after calculating the time difference between England and North Carolina, she was dialing. There were only three people she trusted in the world, three people who needed to be told where she was and why. She knew she might not have time to call them all, but she had to call the most vital.

When a woman answered, she gave the name she and Whit Sanderson had agreed on so long ago and waited.

The wait took a while. The telephone cord reached nearly to the bedroom door, and she had a clear view of the walkway to the cottage. She could hang up if Noah returned and be out of his bedroom before he opened the door. She gripped the receiver and prayed Whit would hurry.

"Celestine!"

"Oh, Whit." She closed her eyes for a moment in gratitude. "I was afraid I wasn't going to reach you."

"Where are you? Are you all right?"

"Yes. No." She laughed, and it almost sounded like a sob. "I was attacked, but I'm all right."

"What happened?"

"I can't go into it now. But I had to leave everything behind, Whit. I don't have a dime to my name. Can you wire me something to help me get started again?"

"You know I can. Where? How?"

"I don't know that yet. Just get the money together. I'll call you back with details."

"If you tell me where you are, I can find out where the closest bank is and make the arrangements."

She hesitated. She knew the name of the village. Trillingden. But Whit didn't need to know that. She could endanger him by giving him too much information. And although she trusted him as much as she trusted anyone in the world, she was too wary to tell anyone more than they had to know. "I'm not sure where I am, exactly," she said.

He didn't press her. "Do you have any identification?"

"Nothing."

"That's going to make it difficult. But I'll find a way."

"Thank you. Thank you so much."

"It's your money, Celestine. It's my job to take care of it for you."

"I'm not going to be able to call Allie or Grandpa Sutter. Can you call them for me? Tell them I'm all right?"

"Of course. Anything else?"

"Yes. Please. I'm with a man named Noah James. He swears he's a consultant for a company called Tri-C International. Have you ever heard of it?"

"Of course. It's one of those giant conglomerates that have their hands in everything. Manufacturing, mining, communications..."

"Can you see if he's for real?"

"His name is Noah James?"

"That's what he says."

"How did you meet him? What's the connection?"

"I don't have time to tell you. And I can't tell you the number here because I don't have it. It's not on the telephone."

"Give me a day or two to make the arrangements. Can you wait that long?"

"I think I'm okay."

"When are you coming home? It's almost time to make your move. But you've got to be here to do it. I can't do anything without you."

She saw movement on the road again. Noah turned down the walkway. "I have to go. I'll call again. Tomorrow."

She hung up before he could reply. She was sitting in the rocking chair by the fire when Noah opened the door. She looked up, as if he had surprised her. "Where have you been?"

"I went for a walk."

"Have a nice one?"

"Just to the top of the hill. It was so dark last night I couldn't tell for sure how close the neighbors were."

"And?"

"As the crow flies, not too far. Half a mile or so through the woods and across the fields behind us. That must be the Farnsworth house. But there's not another one in sight from the road. We really are in the middle of nowhere."

She was struck again by how easy Noah was on the eye. The same light wind now whistling through the chinking of the stones had whipped color into his cheeks and ruffled his hair. He stood in the doorway with his hands thrust into the pockets of his jeans and his eyes probing every corner of the room. She thought he was probably a man who was used to having his own way, a man who took control and didn't relinquish it easily. She supposed that she had confounded him, and the thought pleased her somehow.

But it would be small comfort if he betrayed her.

He stepped forward and closed the door behind him. "How are you feeling?"

She grimaced. "I'll be happy when I have two arms again, but under the circumstances, all right."

"I have to change the bandage. Shall we do it now? Or after dinner?"

She wanted to tell him that she would do it herself. But she knew how futile that would be. He could do a better job, and the quicker her shoulder healed, the sooner she could start assembling a new identity. "Let's get it over with."

"Stay there. It's as good a place as any. I'll get what I need."

She rocked and waited as he rummaged around in his room. She wondered if he would notice anything out of place near the telephone. She had been careful, but had she been careful enough?

He returned with a makeshift medical kit that she knew Betty had put together for him. He adjusted the lamp, then crossed his arms. "You're going to have to take off the sweater. Do you need my help?"

She had been thinking about the telephone call. She hadn't even considered that she would have to undress. Instinctively she clasped the top button of her cardigan. "I can do it."

He crouched in front of her before she could move. "Let me help. It doesn't make any sense for you to take three times as long to do it alone. Either way, I still get the same view."

She realized it would be stupid to protest. She let him unhook the sling strap and gently remove it. She had secreted the scissors in the pocket of her skirt, a pathetic attempt to hide them again. Her fingers closed around them like a good luck talisman.

"That must have hurt." Noah folded the sling and set it on the mantel.

"I'm fine."

"Those will be your dying words."

"Later rather than sooner, I hope."

He smiled. It was a quick flash of warmth that surprised her. Everything about him changed for that moment, and suddenly he wasn't a man to be feared. Just a man. A remarkably attractive man who was about to undress her.

"I can do this part." She reached again for the top button and slid it through the hole.

Noah closed his eyes. "Looks like I'll have time for a nap."

"Think of it as physical therapy. I'll be fully ambidextrous by the time I'm finished." She unbuttoned the second button.

He opened his eyes again. "And I'll be starving."

"Are you going to cook for us tonight? Or did Betty send something along?"

"I'm cooking."

She managed to unbutton the third button. "Why do I have the feeling that you don't know your way around a kitchen?"

"Because I left the wrapper on the ham in your sandwich this afternoon?"

"So you left it on yours, too." The fourth button departed its hole.

"I eat out most of the time."

"What about when you're home? You said you were from the West. Where exactly is home, by the way?"

"Somewhere within two or three thousand miles of yours, wherever that is."

She had only one button left by the time she spoke again. "I am an American."

The expression in his eyes warmed appreciably. "Thank you."

"And now I can drop the accent." She said the words in the same way she would have in the years before she'd been forced to run.

"From the South, I take it?"

She didn't respond directly. "And you're from . . . ?"

"Colorado."

"Always?"

"No. I grew up in Los Angeles."

"Will you help me with my sleeve?"

"Is it tomorrow yet?" He smiled again before he gently lifted her injured arm and began to tug on the sweater cuff.

She gritted her teeth, but she didn't make a sound. His eyes met hers, and concern, or a good imitation, shone in them. ''We have to keep a close watch for infection. I know you don't want any setbacks.''

She thought about how odd it was that the man she had suspected of wanting to kill her was now trying to repair the damage inflicted by a man she had trusted—as much as she trusted anyone. She still didn't trust Noah James or the way he had come into her life, but at the moment she was having trouble dredging up the necessary suspicion. She couldn't recall anyone touching her with more gentleness or compassion. And she couldn't recall being this close to a man and this vulnerable since Stephen's death.

''Why are you helping me?'' she asked. ''Why are you *really* helping me?''

He paused in the act of smoothing away the side of her sweater so that the bandage was clearly exposed. ''I don't know. Because you need it, I suppose.''

''Do you help everyone who needs you?''

''Most of the time I don't know if people need me or not.''

''Because you don't get close enough to find out?''

He made a noise that could have been yes or no, but she pushed on as if he'd said yes. ''You wouldn't have gotten this close if I hadn't had you detained at Waterloo.''

''Better be careful, Celie. You just admitted that Lesley was you.''

''One of my more unappealing roles.''

He finished removing the sweater. The air was cool against her bare skin, and she suddenly felt exposed in every way. She was wearing a bra, but she had unhooked the strap on her injured shoulder to keep it from rubbing against the bandage. She knew that the cup hung open, only partially covering her breast. Noah's eyes flicked to her shoulder, then lower. She didn't know what to say, or even what she wanted to. She could imagine him touching more than her shoulder, more than the bandage, and the thought wasn't unwelcome. His hands were warm and gentle, but for the briefest moment she imagined them giving pleasure, not comfort.

"This is going to hurt." Noah rested his fingers against the bandage. The heel of his hand rested against her breast. "Take a deep breath."

She closed her eyes and pressed her lips together. He made quick enough work of the old bandage, but tears stung her eyes anyway.

"I'm sorry." His voice was husky.

She nodded. "Had to be done."

"Are you all right?"

She opened her eyes. "How does it look?"

"No worse than yesterday. I assume that's good news."

"Probably."

"I'll clean it now, and cover it back up. Are you with me?"

She nodded. By the time he was sealing the wound with another sterile pad and tape, she was breathing more easily again.

He didn't move away. "I'll help you back into that sleeve." He slid his hand behind her, along her shoulder blades, searching for the rest of the sweater. He leaned closer as he searched, nearly close enough to brush her breasts with his chest.

She was acutely aware of him as a man. Not as a mysterious stranger. Not as a rescuer. But as a man who was close enough to kiss. She had the strangest urge to lift her good arm and thread her fingers through his hair. She could feel Noah's warmth; she wanted to feel his strength. She told herself it was relief that moved her so, along with gratitude, but although she was an accomplished liar, she never lied to herself. She was feeling something else, something much more elemental. Something perilously close to desire.

"Got it," he said. He laughed a little and met her eyes, as if to see whether she was laughing at his clumsiness, too. Then the laugh died, and the expression in his eyes warmed. He didn't move away, and he didn't try to slip her arm back through the sleeve.

"I can take it from here." Her words were softly spoken. Almost whispered.

"Take what?"

The question hung between them. Both of them knew what he really meant. Neither of them would admit it.

"You were right when you thought this would be a dangerous arrangement," Noah said at last. He sat back on his heels, but his eyes never left hers.

"I can defend myself against anything."

"Can you?" He looked skeptical. He looked angry, too, but she didn't know at whom.

"Don't take that as a challenge, Noah. Just leave me alone, and I'll do the same for you."

"Like it or not, we're in this together. For a little while, at least." He rose to his feet. "But don't worry that I'll force you into anything you don't want, Celie. My self-control is legendary."

Chapter 7

"How far are we from Canterbury?"

Noah looked up from frying his second round of sausages. He had discovered the hard way that sausages in England were not like those in the States. He had fried sausage at home; he was sure he must have. It had been a simple matter of putting them in a pan and turning them over once or twice. But these sausages, fresh from Betty's favorite butcher, had required boiling first—as Celie had told him after the first batch exploded.

"Three-quarters of an hour or so at most. Why?" He turned down the heat once again, just in case boiling wasn't all they had needed.

"I'm just trying to understand where we are."

"I have a map in the car."

"That would help."

"Did you sleep well?" Noah leaned against the stove and crossed his arms. Celie looked better this morning, not nearly as pale as yesterday. She was wearing the second outfit that Jerry had purchased for her, a modest white dress sprigged with violets and roses. He remembered the tight sweater and slit skirt of Marie St. Germaine and wished that *he* had done the shopping.

"I slept fine."

"You didn't lie awake all night and wait for me to finish you off?"

"You have an odd sense of humor."

"I'm just trying to make a point."

"I slept. You apparently did, too, because I'm still breathing and my heart's pounding away."

"Are you hungry?"

"I'm always hungry."

He had noticed as much. Celie ate everything he put in front of her with the appetite of someone who wasn't sure where her next meal was coming from. Last night for dinner they had eaten overdone lamb chops and peas boiled beyond recognition. She had nearly licked the plate.

"How do you survive?" he asked. "I know you work when you can. But moving from place to place, changing identities . . ." He shook his head. "It has to be expensive."

"I manage."

"I suspect you manage by cutting costs to the bone. Including food."

"I'm an expert with rice and beans."

"Is someone helping you? Someone sending you money?"

"Why do you care?"

"I figure I'm going to worm the whole story out of you one piece at a time."

She played with her coffee cup. He watched her hands with a fascination he didn't want to feel. She had lovely hands, slender and pale, with well cared for, unadorned nails. "I have to get to Canterbury." She looked up. "Will you take me?"

"Why?"

"Because I need to go."

"When?"

"I'm not sure yet."

"And what'll happen if I do? Will you disappear again? Or will I have to fight off Bobby or one of his pals?"

"I won't disappear."

"And Bobby?"

"Noah, I'm the last person who can answer that."

He liked the way she said his name. With just the hint of a Southern drawl. He liked the expression on her face, too. Most of the time she was on guard. Now her eyes were pleading. She needed him.

He didn't want to be needed.

He turned back to the stove. "I'll take you. Just tell me when."

"Thank you."

Her voice was soft, and the sentiment sounded genuine. She didn't trust him, but she was beginning to melt a little. And as each hour went by and she remained safe, she would trust him a little more. What would he do with that trust? How could he keep this woman safe when he hadn't even been able to protect his own wife and son?

He didn't realize she was standing beside him until she took the spatula from his hand. "You really are a pathetic cook, Noah James."

He moved away to make room for her, but not very far.

"Are you sure there's not a wife in the picture somewhere? Somebody who makes your coffee, fetches the pipe and paper?" Celie expertly turned the sausages, even though she was using her left hand.

"Does anybody have a wife like that?"

"I sure hope not."

He wanted to tell her something about himself that was real and solid. "I was married once."

She looked up and frowned. "But not anymore?"

He shook his head. "It ended some time ago."

"I can't picture you married, actually. You're a loner..."

"Like you?"

"I don't know. I don't know what I'd be like if my life hadn't turned out this way."

"You had someone once. You said it was a lover who was killed."

"Yes."

"Then you weren't always a loner."

"He was the first and only man in my life." She looked up. Her expression was bleak. "It was over so quickly. We hardly had time to say hello, much less goodbye."

He felt an unwanted surge of sympathy. "It always seems that way when you lose someone."

"Did you feel that way after your divorce?"

He didn't correct her. He had intimated divorce by his choice of words. "It's a common feeling. Do you know why your lover was murdered, Celie? Wouldn't knowing why help you find out who's stalking you?"

"What could I do about it? I'd have no proof. I have no power. Whoever is doing this has resources far beyond mine. You could tell me his name right this minute and it wouldn't do me a bit of good."

"I have resources."

"This isn't your fight. No, my best bet is to stay on the run. Maybe someday I'll land in a place where I can really start a new life. Someplace where I can't be found."

"Where? Heaven?"

She looked stricken for a moment, but just a moment. Then she began to laugh.

He was surprised. Despite himself, he smiled, too.

"The very place," she said. "Here I've been fighting it all this time, and it's the only absolutely safe place I could go."

"First we should try something a little less drastic."

She sobered, but her tough facade had been breached, at least for the moment. "If you're not out to get me, Noah, you really *are* a nice man."

"I sincerely doubt there are three people on this planet who would describe me that way."

"Betty said you're a good man, someone who's suffered, too."

"Did she? I'll have to talk to her about that."

"What did she mean?"

"I don't know. Maybe she was just trying to make me more palatable."

"As if you aren't palatable enough." She looked as if she regretted the words the moment she said them.

He was intrigued. "Really? Do you think so?"

She looked away. "I'm sure plenty of women have told you so."

"Not in quite those words."

She turned back to the stove and moved the frying pan to a back burner. "Listen to us. We're talking like friends. Next thing you know, one of us will slip up and start telling the whole truth and nothing but. You'll tell me what Betty meant about you. I'll tell you enough about my life to get you killed. This is dangerous, Noah, and worse, it feels like it could be habit-forming. We'd better be careful."

He turned away and retrieved the toast he'd prepared earlier. He buttered it and listened as Celie placed the sausages on the plates he'd set out earlier. The sounds were familiar ones. A clock ticking on the wall above his head. The sound of his knife scraping against the bread. The sound of Celie's spatula against the metal of the frying pan.

The last time he had stood in a kitchen and helped prepare a meal with a woman, the woman had been his wife. Twelve hours later she and his son had been dead.

He didn't look up when he spoke. "Death can sneak up on you, whether you're courting it or not. Lies and deception won't keep it at bay. Talking can be dangerous, but so can breathing. Maybe you just have to ask yourself if living without any of the things you really need is a kind of death anyway."

"That's easy for you to say. It's not your life that's in jeopardy."

"No, it's easy to say because I know what's it's like to live without the things I need. And I don't wish the same thing for you." He saw that she had stopped what she was doing. She was staring at him, her lips parted as if she wanted to say more, but she didn't speak.

He shook his head. "I don't know how I got involved in your life, Celie, and I understand why even less. But I'm glad I did. Just don't shut me out now. You have very real reasons to be afraid, but my friendship isn't one of them."

Celestine covertly admired Noah from the seat beside him in the rental car. He had showered and shaved again for their first outing as a "married" couple. She liked the spicy scent of his after-shave, the way his navy jacket emphasized the breadth of his shoulders, the casual way he rested his palms against the steering wheel with his long fingers extended. Relaxed but in complete control.

She wondered exactly how that felt. She hadn't been in control of her life in years. She had been running so long that she wasn't sure she would know how to stop when she was safe again.

If she ever *was* safe again.

She thought of her phone call to Whit that morning. Noah had gone into town right after breakfast, and she had used the opportunity to call Whit for the second time, this time at his home in Wilmington. She had wanted him to know that she could get a ride to Canterbury if he could wire money there, and he had promised to find a way.

Then the conversation had turned personal. "I got hold of Earl Sutter and Allison and told them you're all right," Whit said.

Celestine had closed her eyes and seen the faces of the other two of the three people in the world who she could really count on. Grandpa Sutter was not her grandfather, but he had been her own grandfather's closest friend. In her grandfather's day Earl Sutter had been the manager of Haven House's vast acreage. Now, at age seventy-six, he still lived on the grounds in a small brick house with a wide front porch that looked over the fields he had husbanded so well. Her aunt and uncle didn't want Grandpa Sutter at Haven House. They had always resented his influence on Celestine, his praise of her abilities, his interference when they attempted to force her to become a person she was not. But at his death Alexander St. Gervais had willed his best friend the house he had always lived in and the five acres surrounding it, and there was nothing that Millie or Roger could do to change that.

Then there was Allison Freeman. Allie had been Celestine's closest friend in the dark days of their adolescence, when they'd both been imprisoned in the strictest boarding school in the South. Black-haired, black-hearted Allie, who had taken the rebellious Celestine under her wing and taught her how to survive the military-style regimen and upper-class pretensions of a school that existed to break the spirit of the South's high-spirited daughters.

Celestine hadn't seen either Grandpa Sutter or Allie in four long years, and she only rarely called them. She didn't want them to be questioned about her whereabouts or, worse, to have their lives threatened. She regretted bringing Whit into her troubles, too, but she'd had no alternative.

After Stephen's death, Whit had demanded that he be allowed to help. After all, he had been Stephen's closest friend.

Noah glanced at her, and she realized she had been staring at him...or staring through him. "We ought to get some facts straight," he said. "I'm sure if the other ladies are anything like Marian, there will be plenty of questions asked."

"What kind of questions?" She spoke with Celie's accent firmly in place. She didn't want to slip up at Marian's.

"Who we are. Where we live. Where we met. Some details about the wedding, probably."

"Do you have any ideas?"

"Well, I can tell them about my consulting job."

"Fine. I'm familiar with that. Why don't I say that I was working as a secretary, but I've just quit that position so that I'll be free to travel with you?"

"Where? Where were you working?"

"Whatever strikes me at the moment. You have no idea how good I am at winging it."

He raised one autocratic brow. "I have some idea. I suspect half of what you say is 'winging it.'"

"Where do we live?"

"We've been living in Kensington. We're moving to... New York."

"Okay. I always wanted to live in the Big Apple."

"Park Avenue?"

"Central Park West or nothing."

He smiled at her. His smile no longer seemed as rusty. She was becoming accustomed to it. "What else?"

"I met you at a party. Mutual friends. I offered to show you London."

"We were married at a small country church. Yorkshire?"

"No. I think we should have been married in the States. Someone at the tea might be from Yorkshire and want to compare notes on people we knew. I'll tell them I'm an orphan and we wanted to be married at your family church—"

"In Philadelphia."

"Done. See how much fun it is reinventing your life?"

"I'll never tell the truth again."

"If they ask you a question about me, refer them to me. Just say, 'Celie would probably like to tell you that story.' I'll do the same for you. And we'd better listen to each other, so we keep everything straight."

"I'll stay glued by your side."

"Don't you wish you'd kept your eyes to yourself in Paris, Noah?"

The eyes in question were suddenly as warm as his smile. She saw that he understood she'd trusted him with yet another detail of her life. "I don't know. Marie St. Germaine was worth all the fuss."

"But not Lesley?"

"Lesley needed a subscription to the Victoria's Secret catalog and a couple of sexy romances on her bed table."

"Lesley would be shocked, sir."

"Actually, I think I like Celie Sherwood the best of the three."

"Why?" They were approaching the Farnsworth house, but Celestine wanted an answer before they went inside.

He stopped beneath a huge copper beech beside half a dozen other cars and turned off the engine. "Because every once in a while Celie gives way and I see the real woman beneath the role. She's my favorite, even though I still know next to nothing about her."

She fought against the warmth his words left behind. "You know everything you need to know."

He touched her cheek. She thought the gesture surprised him as much as it did her. "I don't think so." He shook his head slowly. "I think I need to know a lot more."

"I've told you all I can."

"We'll see." He dropped his hand and turned away to open his door. She had the strangest desire to touch the place where his fingers had been.

The Farnsworth house was centuries old. Half-timbered and sizable, it was set back from a narrow unpaved road and bordered by lacy evergreens. They followed a sternly geometric brick walkway up to the front of the house, where white chrysanthemums bloomed in a carefully laid out border.

Noah lifted a cast iron horseshoe on a chain and let it fall against a door broad enough to keep out the warring bands that had once invaded England's shore.

"You're prompt. I admire that. Particularly in Americans, who are rarely prompt, in my opinion." Marian, in a gray skirt and sweater that were otherwise the identical twins of the ones she'd worn yesterday, stepped aside to let them in. "But perhaps it's because you've married an Englishwoman. You are from England, aren't you, dear? I haven't quite placed the accent. I normally can pinpoint within a mile or two where someone was born."

"I'm afraid we moved so much when I was a child that my accent is confusing," Celestine said. She stepped inside to a short formal hall and felt Noah move in behind her.

"Oh? Where did you live?"

"Sussex. Oxfordshire. Cornwall. We lived in Pakistan and the Yukon for shorter stints, as well. My father's job required him to move every year or two. Life was never dull."

"I suspect it will never be dull with this young man, either. Americans are never dull and never prompt. I suppose one somehow goes with the other." Marian waved her hand toward the room beside them. "Come join our little gathering. Everyone is so pleased you agreed to come."

Marian led the way. Noah took Celie's arm and held her back a moment. "The Yukon?" he asked in a low voice.

"I always wanted to race a dogsled."

"My imagination pales in comparison to yours."

The room where they were to have tea was large and airy, with gleaming pine floors and diamond-paned windows. The rafters were thicker than the span of Celie's arms, and they were garlanded with the same dried flowers that adorned the ones at the cottage. A small fire crackled in a fireplace large enough to pitch a tent inside. Sandwiches and cakes waited on a two-tiered cart, and a sparkling silver tea service flanked by delicate china cups waited on a table beside the fireplace.

Marian took Noah and Celie around the room and introduced them to the dozen or so neighbors who had gathered. Young and old alike stood in clumps conversing, men as well as women, although the women cheerfully outnumbered them. Marian introduced her granddaughters, two well-behaved preteen girls in bright colored dresses. A purring Snow White preened on the lap of one of them, at least temporarily content with having to stay inside.

A little boy of four or five colored in the corner.

Marian stopped beside him. "This is my grandson Edward. Say hello to Mr. and Mrs. James, Teddy."

The little boy looked up, and Celie saw immediately that he had the round face and characteristic facial features of a child with Down's syndrome. He smiled with genuine pleasure and lifted his paper for her to see. She crouched beside him before Marian could demand that he stand. "Ooh... You've chosen such lovely colors, Teddy. Blue is my very favorite."

His smile broadened. "Purple..."

"I like purple, too. Look..." She pointed to one of the violets in her dress. "See, some of these flowers are purple."

She felt movement beside her, and she realized that Noah was crouching with her. "Hello, Teddy."

"Hello." Teddy smiled at Noah, too. Then, before another word could be spoken, he launched himself into Noah's arms. Noah caught him in a hug.

"Whoa there, partner. Where do you think you're going?" Noah got to his feet, bringing Teddy with him, and Teddy wrapped his arms around Noah's neck.

"His father is often away on business. He gets weary of so many women in his life," Marian said. "I'm afraid he can be quite tiresome when there's a man in the house."

Celie watched Noah with the little boy. If Teddy was being tiresome, Noah hadn't yet noticed. He seemed completely mesmerized. Teddy stroked his face, and Noah allowed it, even when Teddy's chubby fingers came very close to his eyes.

"Then you like children, Mr. James?" Marian asked.

"Very much."

"That's always a good sign, I believe," Marian said, addressing Celie. "A man who likes children before he's had his own will be an exceptionally good father."

Celie was watching Noah as Marian spoke. He flinched as she finished. "It takes more than liking children to be a good father," he said.

"Of course. But it's a fine start. You will be a good father, Mr. James. It's quite clear to me." Marian held out her arms to Teddy. "Come, Teddy. Leave Mr. James alone now."

Noah didn't release him. "He's fine where he is. If he wants to stay with me."

"Good. Then you may have the pleasure of holding your teacup in one hand and Teddy in the other. Isn't that right, Teddy?"

Celie was fascinated by Noah's expression. There were adult men—too many of them, sadly—who might find Teddy's limitations upsetting or distasteful. But Noah obviously found the little boy delightful.

There was something more. At the same time that Noah seemed to enjoy holding Teddy, he also seemed pained by it. As if holding him awakened memories of another time. Another child?

"You seem so comfortable holding him," Celie said when Marian moved over to the tea table to begin the ritual of pouring tea. "As if you've had practice."

"I've held a fair number of children."

"Do you have children, Noah?"

Teddy was busy with Noah's tie. By the looks of it, it was an expensive one, but Noah didn't seem at all concerned that Teddy was rolling it into a ball. Noah watched the little boy for a moment before he answered. "No."

"Well, Marian's right. You should."

Several of the women came to escort them to the table where Marian was pouring tea. They spent the next hour eating spiced fruitcake and tiny sandwiches made on thick slices of Marian's own whole-grain bread.

Just as Noah had predicted, questions were the order of the day, but for the most part they were restrained. Not everyone in Trillingden was as forthright as Marian, or as certain of their right to know everything about the newest neighbors. One man, though, seemed fascinated by everything about them. Particularly Celie.

The man, whose name Celie couldn't remember, had been introduced earlier by Marian. He was a late arrival, and he had a habit of moving steadily closer as he spoke. And since he had been speaking for some time, by now he had moved close enough to make her uncomfortable. He had a rasping voice, and he spoke too loudly. "Oxfordshire, you say? Where exactly? I have family there."

Celie was beginning to wonder why he was questioning her so vigorously. "Oh, it was many years ago when we lived there. Near Woodstock, I believe. But I was such a little girl, I couldn't say for certain."

"And Cornwall? Did you say Cornwall?"

Celie decided to turn the tables. She was becoming increasingly uneasy with the man's probing. She had not only missed his name during the introductions, but if anyone had mentioned what he did, she had missed that, too. He appeared harmless enough. She guessed he was nearing fifty, of medium height and weight, with ordinary brown hair and eyes. But he had an odd facial tic that made him look as if he were winking continuously. It also made it difficult to read his expression.

"I've forgotten your name," she said. "I'm sorry."

"Dougie. Dougie Ferguson."

"That's right. And you have a farm nearby?"

"Oh no, dear. I'm new to the area myself. I've just bought the local pub. The Lion and Lamb. You'll have to come visit us, won't you?"

"That would be lovely."

He returned to his original question. "Now, where exactly in Cornwall did you live?"

"Do you have family in Cornwall, too?"

"No. But I lived there once myself. I've lived in a great number of places."

"And have you always kept a pub, Mr. Ferguson?"

"It's Dougie to you. And no. I've done a variety of things." He winked at her. This time she didn't think it was the tic.

Her hands went suddenly cold, and she found the next breath hard to draw. What kinds of things had Dougie Ferguson done? His interest in her life seemed extraordinary, but maybe he was only being polite. She told herself that no one could have tracked her here so quickly, no one would have had the opportunity to approach a local resident with a shady past and offer him money to find her and rid Trillingden of its newest female resident. She was too suspicious.

But she had survived this long because she had learned not to take anything at face value.

"What kinds of things have you done?" she asked. She was proud of her voice. She sounded cool and calm.

"Oh, a few things I'm not proud of, a few I am. But I like keeping a pub the best. The people who come through keep my interest, if you know what I mean."

Celie was afraid she did know. She wondered if someone had come through his pub, someone with an offer Dougie Ferguson couldn't refuse. It seemed absurd. It seemed impossible.

It seemed like another in a long series of nightmares.

"I wish you well," she said. Again she sounded as calm as if she were just passing the time with him. "Maybe you'll find what you've been looking for in Trillingden and you won't need to move again."

"Yes, I believe I've found exactly what I was looking for."

He might as well have said "whom."

A middle-aged woman interrupted them. Celie remembered that she worked at the store in town. Jane, whose last name she couldn't recall. "May I take your cup, Mrs. James?"

Celie handed over the cup and saucer with a grateful smile. At least, she thought she smiled. Dougie Ferguson was still watching her closely. "Jane, didn't you offer to show me Marian's garden?"

Jane, a short woman with thick ankles and sensible shoes, seemed pleased that Celie had remembered. "Why, yes. Are you ready?"

"You'll excuse us?" Celie asked Dougie.

"I'm sure I'll be seeing you soon enough."

Celie wondered if her heart could pound any harder. She saw Noah across the room, with Teddy clinging happily to his legs. She wanted to throw herself into his arms and tell him what she suspected. But Noah couldn't be trusted, either.

No one could be trusted.

She followed Jane through the house, paying scant attention to where they were going. When Jane opened the back door and the cool air of late afternoon stroked her face, she took a deep breath and hazarded a glance behind her. Dougie was nowhere in sight.

Jane led her down a short path. "Marian grows the most perfect roses. Some of them are nearly as old as the house, you understand. And she's wonderfully generous with cuttings. Of course, if you're moving to the United States, you wouldn't be allowed to take them with you, I suppose. Regulations and all that."

"Jane, do you know Dougie well?"

"No, I don't suppose I do."

"He seems nice enough...."

"Yes, but he's a bit of an odd duck, isn't he? Still, he causes no harm. And he's done well at the Lion and Lamb. Cleaned it up. Hired a new cook. We wonder sometimes where he gets the money for all the improvements, but we're glad for them all the same."

"He said the oddest thing. He said he'd done some things he wasn't proud of...."

"I suppose we could all say that, dear."

"But we don't, do we?"

"It's been my experience that Dougie rarely thinks before he speaks. I'm not certain he's quite intact, if you know what I mean. I believe he was injured in a robbery some years ago. A gunshot, I believe, and it's affected him a bit. He does quite well for himself, despite everything."

Celestine was silent. How well did Dougie do? And did he need to do better? Had he spent too much money renovating the Lion and Lamb? Had he been ripe for offers when approached by someone who was searching for her? Or was she imagining things?

Was she imagining this?

"Are you all right, Mrs. James?" Jane sounded concerned.

Celie realized she had been staring into the distance. "Oh, yes. Thanks. But I'm afraid I'm feeling rather dizzy."

"Perhaps we'd better go back inside."

"No." Celie couldn't face another round with Dougie Ferguson. A gunshot? A robbery? Exactly which end of the gun had he been on, and why? Again she wished she could alert Noah. Again she told herself she couldn't trust him. For all she knew, Noah was the one who really wanted her dead.

A picture of Noah with Teddy in his arms filled her mind. Could a man who held a child that tenderly be a murderer? Hadn't he treated her with the same concern? He was a self-described loner, but he had saved her from certain death at Bobby's hands, hidden her and taken care of her. Was he just trying to gain her trust? Did he have an agenda she didn't yet understand? Would he turn on her when the time was right?

"Would you like me to get your husband?" Jane asked, when Celie said nothing more.

"No. No, I don't want to alarm him. I think I just need some fresh air. Do you think Marian would understand if I went home now?"

"Of course she would. I'll drive you myself."

"No. I'm going to walk. It will do me good."

"You're sure, dear? If you're feeling dizzy..."

"It's just what I need. I'll cut across the field. But don't tell Noah for a few minutes, please. He'll only worry."

"Whatever you say."

Celie put her hand on Jane's arm. "Thank you. I do appreciate it."

Jane looked less than convinced, but she covered Celie's hand for a moment. "Stop and rest if you need to. There's nothing to be gained from fainting in Marian's field."

"I'll take care. I promise. I always do."

Chapter 8

There was a path in the general direction of the cottage, a public walkway left from the days when villagers still walked from place to place and needed access through neighboring land. Similar walkways crisscrossed England and were kept passable by landowners. This one veered to the west of the cottage, through the woods that now blocked Celie's view of it. But she knew she was heading in the right general direction.

She had quickly left Marian's house behind her, and now she couldn't see it anymore. The path was cut through tall fields of grain, and she was immersed in it, walking so swiftly that her heart was pounding in rhythm to her feet.

She hadn't gone far before she realized how foolish this decision had been. She hadn't regained her strength. She was still recovering from Bobby's attack. She had lied to Jane about being dizzy, but now it wasn't a lie. She slowed her pace and listened for footsteps behind her, but the only sound she heard was wind rippling through the grain.

Where could she go? Dougie Ferguson might be a perfectly ordinary man making perfectly ordinary conversation. She remembered the way he had closed in on her, the pointed questions about her past, the confession that he had done things he wasn't proud of. Would he have acted so oddly if he was intent on murder?

But if he wanted to be sure she was Celestine St. Gervais, wouldn't he have to check his facts? Wouldn't he have to ask enough questions to convince himself that he had the right woman? Perhaps she and Noah had been traced to the general area and now the hunters were closing in for the kill.

Or perhaps Dougie was just the landlord of a rustic country pub, an eccentric with limited social skills who had merely wanted to make conversation.

She didn't know what to do or where to go. Noah would soon be looking for her. He would drive to the cottage to see if she was there. If she went back there now, then he would find her.

She realized that Noah's finding her was exactly what she wanted. She wanted Noah's help and the comfort of his presence. She was more convinced that he was a man with secrets and less that his secrets were related in any way to her. But she couldn't be sure. He had followed her in Paris. He had tracked her to the repair store in London.

He had let Bobby go.

She took a deep breath to try to clear her head. As much as she wanted to, as logical as his explanations were, she still couldn't trust Noah. Her best bet now was to somehow get to Canterbury, then call Whit and find out what arrangements he had made to send her money. Perhaps under the cover of darkness she could throw herself on the mercy of the vicar of Trillingden's church. Every English village had a church; that was one thing she could count on. She could explain that her life was in danger, tell him bits and pieces of the truth and ask for his help. Once she was in Canterbury, she could take the money and disappear. She had contacts who could find her a new identity and documents to go with it. She could start again.

She didn't want to start again.

Something too close to tears stung her eyes. She had run before. She knew the terrors; they were old acquaintances. She knew the loneliness; it felt like a second skin. But this was the first time in many years that she also felt a sharp pang of loss. She had begun to trust Noah. She had begun to like him. And there was something more, something elemental and far too dangerous, between them that had made her remember she was a woman.

A woman. Not just a woman running for her life.

She tried to think where she could go to wait until it was safe to walk into Trillingden. She hadn't been there herself, but she knew which direction she had to go. She didn't know where the Lion and Lamb was in relation to the village, but she felt certain she could avoid being seen. And if the vicar wasn't in residence, then she could keep walking. There were other villages nearby. And someone, somewhere, would help her.

She rested for a moment against a tree that stood beside the path. She listened carefully and closed her eyes. She thought about Noah and remembered the gentle way he had changed the bandage on her shoulder. She could be at the cottage in minutes. She could tell Noah all the things that Dougie had said and listen to his response.

Or she could disappear once again and keep herself safe until she could go back home and claim Haven House and her parents' estate as her own.

She turned away from the cottage and headed toward the stream and the woods that bordered it.

"She walked home?" Noah knew he was frowning and that Jane clearly wished she was someplace else.

"Yes. That's what she said. She wasn't feeling well, and she claimed she needed the fresh air. She asked me not to tell you right away. I'm sorry, but I couldn't very well refuse, could I?"

He shook his head, because he didn't trust himself to speak. Celie was gone again. He hadn't even considered that she might try to make a break. He had left her alone this morning, half expecting to return from town to find the cottage empty. But she had been right there waiting for him when he returned.

"Perhaps you'd better go in search of her?" Jane said. "She looked rather pale, I'm afraid."

"I'll do that." Noah looked around the room for Marian so that he could say goodbye. Some of the guests had already left. Those who hadn't were gathered in the corner looking at Farnsworth photograph albums. Teddy had just fallen asleep on his oldest sister's lap, displacing Snow White, who was nowhere to be seen.

He found Marian in the front hall saying goodbye to more of her guests. He waited his turn impatiently.

"I'm afraid Celie has gone on," he said when Marian had ushered the others out the door. "Apparently she wasn't feeling well and needed some fresh air. My apologies that she left without saying goodbye."

"The poor dear. Well, I certainly understand. I noticed that she looked a bit done in when she was talking to Dougie. White as my chrysanthemums."

"Dougie?"

"Yes. The new landlord at the Lion and Lamb?"

Noah vaguely remembered being told that someone he'd met today owned the local pub. "Is Dougie still here?"

"No. He was the first to leave."

Noah contemplated that. "You said he was the new landlord? Is he a local man?"

"Not at all. You're not considered local in Trillingden until your family has been here for centuries. No, Dougie's from London most recently. Quite an odd chap at times, but good-hearted, I should think."

"I'm sure." But he wasn't. He wondered if Dougie was the reason that Celie had left so quickly and so quietly. Had he said something that frightened her? Had she run away to protect herself from Dougie?

Or from him?

He said his thank-yous and took his leave.

He had hoped he might find Celie waiting in the car, but there was no sign of her. He considered scouting the immediate area on foot, but decided to drive to the cottage instead. The sun was heading slowly toward the horizon, but if Celie wasn't at home, he didn't have too many hours to look for her before dark. He needed to know exactly what he was up against.

As he had feared, no one was waiting at the cottage door. He walked the outside perimeter calling Celie's name, but there was no answer. He had hoped that she might be waiting nearby until he arrived with the only key, but there was no sign that she had been here. He took a moment to go inside and get her raincoat. The air would quickly grow colder as night fell. He found a flashlight in case he had to search in the dark; then he locked the door behind him again and started across the field toward the Farnsworth house.

Where would Celie go? Noah suspected she always had an escape plan ready to execute. If anything she had told him was true, then she obviously looked at life as a field sprinkled with land mines. If she wasn't constantly vigilant, if she didn't look for clues and act on them immediately, then she would die.

That meant, of course, that sometimes she made mistakes. Innocent people became assassins in her mind. Innocent conversations became death threats. Since she never knew who was stalking her, then everyone she met was potentially a killer. Her killer.

He tried to remember if he had noticed anything out of the ordinary at Marian's. They had stayed together at the beginning, but toward the end they had become separated when Marian asked him to speak to an old man sitting on a chair in the corner. By that time he and Celie had answered enough questions together that he felt he could carry on the charade alone. He had looked for her once, and he had seen her across the room talking to Marian's granddaughters. He remembered that she had seemed relaxed. She had smiled at one of the girls and reached over to pet Snow White.

Had he noticed her again after that? Had he seen her talking to a man? He searched his memory, but he couldn't remember anything else. Why hadn't he been more alert?

The afternoon was growing cooler. He walked faster, but he stopped occasionally to stare into the distance for movement. If Celie was running away, she wouldn't expose herself longer than necessary in the open field. She would veer toward the occasional patch of woods. Or the stream, which was thickly lined with trees. But which woods? And if she was following the stream, which direction was she going?

The question now was her final destination. She had asked him for a ride to Canterbury, so it seemed likely that Canterbury might be her target. Of course, he knew her well enough by now to realize that she might have been trying to throw him off track. Perhaps she was heading back to London. Hitchhiking or begging a ride from someone she'd met at the tea.

"Damn you, Celie."

He slowed his pace a little. Was he making a mistake by searching for her? He had done everything he could to gain her trust, and she had still taken off at the first opportunity. Celie Sherwood—who was not really Celie Sherwood—was not his problem. He had done what he could for her. Now he could let her find her own way to safety.

He almost turned around to head back to the cottage. But Marian's words were still loud in his head. "I noticed that she looked a bit done in when she was talking to Dougie. White as my chrysanthemums."

Was she really in danger again? Did she need his help, even though she was afraid to ask for it?

Damn it, he couldn't abandon her. Not now.

With his mind made up, he started toward the stream. If he was in Celie's place, he would follow the stream toward the village. Once he was there, he would make up a story about why he needed a ride to Canterbury, then tell it to someone safe and respected, someone sympathetic who owned a car.

He tried to gauge how far she might have gotten by now. She was still recovering from the knife wound, so she wouldn't be moving at top speed. And if he was in her shoes, he wouldn't be hurrying too fast. Instead he would wait for dark so that he wouldn't be noticed.

He made his best guess and turned toward a point that seemed like the place to start. As he hiked, he told himself that he would do this for anyone in trouble. He couldn't stand by while someone needed his help. He had no particular attachment to Celie. He felt nothing more than he would feel for any woman in jeopardy.

And all the while another voice inside his head told him that he was becoming as adept a liar as the woman who called herself Celie Sherwood.

Celie didn't know how much time had passed. She was walking in the shade now, and she was beginning to feel cold. The sun had dipped lower, and by the time it reached the horizon, she knew she would be shivering.

But it couldn't be helped. Jerry had bought a coat for her in London, but it was back at the cottage. He had bought her a coat. Clothes. Sewed up her wound, despite the fact that she was a stranger. Betty had fed her, counseled her, fussed over her.

Then there was Noah.

She rested against a tree and wished she wasn't wearing white. She was afraid that anyone who ventured nearby would see her if they looked carefully enough. She wondered if Noah would look for her, or if he would write her off as a bad investment, pack up the little rental car and cruise back to the comforts of the town house in Kensington. He owed her nothing. If he really was a stranger who had accidentally been caught up in her life, then he might be glad she was gone. He no longer had to concern himself with protecting her. He could resume his job and forget about the woman he had cared for with such tender, capable hands.

The stream was just below her, a short climb down to the edge of the water. Noah had helped her down yesterday, taking her hand against her will and patiently leading her to the rocks where she had spun out a new set of lies. There was no one to help her down now. It would be easier to walk along the stream, but she was afraid she wouldn't be able to get down or up again when she needed to without using both hands to steady herself. Even though it was more difficult, she had to walk along the ridge above it and hope she wasn't seen.

She walked about two hundred yards; then she rested again. She was exhausted. The woods were deeper here, the stream shaded almost completely by massive oaks and beeches. She sank to the soft ground beneath one of them and closed her eyes. She thought she would be protected here. No one could see her, and it was safe to rest. She would get up in a little while and cover a greater distance, but in the meantime, she would take advantage of this chance to regain some strength.

The woods were filled with birds. Birdsong was different here than at home. She missed the spontaneity and sass of mockingbirds, the heat-driven languor of North Carolina Augusts, the thunderous roar of bullfrogs when nothing but fireflies and stars lit the summer evening.

She wanted to go home. She wanted it badly enough that she was almost ready to risk everything. Even though she was about to turn twenty-five, home could potentially be the deadliest place on earth until Whit worked some legal magic. But she almost didn't care. She was fast growing too tired to run. She no longer trusted her instincts. She had believed in Bobby, and he had tried to kill her. She had run from Noah....

She thought about last night, when Noah had helped her dress. She'd felt something very like desire for him. And sometime in the night she had dreamed that he was lying beside her. She hadn't been afraid. No, it hadn't been fear she'd felt....

She closed her eyes and fell asleep thinking of Noah, and she awoke sometime later when birds screeched overhead. At first she thought she was at home. She had prowled the woods at Haven House as a little girl, napped in makeshift tree houses, searched for blackberries and pecans in places she wasn't supposed to go. She had been a fearless child, rosy-cheeked and freckled from the sun, and as comfortable outdoors as in.

She stretched and opened her eyes, and Dougie Ferguson was standing just in front of her. His brows knit together in a frown, but his mouth widened into a smile as her eyes grew large with panic.

"And what are you doing out here like this, Mrs. James? Didn't anyone ever tell you the woods are filled with dangerous things?"

For the second time in his brief acquaintance with Celie, Noah was alerted to her location by a scream. The sound was far enough away that he realized he wasn't going to be able to reach her quickly. He had been heading in the right general direction, but he had underestimated how far she might have gotten.

He shouted her name once, then again, to let her know he was coming. His feet pounded the ground as frustration and fear filled him. He wasn't nearly close enough. Not nearly.

The scream wasn't repeated. He almost wished for one, to let him know she was still alive. He ducked under a canopy of trees and pushed aside saplings that seemed to spring up in his path. He couldn't run now. The best he could do was push scrub aside with both hands as he charged through the forest.

"Celie!" He listened, but there was no response. "Where are you?" he shouted again.

"She's here. Over here! I think she's fainted!"

Noah turned at the sound of the man's voice and headed downstream. A minute passed, and frustration filled him. He couldn't see anyone or anything except trees. Then he pushed through a thicket of briars and tangled vines and saw a man kneeling on the ground.

"I don't know what's wrong with her. She was sleeping. She woke up and seemed fine. I don't know what's wrong...."

Noah pushed the man aside long enough to be sure that Celie was still breathing. Then he turned on him. Now he recognized the man as someone he'd met at Marian's. Obviously he was Dougie Ferguson. "What did you do to her?"

"Not a thing. Not a blooming thing! I fish here. It's my favorite place to fish. I came down to try my luck. Brought me pole to Marian's and walked over here from the road after I left." He pointed in the right general direction. "I fished down below for a while, but I didn't have any luck, so I thought I'd try over there."

He swung his arm to another spot below them. "Best way to get there is to climb up, then down again. I didn't even see her sitting there until I was almost on top of her. I must have scared her. That's all I can think of. She was sleeping, and I must have scared her when she woke up. I've scared women before. I can't help me face. I was shot in the side of me head about ten years ago. A man tried to rob the shop where I was a clerk. I got shot when he tried to grab a woman who was there. Got a medal for it, too, and this bloody wink."

Noah grabbed him by the front of his shirt. "Where's your pole?"

"Over there against that tree." Dougie hiked his thumb over his shoulder.

Noah looked over and saw the pole, as well as a small bucket beside it.

"I meant her no harm," Dougie said. "I talked to her at Marian's house. She knows who I am. I didn't know she'd be afraid."

Noah suspected Dougie was telling the truth. He seemed mortified that he had caused this situation, and genuinely worried about Celie. He relaxed his fingers and let Dougie step away. "All right." He knelt beside Celie and lifted her head and shoulders to his lap. "Now, what happened after that? Did she simply faint?"

"She jumped up and screamed, and she whirled around like she was going to run away. Then she ran flat chat into the tree."

"She probably hit her shoulder. It's injured. If she did, she may have passed out from the pain."

"What was she doing out here like this? She shouldn't be off by herself. It's not that kind of world anymore, is it? She needs somebody watching out for her. That's your job, isn't it?"

"Believe me, it's like watching out for a lioness." Noah stroked Celie's cheek. It was smudged with dirt where she'd hit the ground. She made a noise low in her throat, something just short of a moan, then she opened her eyes.

"Celie, you're safe," Noah said. "Perfectly safe. Don't scream again. I don't think my ears could stand it."

She started at the sound of his voice and tried to sit up. He helped her, but held her against his chest before she could move away. "Are you all right?"

She looked in the direction where Dougie was standing, and her eyes widened. "Mr. Ferguson was fishing," Noah told her before she could say a word. "His pole's over there, and his bait bucket. He's not going to hurt you. He's not trying to kill you, Celie."

"Kill her?" Dougie sounded irate. "What are you trying to say? That she thinks I'm trying to kill her? Of course she doesn't. She knows me. She met me at Marian's. I own the Lion and Lamb."

Noah turned her face to his. "You're safe," he said.

She began to weep. Softly. He wrapped his arms around her tighter. "Dougie, will you give us some privacy?"

"Sure. I guess I'm done with fishing for today." He drew himself erect. "You two come to the Lion and Lamb one night. Dinner and a drink apiece on me." He shook his head as he turned. "Kill her...? I risked me life to save a woman once. Kill her...?"

He was still shaking his head when he walked away.

Noah pulled her higher against his chest and rocked her back and forth. "Are you okay, Celie?"

She was sobbing harder. He suspected she was in shock. She was a strong woman who had lived with fear for too long. The fear had boiled over today and swept away her best instincts. She was perilously close to the edge of sanity.

He had walked that edge himself after Lynn's death, and he knew what a terrifying and lonely precipice it was.

He stroked her hair, but his fingers kept tangling in it. He stroked her cheeks with his thumbs and whispered encouragement. No woman looked her best when she was crying, but the tears heightened this one's vulnerability. Her eyes were the softest blue, even when they were overflowing with tears.

"You ran from me, too, didn't you?" He tilted her face higher so that she was looking directly at him. "Dougie frightened you, so you ran from us both. Why? Haven't I proved to you that I don't want to hurt you?"

He saw her answer. She was alone in a world where no one could be trusted. But she wanted to trust him. She wanted it as badly as she had ever wanted anything.

And he wanted her.

The realization was like a stab of pain. He had vowed he would never become intimately involved in another woman's life. He knew about loss. Oh, he knew about it from the inside out, and he knew that he was a coward. He could not survive another loss like the ones he had already endured. And this was a woman who would be easier to lose than to win.

But it didn't seem to matter. Because he had already committed himself to her. Even though he didn't know who she was or what she was running from. Even though she had told him lies and would probably tell him more. Even though she had run from him again, despite everything he had done for her.

Even though she walked the edge of sanity.

"I want you, Celie." He kissed her forehead and clasped her closer. "I want you. I want to help you. I want you."

She lifted her chin. They were inches apart, and tears still trailed down her cheeks. "I have nothing to give you."

"I'll have to be the judge of that."

Her lips were soft under his, and unprotesting. Her hand crept to the back of his neck as if to hold him there. He was overcome with the sweetness and the sorrow of this. She was warm and alive in his arms, and in hours she could be gone again.

The kiss deepened, and it was no longer comforting. Despite himself, he was searching for something, asking for more than a kiss, and he thought that her answer was yes. Needs he'd hidden for years suffused him. Physical needs, and emotional ones, too. He felt a lifetime of possibilities opening up to him, possibilities that he had believed were gone forever. He held her tighter and for a moment forgot about everything except how soft she was and how right she felt against him.

She was the first to pull away. He saw how pale she still was, how drained. He captured her face in his hands and read the same confusion in her eyes that he felt.

"I'm going to get you home now."

"Home?"

"The cottage. Celie, you have to recover before you can run again. I know you're going to run. Don't try to deny it. But let me take care of you until you're strong enough to have an even chance. You passed out. Doesn't that tell you something?"

"Dougie?"

"Did he threaten you?"

"No..."

"I think he's harmless. I think you may have misinterpreted whatever he said to you."

"Jane said he'd been shot in a robbery—"

"He told me. But he wasn't the bad guy. He was shot protecting a woman. I can check it out for you if you'd like. But I think he's telling the truth."

"I thought they'd found me again. I thought they'd followed me here or traced my phone..."

"Phone calls, Celie? Is there someone you call? Someone who's helping you?" He watched the vulnerability fade. It was replaced by the wall she always kept between them. He shook his head. "I get it. You still can't trust me with the truth, can you? You know who's after you, but you're not going to tell me. And you've got someone helping you, someone you've called from the cottage...."

"I can't tell you anything more."

"Won't." He set her away from him, stood and dusted off his pants. "You *won't* tell me."

"You're right. I won't."

He reached down and helped her to her feet. He wanted to be angry at her, but he couldn't be. In the world she lived in, the wrong decision could be fatal. "I can help you. But I don't expect you to believe that. Just let me help you now. Let me get you to the cottage until your strength is back. Then I won't try to stop you if you want to run again."

She closed her eyes, defeated. He knew she was afraid to stay. But perhaps she was more afraid to leave, because she opened them again and nodded. "Thank you."

He didn't know how to answer. He didn't know what she was thanking him for. For a moment of intimacy? For coming to find her? For offering to protect her? Or was it for something as basic as not betraying her? At least, not yet.

"There's a road that cuts across the field back there." He inclined his head to the right. "I'll get you over there, then you can wait until I bring the car around. Can you make it that far?"

"I was going to try to make it to Canterbury...."

"You might have died trying." He put his arm around her waist, and they started across the field.

Chapter 9

Celestine practiced lifting the roll of paper towels with her right hand. Pain shot through her arm and shoulder, but not enough to make her stop. She set the roll on the kitchen counter, then lifted it once more and let it swing to her hip. This time she lifted it with her arm perfectly straight until the roll was shoulder high.

She set it back on the counter and rested.

"Going all right?"

She hadn't heard Noah come in. She turned to the door and shot him a tentative smile. "It feels good to be out of that sling and doing something to help myself."

"Betty warned you not to overdo."

"I'm not. I don't want to reinjure myself. But I'm encouraged. I wasn't sure how much damage Bobby had done."

"She seems to think you'll have full range of motion. But she told me again that you'll need physical therapy to make sure of it."

"That's impossible. I'm just going to have to work at it by myself."

"I suppose it's tough scheduling appointments in your situation. One here. One wherever. One beyond wherever." He shrugged.

"I don't like running, Noah." She leaned against the counter and watched as he opened the refrigerator and took out a canned drink.

"But you won't let me do anything to help you."

"There's nothing you *can* do."

He popped the top and took a sip. This was the first time in the two days since he had found her by the stream that he had broached this subject again. He had left her strictly alone. Except for meals, they had scarcely even been in the same room.

She had spent the time resting and planning what she would do next. Whit had promised her that the money would be available today, and she knew that once she had it, she would have to decide exactly what she should do with it. The rest of his news had been more disturbing. He'd informed her that none of his inquiries had turned up a consultant working for Tri-C by the name of Noah James. He had promised to continue the investigation and warned her to be careful.

She knew that Whit could be wrong. He had admitted that Tri-C was a conglomerate with fingers in a wide variety of pies. Various enterprises under the Tri-C umbrella existed all over the globe. And Noah wouldn't appear on the regular payroll. But Whit's dead end hadn't increased her sense of security.

She wasn't sure what Noah had done with his time for the past two days. She'd often detected the telephone ringing and the soft purr of his computer during the long hours when she didn't see him.

He had rarely left the cottage. Yesterday morning he had gone to visit Teddy. She only knew that because Marian had appeared that afternoon with a picture Teddy had drawn for him. She had seen the picture later, pinned up on his bedroom wall, a smudge of black and orange that only a parent could love. She had wanted to ask him about it; she had wanted to ask him about a great many things. But she was afraid that more intimacy could be her undoing. As it was, he was in her thoughts even when they weren't together. She thought about the kiss, one kiss wrenched from the absurdity of her life. And she wondered what it would be like to open herself to more.

She realized she was staring at him, and she looked away. Noah swallowed at least half the drink before he spoke. "I haven't been completely straight with you, Celie. I've been lucky. I'm a success at what I do. I have more money than I could possibly spend in one lifetime. And I know some powerful people...."

"So do I. And they're trying to kill me."

"Who?"

She shook her head.

"You still don't trust me."

"It's nothing personal." She tried to leaven that with another smile, but he didn't respond.

The drink was gone before he spoke again. "If you won't let me help you any other way, let me give you money. Enough to help you get started again."

"I couldn't accept money from you."

"I can afford it."

"Consulting pays that well, huh? You must be very good at what you do."

"I must be. At least, at most of the things I do." He crushed the can in his hand. "But apparently not at inspiring confidence."

"I wouldn't take your money. Not even if I thought you were all the saints rolled into one. I can't take it. I've already taken your time, your patience—"

"You're right about that. I'm about out of patience." In one easy motion he tossed the can into the trash.

"I don't blame you. And I'm sorry. You'll never know how much I appreciate everything you've done for me here. I'd be dead if you hadn't helped me."

"But you still won't tell me who you are."

She wanted to tell him. She owed him something, but her desire to be truthful was more than that. She wanted him to know exactly who she was. The real Celestine St. Gervais, not a name from someone else's birth certificate. The real woman.

"All right. I'll tell you this," she said, as he turned to leave. "My real name is Celestine."

He turned back. He raised an eyebrow and waited.

"I'll tell you something else. I'm twenty-four, and I'll turn twenty-five this afternoon."

"It's your birthday?"

"That's what the calendar says."

"Happy birthday, Celestine."

"I had a choice on identities.... Back a while ago. One of the possibilities was Celie Sherwood. When I was a little girl, my father sometimes called me Celie. I took that name because it was comforting. I don't think the real Celie Sherwood would mind if she knew."

"And do you have a last name?"

"Yes."

"I suppose I won't be hearing it."

"Please let this be enough."

He crossed his arms. "What will we do to celebrate?"

"Nothing. I haven't celebrated a birthday since... forever."

"Then it's time."

"I'd like to go to Canterbury."

"Oh? And will you be coming back?"

She had told enough lies. She didn't want to tell another. Not now. "I have to disappear again. I could do it today."

"On your birthday?"

"I guess it's not much of a birthday present to myself, is it?"

"I guess not."

"My shoulder is healing. I can move my arm, and I don't need the sling. I need to move on, and so do you."

"Do I? I was beginning to get used to this."

"This?"

"You. Me. Watching the sun warm your skin and the color seep back into your cheeks. Watching you drink your coffee in the morning and eat your soup at noon. Lying awake and listening for the sounds you make at night."

Color was seeping into her cheeks now. She wondered if he was looking for a reaction. "There's no point in getting used to something that can't continue."

"You'll have to decide if you're leaving from Canterbury for wherever it is you're going. I'm not going to try to stop you. Just promise you won't go unprepared. If you need money, let me help. It can be a loan, if that's the way you want it."

"I'd rather drive back with you to London. I can make my plans there and get what I need."

"Then disappear?"

She nodded.

"When?"

She took a deep breath. "Soon."

"Then that's the way we'll do it. But you still need to go to Canterbury today?"

"Yes."

"In about half an hour?"

"That'll be fine."

"We'll celebrate tonight."

"That's not necessary. I don't expect you to—"

"We'll celebrate." He crossed the room to stand in front of her. He pushed a strand of hair behind her ear, searching her face as he did. "You only turn twenty-five once."

"Yeah. And in my case I wasn't sure I ever would."

"I'm standing right in front of you, and you're not reaching for a butcher knife."

"They're too far away."

"You don't jump when I walk into the room anymore."

"What do you want me to say? That I've started to trust you?"

"It would be music to my ears."

His eyes were sad. She knew hers were, too. "Noah, I don't trust either of us. Does that make this any better?"

"You know what? I think it's yourself you don't trust most of all."

Noah had never been to Canterbury, never seen the awe-inspiring cathedral where Thomas Becket had met his maker and pilgrims from all of England had journeyed for enlightenment. During the car ride Celie had claimed that she had never been here, either. But nothing Celie said could be taken at face value.

He parked in a car park and fed coins into the appropriate slots to pay for their space. Then they turned left for a short walk into the heart of the city. Today Canterbury was filled with modern day pilgrims, pilgrims with cameras and shopping bags. The narrow medieval streets were crowded and noisy, and tourism reigned supreme.

"Would you like to see the cathedral when you've finished?" He took Celie's arm and helped guide her around a mannequin dressed as Chaucer's Wife of Bath that was blocking the sidewalk.

"Would you mind? I've always wanted to."

He supposed she really had been telling the truth about never being here before. "I'd like to see it myself."

Two blocks later she stopped and moved out of the heavy foot traffic to stand at the window of a china shop. But her mind obviously wasn't on the display. "I'm going to leave you now. I've got business I have to take care of."

"So I've assumed."

"Shall we meet back here at . . ." She lifted his hand and gazed down at his watch. "Eleven?"

"Do you think you'll be finished by then?"

"I hope so."

"All right. Eleven." He watched her face. She still looked uneasy. He shook his head. "I'm not going to follow you. Go on."

"Thank you."

He proved the truth of his words by going inside the first store across the road. He had chosen it strictly for proximity, but once inside, he regretted not paying more attention.

It was a toy store, and he hadn't been in one like it since Josh's death. He was overwhelmed by memories.

"May I help you?"

He shook his head at the gray-haired woman in blue who looked as if she should be shopping for grandchildren instead of minding the store.

"It's a bit to take in all at once, isn't it?" she said.

"Yes."

"Are you shopping for a boy or a girl?"

"I'm not shopping."

"Oh, I see."

Of course she didn't. He was suddenly so bitter that the feelings came out in a painful rush before he could stop them. "I had a son. He died. I haven't been in a toy store since."

"Oh, I'm so sorry. How perfectly tragic for you."

"He loved to look at toys. He was…" He shook his head.

"What? What was he?"

He turned so he could see her face. Compassion shone in her eyes, but her hands were folded, as if she expected him to continue while she listened calmly. For some reason it was exactly the combination he needed. "He had Down's syndrome. Do you know what that is?"

"Oh, yes."

"He was my stepson, and when I met his mother, she just assumed I'd find his limitations troubling. But I loved him the moment I saw him. There was such sweetness there."

"Yes. I know."

"He was only mine for two years."

"They were good years?"

"Yes."

"I'm glad."

Noah walked over to a shelf where an array of stuffed animals sat and begged with their huge plastic eyes to be taken home and loved. "I met a little boy just a few days ago. Another child with Down's. He reminded me of Josh. The same blond hair, the same smile." He reached for a green-and-purple dragon with a goofy grin. "He likes purple. He'd like this, I think. Josh would have, I know."

"I believe you should buy it for him, then."

He held the dragon in both hands. He had cut himself off from everything and everyone after Josh's and Lynn's deaths. He had buried all the parts of himself that had been able to love Josh so well. So why were those parts alive again? How had he been able to hold Teddy in his arms? How had he been able to tell this stranger the saddest story of his life?

"I'll take it." He thrust it toward her.

"I'm glad."

He was glad, too, even though the pain he had buried along with all the best parts of himself was now alive again.

"It's almost like a present from your son, isn't it?" The woman took the dragon behind the counter to put it in a bag. "After all, if you hadn't learned to love your Josh, you wouldn't be buying this for another child today."

Celestine approached the desk of the bank officer Whit had told her to contact. She waited until he was free, twice refusing a young woman's offer of assistance. When he waved her to a seat beside his desk, she took it and waited for him to look up from the papers in front of him.

"I'm Celestine St. Gervais," she said.

"Miss St. Gervais." He nodded in recognition. He was in his fifties, with a trim white mustache. To Celestine he looked like a summer Santa Claus. And she had been better than good this year.

"I believe Whit Sanderson from Flinders, Billett and Crane in Wilmington, North Carolina, contacted you?"

"He most certainly did. The money has been set up in an account for you. It's at your disposal immediately."

She closed her eyes in relief. "Thank you. Thank you so much."

They finalized arrangements, and Celestine signed the necessary documents. Then she stood and extended her hand, which he took with a smile. "Tell me how much cash you want today and I'll make the arrangements."

She had the cash in her hand before she realized she would have to stuff it in a shallow pocket because she didn't have a handbag to put it in. But she had the money to buy one now. The money to buy a handbag and anything else she needed. She would have to be frugal, but she was safe again. At least until she decided what she had to do next.

She checked a clock on the way out the door and realized she still had half an hour before she had to meet Noah. She needed a handbag, a watch and another pair of shoes, because the heel of one of hers had come loose after her solo hike through the woods. She needed more clothes and underthings, too, but that would have to wait. She didn't have time to do that much shopping, and besides, she needed to travel light.

She found a store with handbags and chose an imitation leather one that was large enough to double as a small suitcase. She found a plain round watch with a cheap metal band and a cloth wallet to put inside the handbag. She searched for shoes but had no luck. Instead she found a shoe repairman, who tightened the heel so that she could take her time finding something she liked.

By eleven o'clock she was feeling satisfied with herself.

She headed for the china shop where she was to meet Noah. He was already there, leaning against a wall with his arms folded watching the passersby.

He didn't see her right away. He seemed perfectly contented surveying the tourist throng, the picture of a man who didn't need anyone or anything.

That impression was a false one. In the days they had been together she had begun to know him, despite his reticence. Some of the image he presented to the world was real. She suspected that even under the best circumstances he was a quiet man, a man who took the measure of any and every situation before forming an opinion. And he was a strong man, one with the courage and intelligence to wrest the best from a bad situation. He had successfully fought off Bobby

and helped her to escape when other men might have failed
to do either. He acted on his convictions, even at personal
risk.

She thought she knew those things about him. Despite
Whit's warning, she couldn't believe that Noah was acting
and had continued the act through all their days together.
But she had also made mistakes. Bobby had been one, and
apparently Dougie Ferguson had been another.

Both those mistakes had been serious. But now, watching Noah, her heart beat a little faster, and she knew that if
she was wrong about him, too, the world would never look
exactly the same to her again. Because she wanted him to be
real. With all her heart, she wanted to believe in Noah
James.

He straightened, turned a little and saw her watching him.
His smile kindled slowly. She liked the way his eyes warmed
to match it. She had the most absurd desire to walk into his
arms and kiss him right there on the ancient streets of Canterbury.

"Did it go well?"

She moved closer before she answered. "It went fine."

"Good." He didn't ask anything else. She supposed he
had learned it was a waste of time, but she was almost disappointed. She wanted to share her good fortune with him.
God knows she had shared the bad.

"What did you do while I was gone?" she asked.

"A little shopping."

"It must have been a little. You don't have any pack-
ages."

"I took them to the car."

She moved out of the way of a group of German tourists. "Do you still want to see the cathedral?"

"Do you want lunch first?"

"Afterward, maybe."

He reached for her hand. It seemed the most natural thing
in the world to share a simple conversation and to walk together through the crowds. She linked her fingers with his.

They ambled along with the flow of the foot traffic, stopping to gaze in windows and down side streets. Celestine tried to remember the last time she had walked with a man this way. She had missed so many of the experiences her peers had taken for granted. But as frightening as the past years had been, and as uncertain, she had gotten some good things from them, as well. She had learned how valuable each moment was. Even if the uncertainty ended someday and she was suddenly handed a normal life, she would never take anything for granted. Not a sunset. Not the scent of summer roses or the feel of silk against her skin.

Not a man like Noah.

They had covered several blocks before he spoke. "I bought a gift for Teddy."

"Did you? What?"

"A dragon."

"Not a real one, I hope. Canterbury seems like the kind of place where real dragons might be had for a price."

"Real enough to suit him."

Since he had broached the subject, she felt she could continue it. "You seemed to know exactly what to say to Teddy, Noah. Not everyone would be so at ease."

She paused, but he didn't answer, so she went on. "Marian told me that he'll be going to school nearby so that he can live at home with his parents while he does. I was glad. Every child needs to be loved. A child like Teddy needs to be absolutely sure of it while he's growing up."

"I had a child like Teddy. My stepson."

"You told me you don't have any children."

"I don't. Not anymore. He died."

She gripped his hand tighter.

He went on. "I'd already forgotten some of the little things about him. Until Teddy brought them all back. He had a stuffed monkey named Dawg that he carried everywhere. Even into the bathtub. He was almost five, and he already knew his ABCs. My wife worked with him for hours and hours every day. Sometimes I'd come home and they'd both be near tears. But she was determined he was going to read and write, tell time. . . ." He paused. "He would have, too."

"What happened?"

"He went to sleep one evening, and he never woke up again."

"I'm so sorry."

"Yeah." He sighed. "I'm sorry I made myself forget. I can't remember the name of his favorite bedtime story, or the color of his bedroom walls, or what it was that he wanted for his next birthday. I put it all away somewhere, and now I'll probably never find it again."

"You haven't forgotten the important things, Noah."

"I don't know."

"My parents died when I was still a child. I've forgotten a lot more than I remember about them. But I remember how much they loved me. And that's kept me going for a lot of miles."

"A lot more miles than most people travel."

"You know what? I'm glad I'm not traveling right now." He squeezed her hand. "Look up ahead."

She gazed up and saw the Christ Church Gate, thrown wide to frame the view of the magnificent cathedral. They drank it in together, standing just in front of the gateway.

"You can almost believe that anything's possible when you see what man can do. When he sets his mind to it," Noah said.

Celestine stared up at the cathedral in its ornate Gothic glory. She felt a little of what the Canterbury pilgrims must have felt all those centuries ago.

"It looks like we have to pay to get inside. I'll—"

She hardly noticed that Noah had stopped midsentence. "Think of all the history here." She shook her head. "I've heard that some of the stained glass windows are nearly as old as the cathedral. I—"

Noah jerked hard on her arm.

She turned, perplexed. "What?"

"Come on." He turned and tugged sharply at her arm again.

She allowed herself to be dragged several steps before she dug in her heels. "What's going on?"

"Trust me."

She did. She knew it in that moment. Something was wrong, and there was no time for questions. Faced with demanding an explanation or giving in, she gave in and hurried along behind him.

There were shops lining the street leading to the gate. Noah yanked her unceremoniously into one, dodging displays and two silver-haired matrons who were making choices between teapots shaped like thatched cottages and red telephone booths. "In the corner." He jerked his head to the side.

She didn't ask why. She did exactly what he said. He stood beside her and turned his back toward the door so that her view of what was going on outside was completely blocked.

"What's happening?" she asked softly.

"What do you think of these?" He lifted a set of tea towels with quotes from Chaucer decorating them. "They'll be perfect for my mother, don't you think?"

She kept her voice low. "Do you have a mother?"

"Somewhere."

She realized that Noah was watching the shop door in a mirror placed on the wall behind her head. She frowned. "What is it?" she asked.

He looked down for a moment. Just the briefest blink in time. "Bobby."

"Oh, God."

"And what will we get for your family?" he asked in a louder voice.

"A hit man."

His eyes flicked to hers again. He seemed to understand immediately that she wasn't joking.

"Where was he?" she whispered.

"Returning from his daily prayers at the cathedral."

She closed her eyes. She was never going to be safe. Never going to be free. Even the house of God wasn't off-limits to those who wanted her dead. "How did he know?"

"He's walking by right now, Celie. Keep your head down."

She didn't move.

Noah began to talk about gifts for relatives she didn't have. She stood there tense and silent as he rambled on about tea towels and ceramic models of Big Ben.

When he stopped talking, she knew the immediate danger was over.

"All right, here's what we'll do," he said after a short silence. "We have to assume he's traced us to town somehow. That means Bobby or one of his friends may be watching the car parks. We can't get the car. We'll have to find somebody else to do it for us."

"Who?"

"Pubs are good for that kind of thing. We'll find somebody who'll do it if we pay him enough money."

"Then?"

"We meet whoever gets the car. Somewhere that Bobby won't be expecting us to go. A residential street would probably be best. Then we get the hell out of Canterbury."

"How did he know?"

"Maybe you'll have to tell me why you're here before I can figure that out."

"No. That couldn't have anything to do with it."

"He traced us here. He was here today of all days. Think about it, Celie."

"No. I know that's not it!"

Noah shook his head. "Then Bobby the giant really is a religious man, and he's here on a pilgrimage. You figure out which explanation sounds like it makes the most sense."

Chapter 10

"It's come to the point where my life is in danger, too. I think you owe me the truth." Noah looked over at Celie—he still thought of her that way, even though now, supposedly, he knew her real given name. She was curled up against the car door, and her hair hid the side of her face. But he didn't have to see her face to know exactly how it would look. Haunted. Desperate. Wounded.

She spoke without facing him. "You've been good to me. But I don't owe you anything, Noah. I didn't ask for your help."

"You might as well have. You asked me not to take you to the hospital that day. Maybe I should have, anyway. Then this would be somebody else's problem."

He regretted the words the moment he'd said them. But he was angry that she still refused to tell him what was going on. And he hadn't been lying this morning when he'd told her that his patience was running out.

"I'll leave as soon as we get back. I'll find a way back to London from Trillingden."

"No." The sigh that emerged was as deep as his frustration. "I'm sorry."

"You have no reason to be."

"I'm not usually cruel."

"You're not usually on the run."

"And I'd like to know exactly why I am now. Which means you're going to have to tell me the truth."

"Do you think so? What makes you think I can trust you? There were three people in this whole wide world who knew I was going to Canterbury today. You were one of them!"

He gripped the steering wheel harder. "I was the one who saw Bobby."

"Yes, and you were the one who had time to meet with him while I was doing my errand. You could have arranged for him to be at the cathedral waiting. Or maybe he wasn't there at all. *I* never saw him!"

"Fine." He barely managed to get the word out. He clenched his jaw to keep from saying something he would profoundly regret.

They drove in silence until they reached the next village. He ignored the road that bypassed the town center and steered the car through the narrow high street until he reached a brick storefront that housed the grocery store and post office.

"All right." He parked and turned off the engine. "It's still early. There's probably a bus you can take out of here this afternoon. I'm assuming you have money now, since you're carrying a purse you didn't have before. So I would suggest that you take yourself out of harm's way, get on that bus to wherever it goes and disappear again. I'd suggest you take a number of buses, so that I won't be able to trace you easily. Because of course I'll want to trace you. I'm trying hard to murder you, even though I've never lifted a hand against you in all the days we've been together."

Only then did he look at her. Tears were streaming down her cheeks, but she didn't make a sound.

He closed his eyes and leaned back against the headrest. The car still smelled like the man who had retrieved it for them. Tobacco, sweat and greed. "I know that you don't know who to trust, but I can't live on the other end of your suspicion. Not anymore, Celie. Either you trust me, or this is it."

He fully expected her to get out. He might very well have, in her situation. But the door didn't click.

"I'm sorry," she said at last. Tears softened her voice. "I'm not working with Bobby. I never saw him until the moment I found you in that alley."

"All right."

"And Bobby *was* at the cathedral today."

"I can't understand how he knew where to find me."

He opened his eyes and turned to her. "I can't help you figure it out until you tell me what you were doing there. You said three people knew you would be in Canterbury. Who were the other two?"

"I have to think about this."

"You have to think about what you're going to tell me?"

"Yes." She took a tissue from her pocket. "If you can't understand that, then I *will* get out."

He considered her words. At the very least she was being honest for a change. "All right."

She took a deep breath and let it out slowly. "Thank you."

"Let's go home."

"What if he's traced us there?"

"If he knew where we were staying he wouldn't have been looking for us in Canterbury."

"If he's gotten this close, he'll get closer."

He started the car engine and pulled back out into traffic. He had no words of comfort to offer her because there were none. She was probably right. And both of them knew it.

Celestine found her way down to the rocks beside the stream. She used her injured arm to balance herself, but it would be a long time before it would bear any weight. The wound would heal completely with time, but she was still a long way from a full recovery.

Noah was inside the cottage working in his room, but she had made sure to tell him where she was going so that he wouldn't be concerned. She felt as safe down here as she did anywhere. Even if Bobby found his way to the cottage, it would be a long time before he spotted her here.

The sun was going down, and the sky was already suffused with coral. She thought of the sunsets at Haven House. Her parents had made a ritual of watching them, no matter what the weather or their other commitments. Every night they had taken drinks to the wide balcony that looked to the west, to watch the sun sink behind the horizon. Celestine had shared in the ritual with apple juice spiked with club soda and the biggest maraschino cherry in the jar. Her father had said that God had been particularly good to them, and they should pay close attention to all his handiwork.

She still felt closest to her mother and father when she could see the sunset. And everywhere she had lived in the years since, she had sought out a place like this one where she could be alone and remember.

There hadn't been time to remember much recently, except that her life was in danger and she couldn't trust anyone. She had become someone, something, that she didn't recognize. There was so little left of the woman who had taken Stephen Montgomery as her lover, a woman who had believed there was still love in the world, despite everything that had happened to her. A woman who had believed in the future.

Four years of running had turned her into someone else, someone who had forgotten how to trust a man, even when he had twice stood between her and a killer.

Or maybe that wasn't it at all, despite what she'd told herself and him from the beginning. Maybe she was afraid that this man, with his cynical mouth and his haunted watchful eyes, would make her long so desperately for all the things she couldn't have that she would forget to run. And they would both suffer for it.

"It's beautiful, isn't it?"

Her breath caught in her throat. She spun around and found Noah standing just above her. She hadn't heard him approach. She supposed if he had been Bobby, she would be dead by now.

"I'm sorry, I made as much noise as I could." He had changed into jeans and a burgundy sweater, and the setting sun shadowed the strong, proud angles of his face.

"Come join me." She moved over so that he could sit beside her.

He didn't move. "You're sure? Until I startled you, you almost looked peaceful."

"I can be peaceful with you, can't I?"

"I don't know."

"Let's try."

He joined her, sitting close, but not close enough to touch her. She liked the way his jeans drew tight around his thighs when he stretched out his legs, the way he restlessly pushed up the sleeves of his sweater. His forearms were dusted with dark hair, and his hands were wide and strong. She had seen those hands closed around Bobby, his wrist, his hair. She had seen Noah fighting for his life and hers, yet she had discounted that vision over and over again.

Because she was afraid. Because her life was ruled by fear and nothing else.

"I have dinner almost ready," he said.

"Will it keep for a little while?"

"It should."

There was very little warmth in his voice. Over their days together he had begun to reach out to her. She thought of the little he had told her about his son today, and her throat constricted. He had suffered, too. Intimacy wasn't easy for Noah James. He was a man who let life parade in front of him. He watched; he didn't participate. But he had been thrust into the midst of hers, and he had responded with courage and compassion.

She made her decision. It was easy after all. Noah deserved to know why she was being stalked. And she needed to tell him. She needed to trust him. Because if she couldn't trust this man, there was no one in the world that she could trust. And if that was true, life wasn't worth hanging on to so tenaciously.

"You wanted to know more about me," she began.

"I wanted to know what you were doing in Canterbury."

"I haven't been completely honest with you."

"You do understatement well, Celie."

"All right. I've hardly been honest at all."

"I knew that part."

He was watching her closely. The space between them seemed charged with more than secrets. "I do know who's trying to kill me."

"But you're not going to tell me because it will put me at risk."

"May I tell you a story?"

"I'm listening."

She saw that he meant it. She could take her time, tell it her way. And he would still be there when she had finished. He had been there for her from the beginning, and, miraculously, he had remained.

She watched the sunset as she began. "When I was a little girl, I was very close to my mother and father. They spoiled me, I guess, because my mother couldn't have more children. I look like her, I think, but I move like my father. I've been told I walk just the way he did, with a little bounce in my step like I can't wait to get wherever I'm going. Maybe that's what you noticed the first time you saw me."

"I suspect the walk looks even better on you than it did on him."

She didn't smile. "My parents died when I was nearly nine. We lived on the water, and they were expert sailors. They liked challenges. They weren't foolhardy, but when they were out on the water they sometimes took chances. The day they died a storm blew up suddenly, and they took one chance too many."

He took her hand. Casually. Like a good friend. But her reaction wasn't the reaction of one friend to another. Not for the first time she wondered what it would feel like to have his hands on more intimate parts of her body.

"Go on."

She sifted through the debris of her life. "Most kids, most orphans, go to live with relatives. In my case, my aunt and uncle came to live with me. My parents were wealthy. My father had inherited his father's entire estate, because my grandfather had disinherited my aunt before he died. My grandfather didn't like my aunt's husband, and apparently she had disgraced the family in a number of ways herself. So he left her nothing in the will except a few words of advice."

"Which I suppose she took."

"No. She was angry, and when my grandfather died she demanded that my father give her a fair share anyway. Like their father, I think he knew that whatever he gave her was as good as lost forever. So he told her that he would always take care of her, but he kept control of the money. She never forgave him."

"She came to take care of you after your parents died?"

"Except for some distant cousins, she was the only relative I had. My father had realized he wasn't immortal, and he'd made a will. All my inheritance was tied up in a trust, except for the amount that was needed for my support and to run—" She stopped. She still didn't want to give Noah any identifying details. "The estate," she finished. "Attorneys were appointed to make all decisions until I was old enough to take it over."

"Sounds like he made a good decision."

"About the estate, but not about me. My aunt and uncle moved in to take care of me, and from that moment on my life was a living hell."

He squeezed her hand.

"They want me dead," she said at last, when she could speak again. "I don't know exactly when they realized that killing me was the only way they could stay where they were and keep what they had. You see, my father was afraid that if something happened to me before I came of age to take over the trust, the entire estate would be eaten up by taxes and attorney's fees. So he stipulated that if I died before that time, everything in the trust would go to my aunt. He was suspicious of my uncle, but I guess Daddy still loved his sister. And he didn't want her to be left with nothing. At some point she and my uncle realized that they could keep everything if I died. And rather than leave that to chance..."

"You think it's your aunt and uncle who are after you?"

"I think they're behind everything that's happened to me. Yes."

"What proof do you have?"

"Besides motive? Besides the fact that they tried to destroy me emotionally all the years I was growing up?" Her voice rose, and she clamped her lips shut.

"I know it's a strong case."

"There *is* no other case."

He brought her hand to his chest, moving closer. He put one arm around her and pulled her to rest against him. "The story about seeing your lover die was a lie?"

"No."

"Now I'm confused."

She swallowed. Pain. Betrayal. The anger that had been simmering inside her since the day of her parents' funeral. She waited until she was calm enough to speak.

"The first attempt on my life came when I was in college. I had managed to convince the attorneys in charge of my money that I had to leave... the South. I wanted to put as much distance between myself and my aunt and uncle as I could manage. My best friend from boarding school was going to college in New England, and I wanted to room with her. My aunt and uncle were against it, of course, but since they weren't paying, they were overruled. I settled in, and for the first time since my parents died, I was really happy. I was a drama major. Does that surprise you?"

"How could it?"

"I studied languages, too. I'm one of those strange people who can pick them up immediately. I discovered that in boarding school. I'm fluent in French and German, and my Hungarian is pretty good."

"Hungarian?"

"Budapest is just one of the places I've called home in the past five years. I was Elena Kovacs there. A second generation American looking for my roots."

He brushed her hair with his fingers. It was a soothing motion, but nothing could soothe her now. She wanted to tell this and get it over with. "What happened in college?" he asked.

"In my senior year I was walking home from class one night. It was after dark, but everyone on campus knew everybody else, and we were all too casual about safety. My roommate was waiting back at the dorm so we could go out for pizza, and I was in a hurry, so I didn't wait for my friends. I decided to duck in between the science and English buildings. The area was poorly lit, but I wasn't worried. I heard footsteps behind me and didn't think anything about it. Then someone grabbed me by the collar and threw me to the ground. Facedown, so I couldn't see."

His fingers gently grazed her cheek, and he turned her face to his. "Do you want to finish this?"

His eyes were dark pools of compassion. She nodded. "He sat on me and wrapped his fingers around my throat. Then he started to choke me. I didn't even have time to scream."

"Someone must have come to the rescue?"

"A biology professor had been working on some project in the science building, and he saw us. At first he assumed we were just a couple of students horsing around, but he decided he'd better check. When he got closer, my attacker ran. I was left with a swollen windpipe and bruises on my throat."

"How did you decide it was anything more than random violence?"

"I didn't. Not at first. But he had no motive to attack me. He didn't try to rape me. He didn't try to steal anything."

"Maybe he didn't have time."

"That's what the police said when they investigated. But one of them, an old sergeant with years of experience, took me aside and asked me if there was anyone who might benefit from my death. Until that moment I hadn't even considered the awful possibility that my aunt and uncle could have planned it. Then I began to wonder.

"They showed up together the next day to take me home. They arranged my withdrawal from the college before I could do a thing to change their minds. My roommate tried to stop them. She was my closest friend, and she knew what they were like. But I was on my way back home before anything could be done. They claimed I needed help to get over the trauma. Help and rest." She laughed, and the sound was bitter.

"I gather they didn't help."

"I was young and frightened. They told me I was needlessly overwrought. That I was emotionally disturbed. They claimed I had always shown poor judgment and crossing the campus at night by myself was just another example. And they questioned whether the attack was real or maybe just rough sex...."

Celestine rested her head against his arm and closed her eyes. Recounting the nightmare of the past years was easier that way. "They worked on me a little at a time. I was trying to recover, but they wouldn't allow it. They continued to hammer away at me. They sent me to a psychiatrist who told me I was delusional. One minute I was frightened they might be right. That I really was crazy. The next I was frightened of them."

"How did you get through it?"

"I decided that I didn't understand enough about my parents' will to know if my death would really benefit my aunt or uncle enough to have me killed. So I went to the attorneys who were administering the estate. At the last minute the man who was scheduled to see me was taken ill. The

firm had just hired a new law school graduate to assist him,
so he saw me, instead. By that time I really was in danger of
losing my mind. I poured out the whole story to him. What
had happened. My fears about my aunt and uncle. My fears
about my own sanity. What the police sergeant had asked
me. By the time I finished I was sure he was ready to call the
men with the butterfly nets. But all he did was take out the
will and explain exactly why it was possible that my aunt and
uncle might want me dead.''

She hurried on. ''He tried to help me, and in the process,
I . . . we fell in love. He discovered that my uncle was attempting to have me committed to a private psychiatric in-
stitution. My uncle claimed I was a danger to myself, and
he'd nearly gotten my psychiatrist to agree. My friend—''

''Did he have a name, this friend?''

She considered his question. ''Stephen.'' She opened her
eyes. ''Just Stephen.''

His lips tightened in something like a grimace. ''Go on.''

''Stephen went out on a limb to try to stop my aunt and
uncle. The older attorneys in his office, the ones who had
been administering the estate all those years, didn't believe
my story. My aunt and uncle appeared respectable enough
by then, and they had the psychiatrist on their side. I was
young and nearly frantic with fear, and I suppose from their
standpoint it was easier to believe that I needed treat-
ment.''

She fell silent. There was only a little more, but the memories were bad enough that now, by recounting them, she
knew she would dream of Stephen's death tonight as she had
so many times before.

''Is that all you can tell me?'' Noah asked.

''Stephen died the day he filed an injunction to try to stop
my aunt and uncle from having me committed. There had
been a number of break-ins in his apartment complex. The
usual kind of thing. Stereos and television sets. Jewelry. The
police said that Stephen must have surprised someone who
was intent on robbing him. But it wasn't like any of the
other burglaries. He was killed with one bullet. The televi-

sion was still in place, and so was the stereo. The murderer had dumped dresser drawers on the bed, to make it look like he had ransacked the apartment, but nothing was missing. The police said that was probably because he heard someone coming and ran out the patio door. But whoever it was didn't even take Stephen's wallet out of his pocket."

"You said you witnessed a murder."

"He died in my arms, but the killer was gone when I got there. I was supposed to be with Stephen. We were supposed to go to his apartment together that afternoon. But something came up, and I told him to go ahead without me, that I'd meet him later. When I got to Stephen's the door was open, and people had begun to gather in the hall. I went in, and he was still alive. He saw me and tried to tell me something. I knelt down, and he spoke again. I put his head on my lap. And he died."

His arm tightened around her. "What did he say? Do you know?"

"Yes. He said, 'Run.' He was telling me to run. My aunt and uncle killed him. I'm sure neither one of them pulled the trigger, but they were responsible."

"Why kill *him?* Why didn't they just kill you?"

"I don't know for sure. Either they'd planned to, and I just didn't show up at the apartment when they thought I would, or they had decided to wait a while so that my death wouldn't raise suspicions. I'm sure if they had succeeded in committing me, I never would have left the hospital alive. But Stephen was standing in their way. They couldn't do anything to me while he was still alive. He believed my story, and he would have made sure they were exposed."

"Who's helping you now?"

"Stephen told me that if anything happened to him, there was another attorney in his office I could trust with my story. He helped me get away, and he's been helping me ever since. He has limited access to my trust, because he handles some of the investments. But he juggles this and that for me when I need it. No one knows. He would be destroyed professionally if anyone suspected."

"And he's the one who just sent you money?"

"Yes."

"So he knew where you would be?"

"It wasn't him, Noah. I know it wasn't."

"And who was the other person who knew you would be in Canterbury?"

"The officer at the bank. A stranger in every way."

"I see."

Celestine could see, too. She knew exactly what Noah was thinking. "You're barking up the wrong tree. Stephen's friend wouldn't betray me."

"Even good friends can be corrupted."

"He's trying to keep me safe. He helps whenever he can."

"Then he keeps track of you?"

"No. But I call him when I need to. He gets word to a few friends that I'm all right when I can't call them myself. If it weren't for him I'd have nobody...."

"Celie, think about it. You call him. He can trace your calls."

"No. I'm careful never to speak to him that long...."

"Ah..." Noah cupped her chin and turned her face to his. "You don't trust him completely, then, do you?"

"There have been other attempts on my life, too. About a year ago I spotted a man following me, or at least I thought I did. I told myself not to panic, that no one could have found me. That night I came within inches of being hit by a car. And six months before that I had another narrow escape. There have been other incidents, too. Maybe they were all accidents, and maybe they weren't...."

"Celie..."

"Can't you see what it's like to be me?" She refused to cry again. Noah had seen her cry more than anyone else in the world. But her distress sounded in her voice. She wanted him to understand.

"It's a nightmare. And I don't know how you've made it this far."

His hazel eyes warmed to the golden hue of the sky. She saw that he believed her. He had listened. He hadn't judged. He was angry that her life had come to this.

She was swept with such relief that for a moment she couldn't speak. Until now she hadn't realized that part of the reason for keeping so much of the truth from Noah had been fear that he wouldn't believe her. It wasn't an easy story to believe. It wasn't an easy story to tell.

Her hand slid into his hair before she could stop herself. "I *have* made it," she said. "And I'm going to keep on making it. I'm going to get through this and find a way to live again. Really live..."

He gathered her closer. She saw the same battle in his eyes that she was fighting. They stared at each other, neither making the first move.

"And if I don't make it," she said, "if for some reason I don't come through this alive, then I would like to know that before I died I trusted one person completely."

"You don't have to say anything else. You don't owe me anything, Celie."

"No. I owe this to myself." She breached the distance between them. She liked the cynical twist of his mouth, but she liked better the way it softened under her kiss.

The kiss was like a match in a drought-dry forest. He slid his hands to her waist as if to push her away, but he didn't—or couldn't. Something, a denial, a plea, sounded deep in his throat. He brought her closer until her breasts flattened against his chest.

She had been half-alive for so long that the sudden rush of warmth and hope was like an alien force inside her. She hadn't risked this flooding sweetness, this abandonment of caution, since Stephen's murder. Now she was overwhelmed by sensation. His tongue touched hers, and her only thought was surrendering to him and to the hours that were left to them.

"Celie..." He lifted his head, but his hands still played restlessly over her hips. "This isn't a good idea. You're still upset." As if to belie his own words, he slanted his lips over hers once more and kissed her again.

She moaned when he moved away. "I don't want to think, Noah. I don't care if it's a good idea or not."

"I care."

"I'm not asking you for anything. There's nothing else you can do to help me. Not any more than you've done."

He drew away, and his hands fell to his sides. His eyes were shadowed. "I *could* do something—if you'll just tell me your full name and where all this happened."

"No. I watched one man die when he tried to help me. I won't put you in more danger than I have already."

"That sounds like you're still planning to leave."

She didn't answer.

"What do you want from me, then? A one-night stand? A brief intermission in the horror show you call your life?"

"A memory. One good memory."

He pushed her away and himself upright. He shook his head as if she'd slapped him. Then, without another word, he started up the slope to the house.

"Noah!" She scrambled up after him. It took her too long, and he reached the house well before she did.

By the time she got there, he was gone. She saw that the kitchen had been transformed. The table had been set for two, complete with candles that hadn't yet been lit. Beside the candles was a cake, and at the place where she usually sat there was a pile of brightly wrapped presents.

"Noah!" She swept through the house, searching for him. He wasn't in his room, but the front door was ajar. She tugged it fully open and stared out into the gathering darkness. "Noah . . ."

He slammed the car door shut and turned. "Can you drive?"

"What?"

"Can you drive? Do you know how?"

"Yes, of course. I—"

"What about your shoulder? The car handles easily. Do you think you can manage the steering wheel for a short distance?"

"Probably, but—"

"Good. Here are the keys." He strode toward her, took her hand and closed her fingers around the key chain. "Take it as far as you want. The only thing I ask is that you call the rental company and tell them where it is before you abandon it. They'll take care of it from there, and I'll take care of the fees. All the papers are in the glove compartment."

"Why are you doing this?"

"What do you want me to do? You want a night of comfort, and then you want to get the hell out of here. You tell me the story of your life, but you won't let me do anything about it. Well, I'm not playing along. Either I'm in your life or I'm out of it right now, Celestine. One or the other. There's nothing in between."

"You don't understand! You can't!"

He stood right in front of her. In the soft light from the cottage she could see the bleakness of his eyes. "No? Don't you think so? Then let me tell you a story. Just a short one. Not too many years ago I was a married man with a son and a wife I adored. But I didn't take care of them the way that I should have, and one day they were both gone. Just like that." He snapped his fingers. "So maybe I don't understand what you're going through, but I do understand something. I will never stand by and watch a woman I care about suffer because I didn't do enough for her. I would give up my life in a heartbeat before I'd let that happen again."

He stepped closer, until there was no space between them. "So make your choice, Celestine. Either run or stay. But if you stay, we're in this for the long haul. And whatever happens, we'll face it together. You decide."

Chapter 11

Noah watched Celie's face. She was emotionally and physically exhausted, and she couldn't hide either condition. He wanted to stand there, resolute, and demand that she make her choice. But another part of him, a weaker part, wanted to kiss the lies out of her and pledge that no matter what she said, they would still have this night together.

She held her arms out to him, and he knew it was the closest thing to a promise she could manage. He hauled her against him with a groan, and his mouth came down on hers.

She was trembling. One arm crept around his neck, and her lips opened under his. He had never tasted anything sweeter or more poignant. He wanted to believe that this was the start of something. He had made his stand and believed every word of his own noble speech.

But he knew that this could still be goodbye.

He nudged her inside and kicked the door shut behind them. "What am I going to do with you? What am I going to do *about* you?'' He kissed her again, harder this time, taking care not to hurt her shoulder.

"Don't do anything. Just let it happen."

He knew that was exactly what he shouldn't do. But he was past the point of making choices. This one had been made, and already his body was straining toward fulfillment. She had bewitched him from the first, before he knew that she was everybody and nobody. A woman without a name.

She broke away, and for a moment he thought that she had changed her mind. She turned and started toward his bedroom. In the doorway she faced him again. He hadn't moved. He hadn't known what she was going to do. But now one hand reached for the top button of her sweater, and she freed it.

"Let it happen, Noah." She freed the second button.

He moved closer, but he was mesmerized by the sight of her as she undressed. Her hand moved with the grace of Marie St. Germaine. Her blue eyes were as steady, as determined, as Celie Sherwood's. But the woman undressing for him was someone named Celestine. And tonight, for the first time, he understood what had made her the woman she was.

"I could use some help." Her voice was low-pitched and sultry. She was a seductress now, determined to get her way in this. The need was there. He saw it in the slight trembling of her fingers, in the unsteady smile. The passion was there in the way she leaned forward, as if she could draw him to her with the sensuous swaying of her body.

"You're doing fine." His voice belonged to someone else, not to Noah Colter, who controlled every situation before it could control him. He had always been a watcher, and more so in the years after Lynn's and Josh's deaths. But watching had been a way to distance himself from others. Now, watching Celestine, he wanted to be as close to her as a man could be to a woman.

She unfastened the third button, then the fourth. She stopped, her hand poised against her breasts. "Why don't you show me how well I'm doing?"

He moved toward her. She stood quietly, hands at her sides now. He reached for the fifth button. Her bra was in view, a simple white cotton affair that Jerry had bought at a discount department store. She deserved silk and lace, something that smoothly hugged the gentle curves beneath, something classy enough to suit the elegant swell of her breasts and hips. The button came undone, and the pale skin of her torso gleamed in the fading twilight.

She rested her hands on his shoulders. He was acutely aware of her touch. Even through his sweater, her hands felt warm and heavy. He could feel each separate finger, the slightest flicker of a fingertip. His breathing faltered. "I don't want to hurt you. You're far from recovered."

"I won't let you hurt me, Noah."

He knew she was talking about more than her shoulder. He reached for the next button, then the next. He spread the sweater open, and his palms grazed her skin. Her eyelids drifted shut, and her fingertips dug deeper. "You're not as tough as you pretend." He kissed her eyelids, her forehead, but not her lips. "You're an open wound, Celestine. Your life has been one assault after another...."

"Then heal me tonight. Not forever. You can't do that. But for now."

She tipped her head back and offered her lips to him. He took them with a groan. He was lost now. If there had been a moment when he could have stopped this, it was long past. He was not the man he had thought himself to be.

She shrugged off the sweater, and it fell to the floor at their feet. He found the catch on her bra and made quick work of it. She let him slide it over her shoulders until it had joined her sweater on the floor.

From the first moment he had seen her, he had wanted to feel the satin sweep of her skin against his hands. Her breasts were small and round, perfect in every way. He had buried the desire to touch her deep inside him, confused that his own dark needs could be so powerful. Now he gave in to them. She felt as he'd known she would, fragile, yet solid, as smooth as marble and as warm as a smoldering ember.

Her hands fell to his waist, then inched beneath his sweater. Against his bare skin her fingertips were even more provocative. His blood was pulsing through his veins with a stunning intensity. He was a cautious lover, a man who could please a woman and find pleasure without giving too much of himself away. But now there was nothing subdued about what he was feeling. He wanted to sweep Celestine off her feet and carry her to his bed. He wanted to make love to her on top of the covers, without removing more of their clothes than was necessary. He wanted to plunge into the very core of her and claim her as his mate. His desire for her was so primitive, so basic, that he could not recognize it as belonging to him.

But it was also undeniable.

He tugged his sweater over his head and threw it to the floor. Her eyes gleamed brighter. She moved her hands over his chest, then circled his neck and pressed her breasts against his bare skin. He drew a sharp breath and clasped her close. She was unbearably soft, as soft as a whisper. He found the catch of her skirt and listened as it slid over her hips and pooled on the floor.

"Are we going to make love here?" Her voice was soft, too, as sultry as a Georgia night, as honeyed as a Carolina morning. She was Celestine now, and everything that meant. He knew that this time, this once, he held the real woman in his arms.

He scooped her off the floor easily. For all the burdens she had borne, she was a small woman. By all rights she should have died instantly with a twist of Bobby's hands. But she was more than flesh and bone. She had a spirit that was more powerful than all the attacks against it.

The bed seemed unbearably soft when he laid her against the covers. She watched him, making no attempt to cover herself as he undressed. Her panties gleamed white against the flowered comforter, and so did the bandage that adorned her shoulder. She didn't smile, as if she were afraid to break the spell that bound them together.

When he finally lay beside her, she opened her arms to him. He tangled his hands in her hair and learned the contours of her face with his lips. "I'm going to be careful. But you'll have to help me."

"I'm ... not protected, Noah. And I can't risk—"

He silenced her with a kiss. "I can take care of it," he said at last. "I wouldn't let anything happen to you."

She sighed. "I know.... I know that."

He felt her trust like a flash of sunlight. "I'm going to keep you safe. In every way."

"I know you want to. I know..."

He traced the contours of one breast with his fingertips, and her words trailed into a soft, sweet moan. "Your nerves aren't even skin deep," he whispered. "They're on the surface. That's how you've stayed alive. And now that's going to make this so much better."

He flattened his palm against her breast, cupping it and gently stroking her. Her skin seemed to heat as he touched her. Her breast grew swollen and taut against his hand. He flattened his palm against her abdomen and then lower, moving slowly, so slowly that he wondered where he found the control.

Her hands were featherlight against him, but he had never been so acutely aware of a woman's touch. He wanted to be touched everywhere; he wanted to touch everywhere in return. In moments he could not distinguish between her pleasure and his. When she moved against his palm and gasped, he felt that small ecstatic sound within him. When her hands closed around him, small, warm hands that seemed to know exactly what would take him higher, his own gasp seemed to quicken her response.

He kissed her, and the kiss had no beginning or end. Her taste was as sweet, as elemental, as spring rain or sun-heated air. He found the different textures of her body and learned them all. The lush curve of her bottom, the sleek length of her legs, the dark, moist center of her desire.

His heart slammed against his chest, and his muscles contracted painfully as he denied himself what he most wanted. She had not done this often. Mixed in with a tumultuous natural passion was the hesitancy of inexperience. She had named one lover. But he doubted that she could name two. She had run so long, so far, and there had been no room in her life for a man.

There had not been enough trust.

He rolled to his back and sought what he needed from a case on his nightstand. Then, when he was protected, he brought her over him to lie against his chest. "Celestine..." He closed his eyes as she kissed him again. He could feel every alluring inch of her pillowed against him. He wanted nothing so much as to turn her on her back and thrust into her, to stake his claim to her heart and her life. Men had taken women that way from the beginning of time, and his response to her was that primal. But he knew better and cared too much. He was afraid of hurting her or frightening her. He knew this had to be in her time and her way.

She lifted her head and gazed into his eyes. "What can I do to make this good for you?"

If he hadn't been so touched and so aroused, he might have laughed. But he saw the very real concern in her eyes and knew she was serious. "Anything. Anything at all."

"I want to make love to you...."

"Good." He nearly strangled on the word.

"Slowly. Completely."

"Now." He rested his hands against her hips to help her. She took him inside her body both slowly and completely. He held his breath, groaning deep in his throat as she moved. He had forgotten that a man and a woman could fit together this way, that sex could be more than a convenience or a way to forget the emptiness inside him.

She moved, and he was flooded with heat. He remembered this now, this coming together when there was more than physical desire to prompt lovemaking. He had made himself forget this instant tenderness, this chasm of feeling that could open beneath a man with every move a woman made. He had felt this ecstasy, this union, once, but now he felt no guilt for feeling it again. Lynn would have understood this. She would have wanted him to be alive.

And he hadn't been alive for so long.

"Noah." Celestine's eyes were closed. Her expression was strained.

"Just let it happen," he said.

She tried to move, and he realized that she could only brace herself on one arm. "Hold on," he whispered. He turned her gently to her back, still deep inside her throbbing warmth. "Are you all right?"

"I didn't even know." She opened her eyes and stared up at him. They glittered with unshed tears. "I thought this was just sex."

It was something else, but he wouldn't give it a name. Not now, when there was still so much standing between them. He began to move. She didn't close her eyes, and she didn't look away. He watched the entire kaleidoscope of ecstasy in her expression and knew it was matched by his own.

If she had ached quite this way, throbbed deep inside quite this way, then she couldn't remember it. Celestine lay beside Noah and listened to his breathing slow. But he wasn't sleeping. She could sense that he was still awake, even though they hadn't spoken.

She was too confused to name what had happened between them. If she had been forced to find a word for what she had felt before their lovemaking, that word would have been *desire*. Desire for physical release. Desire to be touched. Desire to be wanted. She hadn't thought herself capable of love. Not now, when her life was still in jeopardy.

Perhaps what she felt was only gratitude. In Noah's arms she had experienced things she had thought impossible. She had trusted him completely. She had given in to her most secret desires, and he had fulfilled them all. But *gratitude* seemed a poor word for something as shattering as what she had felt. And for what she was still feeling.

"Are you awake?"

She opened her eyes and found his face close to hers. "Was that supposed to make me go to sleep?"

"It's been known to work that way."

She tried to read his feelings, but what had been so open was now closed to her once more. "Well, you're wide-awake."

"I didn't want to miss any time with you."

She smiled. It seemed to come from somewhere deep inside her, some place that hadn't been accessible until now. "I'm glad."

"Stay here."

"Why? Where are you going?"

"I'll be right back."

The room was nearly dark now, but she drank in what she could of his lithe, easy stride as he left the room. Only when he was gone did she remember the presents. And the cake.

She swallowed a sudden rush of tears. She couldn't even remember the last time her birthday had been anything except a way to mark another year that she had survived. And Noah had no way of knowing exactly how important this birthday was.

His arms were filled with presents when he returned, as she'd known they would be. He turned on the bedside lamp and sat cross-legged in naked splendor against the headboard.

"Please don't sing," she begged. "I'll cry."

"I don't sing. I'd make anybody cry."

She sat up, too. She had never been naked with a man this way. But she felt no embarrassment with Noah. Besides, her body held no secrets for him now. "You didn't have to do this. I wouldn't even have told you if I'd known you'd do this."

"I haven't told you how beautiful you are."

She looked up. She realized she was blushing. All over. "You don't have to. I know I'm pretty ordinary. But it's worked in my favor, so I'm glad. I have a face no one seems to remember."

"Completely untrue. I found it memorable as hell."

"It was my walk you found memorable."

"Everything about you is memorable. Especially now."

She reached for his hand. She didn't know what else to do.

"You can't open your presents if you're holding my hand."

"Then why don't you help?"

"No. I want to watch you."

She smiled; then she started on the first ribbon. "Did you shop in Canterbury?"

"Yeah. And we're lucky our friend from the pub didn't think to use the car key to open the trunk."

"That would have taken a leap in logic. And I don't think he had that in him."

"I would have felt particularly bad if he'd made off with the one you're opening."

"Oh?" She spread the wrapping wide and lifted the top off a plain white box. "Oh!" She looked up. "Noah, it's…"

"Take it out and see."

She already knew exactly what it was. She shook out the folds of emerald silk and stared at a nightgown with thin rolled straps and a neckline that had nothing to do with necks and more with belly buttons. She looked up at him. "Were you anticipating?"

"No. But I'd passed too many long nights wondering what you looked like lying in bed up there. And I couldn't seem to get you out of Betty's old flannel nightgown in my mind."

Delight filled her. She leaned over and kissed him; then she clutched the nightgown to her breasts. "I'm going to put it on right now."

He slid it from her hand. "No, you're not."

She laughed. "Thank you."

"Open the next one."

"You've really overdone it here."

"I'd forgotten how much fun it is to buy for a woman."

She stopped tugging at the next ribbon and looked back up at him. His eyes were serious. "Had you?"

"Yes."

She realized what he was telling her. Since his divorce, there hadn't been a woman in his life who was important enough to buy a simple present for. "I'm glad you had fun."

"Open it."

She removed the wrapping and stared at a dress. She guessed immediately that it was cashmere, finer than anything she had worn in years, blacker than sin and designed for it. "They had this in Canterbury?"

"It reminded me of the dress you were wearing the first time I saw you."

She shook out the fabric and held it against her breasts. "It's much nicer. It's wonderful. Thank you."

"If it fits like the other one, it'll be a success."

"I owe a lot to that dress, don't I? If you hadn't followed me, we wouldn't be here now."

"There's one more." He held the package on his lap for a moment, an incongruous splash of color against his flesh.

She smiled at the picture he made. "Noah, if you don't want to give it away, you can keep it."

"I'm afraid you're going to laugh."

"More of a chance I'm going to cry."

"Don't do either." He held out the present, and she took it. It was simply wrapped, a small red-and-gold gift box tied with a plain white ribbon.

She slipped off the ribbon and lifted the lid.

"Take it out."

She lifted out a block of wood and saw that it wasn't a block of wood at all, but puzzle pieces cleverly designed to fit together and form a cube. She spread them out on top of the lid of the first box she'd opened and then she saw. "Oh, it's Noah's ark." The pieces were finely crafted from a pale wood. The ark was the largest piece, followed by Noah himself and a sextet of animals. There was even a gang-plank.

"It's darling." She arranged the animals, two by two, with Noah at the head. "I love it."

"I saw it at the toy store where I got Teddy's dragon."

She looked up and saw that he wasn't smiling. "I'll treasure it."

"I wanted you to have something that reminded you of me."

She couldn't answer. She didn't know what to say.

"Something more than tonight," he said.

She cleared off the bed, carefully reassembling the puzzle and putting it back in its box, and replacing the dress and nightgown in theirs. When everything was on the floor beside her, she spoke. "I love the ark. I'll treasure it. But I won't need a toy to remember you, Noah."

"You're not going to let me help you, are you?"

"I don't want to talk about that. Not now. Please?" She rose on her knees and rested her hands on his shoulders. "Let's not talk at all."

He resisted for a moment. She knelt in front of him, pleading with her eyes. She couldn't face another confrontation with him now.

"There are people in this world who think I'm an immovable object," he said. "None of them has met you."

"This has been the most wonderful birthday of my life. May I thank you properly?"

"Improperly would be more to my liking."

"Noah..." She traced the corner of his mouth with a finger. "Would you like me to put on the black dress...and nothing else?"

The smoldering fire in his eyes kindled into flame. "I'd like that."

"I'm sorry I cut my hair. But you could pretend...."

"I don't need to pretend you're someone else. I wish that you didn't, either."

"Not someone else. Marie St. Germaine was a part of me. I was fond of her."

She moved away, stood and retrieved the dress. She slowly lifted it over her head, swaying provocatively as she did.

Then, as Noah watched, she inched it over her body, letting it slide sensuously over her breasts, her hips. It ended well above her knees and hugged her tighter than the other dress ever had. It was a dress a woman would only wear for one man.

Her man.

She fluffed her hair and posed, one leg extended, so that her slight figure was shown to its best advantage. "So, what do you think?"

He swung his legs over the bedside and came to stand in front of her, aware that what he "thought" was plainly visible. He didn't smile, and he didn't speak. He cupped his hands under her breasts, and she drew in a sharp breath.

He spread his hands, and his palms began a slow slide to her waist, smoothing the fabric that hugged her body so well. He stopped at her hips, then crouched in front of her, running his hands down her thighs to the hem and under it. Then he pulled her closer. "There's only one thing I'd rather see you do than put on this dress."

Her voice emerged breathy and low. "And that is?"

"Take it off."

He was sleeping soundly when she woke up the next morning before dawn. In sleep he didn't look so austere, so guarded. He looked like a man who was satisfied that the world was a safe place to rest, a place to hold a woman in his arms and dream.

It was neither, of course. And perhaps he knew it. She thought he had guessed that opening her arms to him last night had been the worst lie of all. She had not promised to stay with him, to let him help her face her demons. Opening her arms, gathering him close, had been a betrayal. Because now she was going to run again.

She got up carefully, and he slept on. The room was cold, but at least it jolted her completely awake. She stooped to collect her birthday gifts. As always, she had to travel light, but she couldn't make herself leave anything behind that he had given her. Over the years she had learned not to be attached to possessions, but she was already profoundly attached to these.

She gathered her clothes from the floor near the doorway and dressed in the kitchen, where the earliest light of morning was beginning to creep through the windows. The ruins of their midnight supper still cluttered the table, and crumbs from the bakery birthday cake littered the floor. Just hours ago they had laughed together over nothing, ravaged most of a roast chicken and fed each other cake like the bride and groom at a wedding reception.

She wondered if he had known, as she had, how little time they had left together. Because by the time they had sat down at this table last night, she had understood exactly what she had to do next. And by the time he had made love to her for the last time, she had known exactly how she was going to do it.

She took one last look around. Everything seemed so special suddenly. It was a room that held memories. And in the past days she and Noah had added theirs to the others that had been made in this room.

On a whim she reached up and plucked one of the dried flowers from the vine that twined low around the rafters. Noah had discovered from Marian that these were "hop bines," and that they often adorned pubs and houses in Kent, where hops had once been a major source of income. He had told her that prosperity and happiness were supposed to favor anyone who walked under them. The vines were replaced every year at harvest time, so she supposed no one would miss this small sentimental memento.

She was taking so very little with her, but it was more than she had ever had before. And she was taking her memories of last night.

In a few minutes she was ready to leave. Everything she owned fit in the handbag she had bought yesterday. She wanted to stand in Noah's doorway and whisper a last goodbye. But she knew she was in danger of waking him if she did.

At the end she left him the only thing that she could.

She wrote him a note asking him not to be angry. And then she placed it on a side table where he would be sure to see it, and weighted it with the gold wedding ring.

Chapter 12

The television got only one station, unless you counted the X-rated movies that were a pay-per-play service of the motel. Celestine hadn't been tempted to call the front desk to hook up to one of those. She'd gotten all the erotic entertainment that she needed listening to the couples next door, who rented that bed by the hour and made excellent use of their time.

She hadn't expected quality when she had taken this room. But no roaches crawled the walls here, as they had at the first place she tried. The sheets were yellowed with age but clean, and there was a peephole, along with a sturdy chain on the door. She had rented the room on the strength of that. Now, as someone pounded on the door, she was glad she had.

The knock sounded again. Louder this time. She hurried to the peephole and closed one eye to peer at her visitor. Then she threw back the chain.

In a moment she was in the visitor's arms.

"Allie..." Celestine whisked her best friend inside and closed the door behind her. "Allie..." She began to cry.

Tears plowed down her cheeks as she hugged the other woman and thumped her on the back. "I didn't think I'd ever see you again."

"Jeez, Celestine, could you have chosen a bigger dump?"

Celestine wiped her eyes and moved reluctantly out of Allie's hug. "You're dissing my humble home."

"Humble is right! God, there's a pawnshop to the left, a pawnshop to the right. You ever need a gun or an engagement ring with a diamond chip, you're in the right place."

Celestine slipped the chain back into place. "Maybe I do need a gun."

Allie grabbed her again. The hug was more like a shake. "Now, sweetcakes, don't talk like that. Nobody knows you're here. You're going to be okay. You are. Pretty soon everything's going to be okay."

Celestine drank in Allie's face. All the changes of the past four years stared back at her. Allie's dark hair was shoulder length and as shiny as patent leather. Her wicked brown eyes were dancing now as she cataloged the changes in Celestine. She had a pert schoolgirl nose, but her wide, full mouth and hourglass figure hinted at an interest in more adult passions.

Allie had been the worst of the bad girls at their boarding school, and more than one boy had fallen in love with her on sight. In the years since Celestine had left the country, Allie had graduated from college and taken a job in North Carolina as a sales representative for a pharmaceutical firm. Celestine imagined there were physicians all over the eastern third of the state who waited impatiently for her visits.

"Well?" Allie asked.

"You're gorgeous. I'm in awe."

"Oh puh...lease!" Allie dimpled. "Not so bad yourself. Maybe ping-ponging across that little old globe agrees with you."

Celestine's hand went to her hair. It was shorter now and much lighter, a tousled, layered style that went with her casual California-style clothes and the tan that was the result of hours under lights at an Edinburgh salon while she had waited for a new passport and papers. No one who had known Celie Sherwood would recognize her at first glance. She wondered what Noah would think of her if he could see her now.

Noah, who had haunted her dreams for the month since she had left him in Trillingden.

Her hand dropped to her side. "Running doesn't agree with me. I can't do it anymore."

"I'm glad you're back. Don't be afraid."

Celestine gestured to the chair with the torn plastic seat in the corner beside the bed. "Make yourself at home. I got us sodas from the machine."

"I guess that's safe. Can I sterilize the rims?"

Celestine popped the lid on one of the drinks and handed it over, taking the other for herself. "I wish I could stay with you. I'd love to see your condo."

"Remember all the nights when we used to stay awake and talk about what we'd do when we were free? The places we'd go? The things we'd buy?" Allie lifted her can in a toast. "To dreams coming true. You've probably been everywhere we talked about. And I've found one good old boy right after the other to buy me the things I wanted."

Celestine propped pillows against the bed's rickety headboard and opened her drink. "One right after the other?"

Allie shrugged. "You were the one with the classy tastes. Not me."

"Hasn't there been anybody who was special?"

"You were the one who believed in fairy tales." Allie smiled to soften her words. "You were always waiting for some knight to come and take you away from everything. I was always willing to settle for an itty-bitty bauble before he rode off."

Celestine smiled, too, but she supposed what Allie said was true. Allie had been born the only child of a single mother, and compared to the other girls they had gone to school with, Allie had been one step from the welfare lines. After her mother's death, her relatives had grudgingly paid for the expensive boarding school so that they wouldn't have to put up with her, but she had rarely had spending money. A long time ago Allie, much like Scarlett before her, had vowed that she would never go hungry again.

"And what about you?" Allie propped her bare feet on the bed and wiggled her painted toenails. "I know you thought Stephen was all decked out in shining armor. Any other Round Table refugees come your way?"

Celestine played with the faded comforter. "There was a man in England. . . . An American, actually."

"Well, I don't see him here. . . ."

"I left him. I couldn't involve him any more."

"Any more?"

"He rescued me. There was another attempt on my life."

Allie sat forward. "No. You didn't tell me that."

"What was the point? What could you do?"

"Those bastards." Allie punched her fist into the bed. "Those freaking bastards!"

"I'm going to beat them, Allie. That's why I'm back. I'm not going to run away again. I've done some sleuthing, and I know there's a hearing coming up to start the proceedings to declare me legally dead. Millie and Roger will do anything to keep me away from what's mine. But, I'm twenty-five now. The estate is mine now, or it will be as soon as I walk into that courtroom on Friday and tell the judge who I am."

"That's your plan?"

"That's my plan."

Allie sat back and picked up her can. "Are you sure you can risk it?"

"No. But I'm going to."

"Why?"

"Because I want a life. And the one I have isn't worth living."

Allie sipped her drink and watched Celestine as she did. "Does Whit know?" she asked at last.

"No."

"How come?"

"Because I don't trust him."

"Sweetcakes..." Allie shook her head. "If you can't trust old Whit, who can you trust?"

The question was excellent. Celestine had asked herself the same thing over and over again. But in the end, she couldn't ignore Noah's warning. Whit had been one of only three people who had known she would be in Canterbury that day. It was possible that Bobby had traced her another way. Perhaps he had followed leads to Kent. The taxi driver who had picked them up near Covent Market, the Kensington neighbors, the rental car agency. Perhaps it was only a coincidence that he had chosen to search Canterbury the day she and Noah had gone there. But it was too large a chance to take.

She tried to explain her logic. "I don't think anyone will expect me to show up at that hearing. I think everyone expected me to come back on my birthday if I was going to come back at all. My aunt and uncle waited until I didn't return to start the process to have me declared legally dead. Usually it takes seven years, but they're claiming my mental state deteriorated so badly after Stephen's death that I probably committed suicide. And they're using the fact that I didn't return on my birthday as circumstantial evidence."

"But they know you're not dead. They've been trying to have you killed."

"The judge doesn't know that. And Roger and Millie won't expect me to come back right now. They're hoping they can get the legal wrangling done before I decide to return. If I ever do."

"How do you know what they think?"

"I don't. I'm guessing."

"Okay." Allie crossed her legs. "This is the deal. What's going to stop them from having you killed when you show up? Oh, not in the courtroom. That's a little much, even for them. But sometime between then and the time the estate's legally turned over to you. Because they'll try to block that or delay it. They'll say you're still crazy or incompetent, and there'll be weeks in there when everything's up for grabs."

"I'm going to have Whit draw up my will. We've talked about it. I'll leave everything, the whole kit and caboodle, to the biggest charity I can find. One with a staff of cutthroat attorneys. Even if I die two minutes after showing the judge I'm alive, the estate should still be mine, even if the paperwork isn't completed. My will should be in force, and the stakes are high enough that there'll be one heck of a good fight if it's challenged. When the smoke clears, Millie and Roger won't get a thing. And to top that, I'm going to tell the judge exactly why I've been running and what I'm afraid of. That way, even if he thinks I'm crazy, if I die before all the paperwork's done, he'll be sure to order an investigation."

Allie gave a long, low whistle. "Bitching."

"There's a catch."

"There's always a catch...."

"I need Whit to do the paperwork." Celestine had thought this over carefully, too. Her life depended on how she played her cards. She hadn't had a good night's sleep since she had fled Kent.

"How come?"

"Because he has all the details of my parents' estate. I can't afford any mistakes in the basic information. My life depends on it. My will has to be ironclad, or I'm dead. If I go to some attorney off the street, he'll have to go to Flinders, Billett and Crane anyhow to get all the facts, and not only will that take more time, it will signal Whit that I'm here and alive. So it's better if I just get him to do it outright. Then, once the facts are in place I can have the will checked over by an expert."

"How are you going to get Whit to write it?"

"That's why I need you, Allie." Celestine leaned forward. "Will you help me?"

"I'd walk across hot coals for you. You know that."

"Will you go to Whit and tell him I need the will? Don't tell him where I am, or what I plan to do with it. Just tell him to draw it up the way we've discussed in the past. Then get a copy that I can take to court."

Allie looked disappointed. "That's it?"

"That's it."

"I was hoping for something a little more Mata Hari. At the very least I expected to sell my body."

"Will you ask him?"

"Damn right I will."

Celestine reached down and squeezed Allison's foot. "Thank you."

"I've got to go in a minute. I don't think anybody followed me. I was careful, in case Millie and Roger are having me tailed, but I don't want to take any chances."

"This isn't your kind of place."

"Are you kidding? This is exactly the kind of place your family expects me to go for a good time. They always thought I was a tramp."

"They're less than nothing."

Allison's expression turned serious. "There's something you should know. Grandpa Sutter's been sick. I was out there last week to see him. I visit once in a while. For your sake."

"Do you really?" Celestine had successfully fought off tears through the whole recitation of her plans. But now her eyes filled. "You do that for me?"

"Yeah, when the company moved me to Wilmington, I realized that was one thing I could do to help. So I go there once in a while, listen to his stories, drink a few beers with him...."

"He shouldn't be drinking."

"Tell him, not me. That's one stubborn old man."

"I know. I wish I could see him."

"You can."

"How? I can't go back to Haven House. That's the last place I can go."

"He moved in with his daughter a couple of days ago. Just until he's on his feet again. He called me to tell me where he was. No one would suspect you'd have that information, so they won't be watching his house. His daughter and her husband work nights. You could get in, see him, then disappear again before anybody was the wiser. It would mean a lot to him."

"Leave me the address. I'll think about it."

Allison rummaged in her purse and pulled out a slip of paper. "I didn't tell him you were back, or even that I thought you were coming back. I don't tell anybody anything. Not even Grandpa."

"I trust him like I trust you. With my life."

Allison got to her feet. "Can I call you here?"

"Better not. I'll call you from pay phones."

"Your life is a B movie."

Celestine walked her to the door. "I'm going to get through this. And one day soon you can call me all you want. I can see your condo—"

"We can pick up men together."

Celestine's smile faltered. That prospect, or even a more respectable version of it, had no appeal. The only man she could think about right now was Noah, and even if she could find him again, she knew how he would feel about what she had done.

"Be sure you lock this door behind me," Allie said. "This place is a rat hole. There's no telling who's lurking out there."

"There never has been, has there?"

Allie smiled sympathetically. She brushed the knuckles of one hand against Celestine's cheek. "Hang in there, sweetcakes. And keep in touch. Your day's coming up."

Celestine locked the door after Allie had gone and stood with her back to it. Soon all this would be finished. But now she was just tired and lonely.

She wondered where Noah was tonight. Had he thought about her since she'd left him sleeping in his bed? Or had he vowed to forget her after she had run again?

Wherever he was, that was the only place she wanted to be, too.

Grandpa Sutter's daughter Rhonda lived in Morehead City in a clapboard house that looked as if it belonged on a naval base. The house sat on a street of similar houses under a canopy of old trees that were nearly as helpful as airconditioning on a hot summer afternoon. There were no cars parked in the drive or carport, but a light shone in the living room, visible through a crack between the draperies. Celestine had driven by the house twice, looking for the safest way to approach it. She had chosen a rental car with dark tinted windows so that the inside of the car wasn't visible to a casual observer, but she still felt exposed.

She had finally settled for parking her rental car three blocks away. The neighborhood lent itself to crossing on foot. It was a family neighborhood, with dogs barking and the sounds of television drifting through open windows. There was enough movement, doors slamming and cars passing, that she thought her presence wouldn't be questioned. She zigzagged a path toward her target, crossing a vacant lot and walking on the darkest side of every street until she was one street away.

She knew Earl Sutter well enough to know that even if he was home alone, he wouldn't lock his doors. She cut across the lot that adjoined his and made it to his yard without incident. She tried the latch on the breezeway, which extended nearly to the short chain-link fence surrounding the house. Just as she had guessed, the door swung open without fuss.

The door leading into the rest of the house was open. She slipped through it, walking through a small, utilitarian kitchen adorned with cheap prints of kittens in tutus and tuxes and into the living room. There was a man sleeping in a rocking chair under the light of a sixty-watt lamp. He was four years older than he had been the last time she had seen him, but he was every bit as dear.

"Grandpa?" She was afraid to startle him by approaching any closer. "Grandpa?"

He opened his eyes and squinted in her direction. "Who's there?"

"It's Celestine." She crossed the room and knelt at his side. "It's me."

"Celestine?" For a moment he looked as if the name meant nothing to him. Then, as he woke a little more, his eyes began to focus. "Baby doll, is it really you?" He touched her hair and frowned.

"It's me. Forget the hair. It's just blond to make me look a little different."

"There's nothing wrong with brown hair. The good Lord gave you that hair."

"How are you feeling, Grandpa?" Celestine reached for his hand. For the first time in all the years she had known him, he really looked old. What was left of his hair was white, and he looked shrunken and frail. "Allie said you've been sick."

"That's how you found me." He leaned forward and wrapped his arms around her. "That Allie's a good girl. I knew she'd tell you where I was if you came back home."

"What's wrong with you?"

"Nothing much. Pneumonia, that's all. Had to quit smoking. Wished I was dead for a while."

She laughed a little and kissed his cheek. "And you're getting better?"

"Slower than I'd like. But I'll be able to go home soon. Rhonda doesn't want me to, but what the hell does she know?"

"Rhonda adores you. I adore you. You have to take care of yourself."

"She worries about you, Rhonda does."

"I'd love to see her, but I can't risk it. I don't want anybody but you and Allie to know I'm back. Not until it's safe."

"I didn't know if you'd come. I'm not sure you should have. That Roger's already counting the money he's going to get when the courts declare you dead. He'd do anything to keep you away."

"I know he would."

"You're all right? Really all right?"

"Yes. A little scared. But hopeful, too."

"What are you going to do?"

She recounted the plan that she'd explained to Allie. He asked questions as she went, shaking his head. "I can't believe it's come to this. Your grandfather would skin that Millie alive if he knew what she's been up to. She was a bad seed. That's all. Never been another St. Gervais like her."

"I'm going to have the last laugh."

He squeezed her hand. "What can I do?"

"Wish me luck. Not a thing more." She kissed his hand and released it. "I've got to go. I probably won't be able to see you again before the hearing."

"You shouldn't have come tonight. They're probably watching me here. They sure as hell watch me when I'm back home."

"It was worth the risk."

"Don't tell me where you're staying. Ain't sure I could stand up to torture. They might offer me a cigarette to turn you in."

She laughed, and he smiled fondly. His expression changed to concern. "You'll be careful, baby doll? Really careful? 'Cause they ain't fooling, those two."

"Nobody knows that better than me." She rose and backed away. "I'll call you just as soon as this is over. We'll go out for shrimp. You look like you could use some feeding up."

"I can still eat more than you, even without all my teeth."

"We'll see." She blew him a kiss. Then she left the way she had come.

Rhonda's street was poorly lit, which was a bonus. The neighbor whose yard Celestine had crossed was outside now, emptying the trash, but his porch light didn't extend as far as Rhonda's yard. She stood to one side under the spreading limbs of a live oak and waited for him to go inside, but he dawdled, taking out his hose to spray down a flagstone patio and tidying up lawn furniture before he finally went inside.

Once he was gone, she stepped over Rhonda's fence and edged along the inside of an eight-foot cypress barrier separating the man's yard from a neighbor he probably didn't

like. Out on the street, she chose a different route to her car, just to be safe. She cut through another yard, turned down an alley and followed it to a small concrete block church that sat on a residential corner. She waited in the shadows for several cars to pass, then cut through the parking lot to the next street.

No one was about. She felt relatively safe, although safe was a feeling she couldn't easily recognize. As before, no one appeared to be watching her. There was only one other car parked on the street, a plain dark sedan in front of a house with a driveway under repair. She could see her rental car down at the end of the block where the street lamps were smothered by tree limbs. She had chosen the spot because she would be most inconspicuous there.

The September night was comfortably warm, and the sky was bright with stars. By the time she reached her car, she had breathed in the essence of everything she had missed so much all the time she was away. The ocean air, the sultry breeze, the gritty crunch of sand under her shoes. Although it was dark, a mockingbird had favored her with his song, and somewhere far away she had heard the caw of gulls.

She was back, just miles from Haven House now. She had almost made it. She was almost safe.

She looked around again to be sure no one was watching; then she unlocked her door and slid into her seat, locking the door behind her. Before she could turn to fasten her safety belt, a hand gripped her shoulder. Before she could scream, the hand covered her mouth.

"If I could find you this easily, Celestine, what about the people who want you dead?"

Chapter 13

"Noah!" The word emerged as a muffled scream. Celestine swatted his hand from her mouth, and he let her.

"Don't you check your car before you get in?"

She didn't answer, but he could hear her gulping air, as if she needed to store a year's supply.

"You didn't even notice that the light didn't come on when you got in. I unscrewed the bulb. You could be dead right now." There was a part of Noah, smaller than it should have been, he supposed, that wanted to comfort her. He knew he had scared Celestine almost beyond endurance. But he was also toting a couple of bushels of anger, and he'd been in a month-long mood to spread some of it around.

She was still breathing hard when she finally spoke. "How did you find me?"

"You left a trail a mile wide and twice as long."

"I never even told you my full name!"

"Celestine Marie St. Gervais. Daughter of Melanie and Simon St. Gervais. When your grandfather died, your father inherited miles of the Gulf Coast, as well as holdings in shipping, tobacco, lumber. Then there was the family es-

tate, Haven House, near Beaufort. Three hundred acres with mansion and North Carolina history to boot. Did you sleep in the room that was haunted by the ghost of a Union soldier, or the one with the lady in blue who stands at the window looking for her lover lost at sea?''

''Congratulations. Now I don't have to tell you anything else.''

''Not that you would have.'' He was still waiting for her to look at him, but she continued to stare blindly out the windshield. ''What did you do to your hair?''

''It's pretty obvious, isn't it?''

''It's cute. You look like a high school cheerleader.''

''Every woman's fantasy.''

''Every man's fantasy is to help a woman in trouble. Particularly one he's grown attached to.''

She looked at him then. Her eyes were still wide, and her shoulders heaved. ''I couldn't involve you!''

''You did. Thoroughly. And now I've involved myself beyond thorough. So the question is this. Do you want me to leave? Because if you say yes, that'll be it. You won't see me again. Or do you want me to stay and help? Because I can. I already have information you need.''

''What kind of information?''

''Answer me first. I'll give you the information no matter what you say.''

''Noah...''

Her eyes glittered suspiciously, but he didn't touch her, and he didn't smile. ''It's the zero hour, Celestine. No more games. No more lies.''

He had almost given up on an answer when she spoke. ''I couldn't stand it if something happened to you.''

His anger drained away. By now he knew the whole story of Stephen Montgomery. Celestine hadn't lied about Stephen's death. She had just played down the horror of finding her lover bleeding to death and the futile attempt she had made to save him. The medics had found her trying to breathe life back into Stephen's body. They'd been forced to wrench her away.

He reached for her, and she resisted. "Celie..." He tugged her toward him anyway, silently cursing bucket seats. "Don't you see? I can't let anything happen to *you*. I would feel the same way. Let me help you. Together we can get you through this."

She began to cry. He held her, and she sagged against him. He was afraid there were years of tears stored inside her. She had lived the life of the damned. For much too long she had been afraid that every hour would be her last.

"I'm not Stephen Montgomery," he said when her tears were nearly spent. "We're not going to be fighting this alone. I've got men watching this car right now."

"What?" Her head came up. He knew better than to kiss her. She was wounded, as vulnerable as she would ever be. But her lips were so close to his, and he seemed incapable of rational thought.

"Damn." He kissed her anyway. Her lips were as sweet as he remembered and even softer. His arms closed around her and tightened. He was instantly aroused. He'd been aroused when he'd seen her walking toward the car. The lilting, sexy thrust of her hips had been unmistakable.

"We can't do this." She pulled away sharply.

"We already did."

"Who's watching us? You said you have men?"

Noah knew this wasn't the time to tell her the truth about who he was. His last name and background seemed irrelevant right now, and, more important, they would cloud the issue. He would have to explain why he hadn't been honest from the beginning, and she didn't need to absorb his life story, too. He settled for a piece of the truth. "They're security professionals. Some of the best. Tri-C let me have them for a while."

"Why?"

"I've done some favors for the right people. Now they're doing one for me. There are two men. They're going to make sure that nobody lays a hand on you between now and the day you go to court."

"How do you know about that?"

He shook his head. "You're here. There's a court hearing in two days. You put it together a different way and I'll be glad to listen."

"You know everything, don't you?"

"Except your answer. Are you going to let me help you or not?"

He watched different parts of her warring silently. It was a battle he was familiar with. He played his ace of spades. "If *I* found you, Celie, who else can? Who else *will?*"

The fight drained out of her. She sat back against her seat and closed her eyes wearily. "If you die because of me . . ."

"I'm not going to. I'm planning to be there the day you take over Haven House and everything that belongs to you."

"How did you find me?"

"You made calls to Whit Sanderson from the cottage. A baby could have traced them. I got to Wilmington and spent a day reading old newspapers. Then I asked a few questions. It was painless. The painful part was wondering if you were going to keep running or come back and make a stand. But we've been watching the old man's house for a week, and following your attorney and your friend Allison, as well as a few other people. Allison took off like a bat out of hell late this afternoon, and we lost her. We guessed she was trying to fool anybody tailing her. Did she come to see you?"

"Leave Allie out of this. Please. And Grandpa Sutter, too."

"And Sanderson?"

"I don't know about Whit."

"Have you thought twice about me since you left England?"

She turned her head, but her eyes were shadowed. "Yes."

He nodded. He supposed that was good enough. "I've rented a house on Atlantic Beach. I'd like you to come back with me. Where are you staying?"

"You wouldn't believe."

He smiled. He wished there was more light so that he could read all the nuances of her expression. "Someplace better?"

"I don't even have to go back and get my things. I've got what little I own in the trunk. In case I couldn't return for some reason." She smiled a little, too. "And because it's the kind of place where nothing's safe if you don't have your eye on it."

"You don't happen to have a certain green nightgown I never got to see you wear, do you?" He asked the question casually, but he was surprised at how much the answer was going to matter.

"Yes, I have it. And a black dress I only wore for a minute. And—" Her voice caught. "Noah's ark."

He put his palm against her cheek. His fingers plowed through her hair. Blond hair now. Shorter and unbelievably sexy. "I'm going to drive. One of the men will bring your car later, after he's made sure no one is tailing it. Stay right here, and I'll bring mine. Slide over to this seat, then get in when I open your door. Okay?"

"Okay," she whispered.

He bent over and kissed her again. Then he opened his door and locked it behind him.

If Noah hadn't told her that there were men watching, Celestine wouldn't have known it. She had developed acute instincts, but apparently they weren't good enough. The men were obviously top-notch professionals, as capable of disappearing into the background as she was of disappearing, period.

She gave up trying to spot them and settled into her seat. Noah's car was luxury itself. Leather seats as soft as butter and a stereo system that was as good as a front row seat at the London Philharmonic.

She was trying not to stare at Noah as he drove. She hadn't forgotten his face or any other detail about him. But the real man was so much better than her fantasies. He was wearing a summer weight sport coat and charcoal slacks. He had smiled at her once, but now his face had settled back into serious lines.

"I've never been to this part of North Carolina before," he said.

"It's building up too fast. Too many miniature golf courses and condos."

"Some of them have gone up on your land."

Noah knew everything. Celestine wondered if he knew when her first tooth had come in, too. "I've never been allowed to make the decisions about what happens. The men my father left in charge feel their only duty to the estate is to make more money for it. They get a percentage, of course, so they sell when it's profitable. I've cried over their choices more than once."

"You won't have to cry anymore."

She changed the subject. "Noah, you didn't have to come after me. Why did you?"

He didn't answer for a moment, as if he were sifting through answers. "You told me enough to make it easy. You left phone records. You dropped names. You wanted me to come."

"I didn't!"

"You did."

She turned her face to the window. They were crossing the wide bridge to Atlantic Beach, and Bogue Sound sparkled under starlight below them. "I was protecting you."

"You were trying to make it easy for me to back away. You gave me just enough clues so I could find you if I wanted and just few enough so I'd have an excuse not to, if that was my preference."

"So you felt obligated?"

"I felt compelled. I felt frantic!" He hit the steering wheel with his hand. "You've frustrated the hell out of me, woman. I was so angry sometimes that I almost walked away."

"Why didn't you?"

"Because you needed me."

Disappointment seeped through her. She had hoped it was something else, something more. Now she wondered if it was guilt. Only guilt.

The night they had made love, Noah had told her that he hadn't taken care of his wife and son, and now they were gone. He had told her very little about himself, and she had asked little, because she hadn't been able to answer his questions in return. But now he knew everything about her, and she still knew next to nothing about him. She determined to find out more.

"Tell me about your wife and little boy."

"Why?"

"Because whatever happened to them has had a big effect on you."

"They died."

"But I thought—"

"You thought I was divorced. I never said I was."

"You let me go on thinking it."

"There wasn't any reason to set the record straight. It didn't matter."

"It didn't matter, or I didn't? Didn't you think I deserved to know the truth?"

"Apparently I thought the truth was as irrelevant as you did." He turned at the end of the bridge and started west on the main road that ran along the island. "There's a lot and a little to tell, and none of it's worth telling now. We're going to concentrate on getting you through this alive. And then we're going to sit down and straighten out everything else."

"What exactly *is* 'everything else'?"

"Everything that doesn't get straightened out before then."

Her frustration had reached its limit. "I want to know right now if I'm anything more to you than someone to rescue. Are you here because you just had to get it right this time? Tell me that much, damn it."

"Nothing that happens now can bring Lynn to life again. I can't bring her back from the grave by my good deeds.

You're not a substitute. Is that what you're trying to find out?''

She was shocked into silence. Then remorse throttled her. "I'm sorry. I didn't mean . . ."

"You want to know if you mean anything to me. You do. But we aren't going to talk about that right now. Everything you are is hanging in the balance. I'm not going to push you or pull you in any direction. I'm just going to keep you alive."

"I see."

"I doubt it."

She gave up. She rested her head and closed her eyes. She had been on guard for such a long time, and now Noah was going to take over for a while. She didn't know how he really felt about anything. She knew very little about him at all. But she had learned one irrefutable fact. He could be trusted. With her life, if not with her heart.

She didn't know how much later it was when she realized the car was no longer moving. She opened her eyes and squinted into the darkness of a garage.

A car door slammed, and she heard footsteps. Then Noah rapped gently against her window. She unlocked her door and sleepily swung her feet to the ground. "Where are we?"

"In a safe place. Alone."

"I'll miss all the folks parading through the room next door."

"What?"

She stood. He put his arms around her for a moment to steady her, and she stared into his eyes. "That morning in Trillingden. I didn't want to leave you."

"How's your shoulder?"

"It's nearly healed. A little sore sometimes, but that's the worst of it. I had a doctor check it, and he said that whoever sewed it up should have been a plastic surgeon. I'll have a faint scar."

"You have enough scars to go around." He brushed her hair back from her face; then he ruffled it. "Celestine . . ."

"Uh-huh?" She was waiting for him to kiss her. She wanted it desperately.

"I'm not expecting anything from you. You don't have to pay me back for anything."

"Don't I?"

"That's not the way it should be between us."

"Well, what if I want you? Just hypothetically. It could happen, you know. Out of the blue, I might suddenly find you attractive."

"In that case, you ought to let me know. In case I suddenly find you attractive, too."

She slid her arms around his waist. "Is there any chance you're finding me attractive now?" She'd meant the question to be a tease. But she heard the plaintive undertone and knew that he did, too.

He pressed himself against her, and the evidence was irrefutable. "Just the slightest chance," he said.

"My nightgown's still in my car."

"Then I guess we'll have to wait." His mouth twisted upward, as if the smile were painful. "Unless you think we could make love without it."

"We managed once before."

"More than once, I think."

"Noah, I missed you."

"Then something good came of this, didn't it?" He bent his head and brushed his lips against hers. Once. Twice. He lifted his head. "But something better can come of being together again." He stepped away and took her hand. "Come on."

He unlocked the door into the house and ushered her inside. She saw at a glance that the house was huge, as different from the cottage in Kent as England was from North Carolina. The house sprawled, beach-dwelling style, in all directions. The walls were natural wood—cedar, if the pleasant pervading smell was a clue—and large expanses of glass. Decks spread out from every doorway, and the decor took a cue from the dunes and ocean beyond, using seascape colors and natural materials to bring the spectacular view indoors.

"I know it seems exposed," he said, "but the way it's situated, there isn't another house in sight. And no one can see us."

She walked to the French door leading to a deck overlooking the beach. Vines crawled along its border, and stunted, wind-tortured trees blocked the rest of civilization from view. She could hear the ocean just beyond a set of high white dunes. In the daylight, she knew, she would be able to see its sparkle.

She felt Noah's arms creep around her waist, and she leaned against him. "You're almost home." She felt his lips against her hair. "It was the best I could do."

She turned in his arms and cupped his head with her hands. "It's like waking from a bad dream."

"Let me help you wake up." He kissed her again, this time with clear intentions. They stepped apart long enough to shed their clothes; then they fell into each other's arms. The bedrooms were too far away, and the rug at their feet just soft enough.

She was nearly home, but in Noah's arms home suddenly seemed like more than ocean breezes and a house she hadn't seen in five long years. She took him inside her as if the moment of homecoming were now. He scooped her in his arms and held her close before he began to move.

And when he did, she forgot about everything else except what she had nearly thrown away.

Celestine was tanned all over. Noah felt a shiver of jealousy before he realized that the tan was probably artificial. Her skin was the tawny gold of wildflower honey, and her hair the soft streaked gold of morning sunlight. He wondered where she had gone after taking his car in Trillingden. She had abandoned it in the village so that it would be easy to find, but no one had seen her do it. His survey of nearby towns hadn't turned up anything, either.

But she had left a clear trail to her former life. Now they were together again.

Celestine stirred in her sleep, arching one arm above her head. She was easy to sleep with. She didn't sleep deeply, and she rarely moved. He supposed she had trained herself to wake at any disturbance. She seemed comfortable now, dreaming, perhaps, about something that pleased her.

She pleased him. He had expected her to be gone when he awoke that morning in Trillingden, and she hadn't surprised him. What he hadn't expected was the deep sense of loss that had followed. He had guessed that he would be able to find her again, but in the month that it had taken, he had thought about little else.

Her eyes opened, and her hand found his cheek. "Didn't I wear you out?"

"Not nearly."

She smiled sleepily. "I was dreaming I was home, and you were in bed beside me."

"How long has it been since you've been home?"

"Forever."

"How would you like to go back now?"

Her eyes opened a little more. "Go back?"

"Your aunt and uncle are out of town."

"How do you know that?"

"I've made it my business to know everything they do."

"Where are they?"

"Your aunt has jet-set pretensions, and there was a party in Washington this weekend that she couldn't miss. They'll be back tomorrow afternoon."

"What did you mean, go back now?"

"We can be there in twenty-five minutes. There's a dirt road bordering the property. I'm sure you know the one I mean. We can drive there and park, and you can get a good view of the house in the moonlight. That's the best we can do for now, and you've got to promise you won't try to get out of the car. But at this hour, I think we're perfectly safe."

She closed her eyes. "Do you know ... Have they done anything to it?"

"I think the house is intact. It's protected by your father's will, and they've been forced to respect that."

"You would do this for me?"

He would do this and more. He was beginning to think he would do almost anything. He kissed her in answer, a lingering gentle kiss. "Would you like to go?"

"Oh, yes."

"Then I guess you'd better dress."

Her hands clasped his neck as he started to move away. "We'd be safe now because it's so late?"

He propped himself on one elbow to gaze down at her. "I'm almost sure."

"Wouldn't we be even safer if we waited just a little while?"

"Why, do you need some more sleep?"

She smiled Marie St. Germaine's smile. "No, Noah. I need some more you."

Chapter 14

Celestine had stirred her coffee already, but Noah watched her pick up the spoon and stir it again. He imagined it was already cold, since she'd been staring and stirring for a good ten minutes.

"You need some sleep." He tucked his hand under her chin and lifted it so that her eyes were level with his. "You're done in."

"I'll sleep for a week when this is over."

"Now that's something for me to look forward to."

She flashed him a brilliant smile. "I'll take breaks."

"Good thing." He watched the smile fade and her mind turn somewhere else.

He wasn't sure now if taking her to see her ancestral home had been a good idea. In the earliest hours of the morning she had stared at the old plantation house as if it were a ghost rising from the mists. It had been a spectacular sight. The house was huge, with twenty or more rooms, and porches and balconies on every side. He had counted six chimneys and four gables, plus enough windows to keep a janitorial service in business for weeks. A parade of live oaks led up to the front veranda, where pillars as massive as the trees provided the backbone to hold up the ancient cypress shingle roof.

She hadn't said much. She had stared at Haven House until he announced that they had to go. "I don't know if I can live there again," she said as he turned the car around.

"Why not?"

"Because they've lived there so long, I'm afraid I'll think of them in every room."

He knew she was thinking of her aunt and uncle. "We'll have an exorcism. We'll sweep out everything that reminds you of them."

"We might have to burn down the house."

Noah had driven her back to the beach house and held her close, hoping to drive out thoughts of the past. But he supposed that now she was thinking about her aunt and uncle again. He took her coffee cup and switched it for another, filling it from a thermal pot and pushing it toward her. "There's no point in worrying, Celestine. You'll have time to worry about moving back in when this is all settled."

"The day Millie and Roger moved in after the accident, they packed up everything that belonged to my parents, everything that wasn't valuable, of course, and gave it away. I begged Millie to let me keep my mother's costume jewelry. My mother used to let me play dress up with it, and I knew it would remind me of her. Millie packed it anyway."

Noah was not a violent man, but he had satisfying visions of his hands around Aunt Millie's throat. "I'm sorry."

She stirred the fresh coffee. "Don't be. I found the jewelry before she could get rid of it and hid it in the attic. Then I put some of Millie's jewelry in the boxes and sealed them up again. I was truly a rotten child. To this day she probably doesn't know what happened to her pearls."

He hooted with satisfaction.

"I called her Millie from the first, and she hated it. Roger was never Uncle Roger. No matter what they did to me, I refused to call them anything else. They weren't family. Not in any way that mattered. Little victories. But victories."

"I told you I'd learned a few things. Would you like to hear them?"

She looked up, and her hand stilled. "You know I would."

"Millie and Roger, for starters. They've socked away quite a little nest egg on their own. That suggests to me that they aren't completely sure they're going to win this game. And if they don't, they'll have money to fall back on."

"Where did the money come from, or don't you know?"

"You won't like this part."

"That doesn't surprise me."

"They've managed to sell off some of the antiques and artwork that legitimately belong to you. And Roger's not stupid. He's on the spot. He can juggle what money he has access to, make false reports, move funds from one account to another. The people in charge of the bulk of the estate are good, but Roger is better."

"How much?"

"When you figure what you're going to be worth? A small percentage."

"How much?"

He sighed. "As near as we can figure it, about half a million."

"How did you find this out?"

"I have connections."

She drummed her spoon against the saucer. "What kind of connections?"

"The kind that are now monitoring what goes in and out of Roger's bank account in D.C. That's where he hides the money."

"Well, I'm just so relieved to hear that my dear departing relatives won't be destitute after I stick it to them." Her accent was exaggerated. The air was poisoned by it.

"You'll get the money back. We can probably prove every cent. And the I.R.S. will be delighted to hear about Roger's shenanigans."

"I'll worry about that later." She frowned. "Is there more? You said Millie and Roger 'for starters.'"

Celestine's relatives had been the easy part. Noah wasn't sure how to break the rest of what he'd learned.

He tilted his chair on its back legs and crossed his arms over his chest.

"More bad news?" she said. This cup of coffee, too, was growing colder.

"It didn't take me long to find out who you were. Then I had a lot of time on my hands while I waited for you to come back. So I did some investigating."

"I can see you did."

"I had everyone you've ever been close to checked out."

"Apparently my life is an open book."

"Be glad it's still open."

She winced.

"Who exactly do you trust, Celie?"

Her face lit up. He knew it was the name. She smiled a little every time he called her that. "I trust you."

"I'm glad. Now, in order, who else do you trust?"

She appeared to think about it, weighing names. "Allison and Grandpa Sutter are tied for first place. I can't possibly separate them."

"Okay. Is that all?"

"Grandpa Sutter's daughter Rhonda. She's a sweetheart. She tried as hard as she could to mother me after my own mother died. That was when Millie's back was turned, of course, because Millie made it clear that Rhonda wasn't good enough to associate with a St. Gervais."

"Anyone else?"

"A few college friends, though I've lost touch with them. Some people I met along the way. But they don't matter now."

"You didn't mention Whit Sanderson. Last night you said you didn't know about him...."

"You planted the seed of doubt. It's flourished."

"Good."

She didn't wait for him to continue. "Why? What do you know?"

"Your friend Sanderson has a gambling problem. He's an Atlantic City regular. He flies to Vegas once a month for a long weekend." He shrugged. "He's moderately good, as a matter of fact. He doesn't make money, but he hasn't lost his shirt yet. I'm not sure why. Either he's better than my Vegas contacts seem to think, or he's getting help from a source he doesn't report on his income taxes."

"A source like Millie and Roger?"

"Possibly."

"Stephen thought the world of him!"

"Desperate men do desperate things. Sanderson might have been in danger of his whole world tumbling down around his ears." Noah saw that Celestine didn't want to believe any of this, but neither was she ruling it out.

"Noah, do you have contacts everywhere? How are you getting all this information?"

Once again he wished he had just been honest from the start. "Over the years I've learned how to use people to get information. It's important in what I do."

"Is that all the bad news?"

He hesitated. "You're going to like this part even less."

"Might as well go for it. You seem to be on a roll."

"Did you ever wonder how Earl Sutter got to be so thick with your grandfather that Alexander St. Gervais left him so much in his will? A house? Prime acreage? An income for life?"

"There's never been a reason to wonder. Grandpa Sutter's a wonderful man. The best in the world. He was a loyal friend to my grandfather, and Grandfather repaid him."

Her feathers were ruffled. Her eyes shot fire. She'd had little reason to feel loyalty to anyone, and now he was attacking the few people she had believed in. Noah had known to expect this, but that didn't make it any easier. "Don't shoot the messenger, Celie."

"If you're going to say something bad about Grandpa Sutter, don't."

He continued to lean back in his chair and watch her.

She threw her spoon on the table at last, and it bounced halfway across before it came to a halt. "All right, damn it. What?"

"Are you familiar with the history of Haven House?"

"More or less. Millie and Roger were more interested in gutting the estate than in extolling the St. Gervais lineage, but I remember some stories my father told me."

"Did he ever tell you how the Sutters came to be associated with Haven House?"

"Not that I recall."

"During the Depression your family was in danger of losing nearly everything they owned due to poor management as well as general hard times. Your great-grandfather Raoul was a dreamer, not a businessman. Ike Sutter, Earl Sutter's father, came to the door one day looking for work. He had his wife with him, and Earl, who was just a small boy. Ike took a good look around and saw some things that needed to be done right away. He told your great-grandfather that he'd take over the management of the plantation in exchange for nothing more than room and board. But when times were better, if Haven House was prospering under his guidance, he wanted a percentage of the place, not a salary. Raoul was so desperate for help, he agreed."

"I never heard any of this."

"Raoul died years later without making provision for Ike or Ike's family in his will. And there'd never been anything about percentages in writing. Their agreement had been made on a handshake. Your grandfather and Earl had grown up together, and Alexander promised Earl that he would always have a home there. So Earl stayed on to take over the property, but he got a salary, a house to live in, and that was that."

"He stayed, though, didn't he? He wouldn't have stayed if he thought he'd been cheated. He must have been paid well."

"But maybe not as well as he should have been."

"What could any of this have to do with me?"

"If Earl Sutter's been nursing a grudge against your family all these years, he might have been willing to pass on information about you to your aunt and uncle. He might secretly enjoy watching what's left of the St. Gervais family claw each other's eyes out."

"No!" She slapped her hand on the table. "Not a chance. He loves me. And you're forgetting that my grandfather left Grandpa Sutter a big chunk of property, a house, a healthy income for life."

"Greed doesn't clarify the way a person looks at things, Celie. It distorts it."

She was silent for a while. He wanted to comfort her, but he knew better. "You've forgotten something else," she said at last. "Grandpa Sutter didn't know I'd be in Canterbury that day. Only Whit knew that."

"No. Whit's the only person besides the bank officer who we're sure about. But Whit talked to both Allison and Earl Sutter on a regular basis. He could have said something to either or both of them about Canterbury. Particularly if they were pumping him for information."

"I can't believe this."

"You don't have to believe it. You have to take it into account. That's all."

She looked up from the table. "I suppose you've dug up dirt on Allie, too. There's plenty there, I'm sure. She doesn't care what anybody thinks of her. But she's been my best friend since the day I met her. She befriended me when I was at one of the lowest points in my life, and she's been right by my side from that moment."

"There's not much your friend Allison won't do for money," he said carefully.

"Except hurt me. And she hates Millie and Roger almost as much as I do. They were always hideous to her. At my graduation Millie told her right to her face that she was a bad influence on me and ought to be locked away. Allie wouldn't cooperate with them for any amount of money."

"Just consider it. That's all."

"No."

"I hope you're right and I'm suspicious for nothing."

"I know I'm right. Neither Grandpa nor Allie would hurt me. Not for anything."

"*I'm* not trying to hurt you." He leaned forward and stretched his hand across the table. "I'm just trying to keep you safe."

She sighed and placed her hand in his. "I know."

"Tell me what you're planning to do."

He listened while she outlined the plan that she had obviously spent a great deal of time developing. She wound to a close. "I saw Allie yesterday. That must have been when she gave you the slip. She came to my motel. I told her what I've just told you, and I asked her to have Whit finish drawing up my will."

"I think I should second that request. In person."

"Why? She'll do it. She probably already has."

"I want to meet Whit Sanderson face-to-face. Today. And I want him to know I'm watching everything he does."

"I suppose you'll want to meet Allie and Grandpa, too?"

"It wouldn't hurt. Why don't you invite Allie to lunch? She travels the area. You should be able to arrange someplace inconspicuous to meet her, and I'll be sure you're protected."

"One of your invisible men?"

"He won't be so invisible at that point. He'll be at the next table. I'll pick you up, and you can introduce me to Allie."

"I'll call her." She stood, as if to look for a telephone, but he held firmly to her hand.

"Don't use the telephone here. I have a cell phone. Use that."

"Why?"

"Because the call can be traced to me, but not to this address."

"You think of everything, don't you? Well, don't waste too much time. Millie and Roger want me dead, but they're in this alone. You're trying to protect me from the people who love me."

"Not from all of them." He watched her eyebrow lift in question, but he didn't elaborate. He had told her there would be time later to straighten out everything that was between them. He only hoped he was right.

Whit Sanderson's office suite in Wilmington was pleasant, with ocean prints, instead of an ocean view, and one secretary who handled his appointments. From the size of the practice, Noah guessed there were other, better suites for associates, and he supposed that Sanderson was trying to work his way into one of them. But if his gambling continued, it was doubtful that he would keep his job. Flinders, Billett and Crane was an old firm with an established reputation. They wouldn't take kindly to any hint of scandal.

Noah only had to wait a few minutes before he was ushered into Whit's private office. He had made this appointment as Noah James, and he was sure that Sanderson had realized that he was the man Celestine had asked about. The young attorney stood when Noah entered. He was short, with hair cut close to his head and a slight paunch that might be a result of too many Las Vegas nights. He gave Noah the same visual going over that Noah gave him; then he motioned to a chair in front of his desk.

There was no ocean view here, either. Just walls of cherry bookcases and a matching desk that was as old and solid as the firm's reputation. "I know who you are," Whit said at last.

"Do you?"

"This is about Celestine, isn't it?"

"Absolutely."

Whit leaned forward. His eyes narrowed. "Is she all right? Because if she isn't . . ."

"What? If she isn't you'll drown your sorrows in a couple of bottles of champagne and another game of blackjack? Las Vegas or Atlantic City this time, Sanderson? It's hard to keep up."

Whit sat back for a moment; then he leaped up and shot around the desk so fast that it took Noah a precious second

to figure out what he was doing. He got to his feet just as
Whit grabbed him by the jacket. "What have you done to
her?"

Noah shook him off easily and grasped him by the arms.
"She's fine. Now we're going to talk about you."

Whit wrenched himself loose, but he didn't retreat. "My
game's not blackjack. But yours is obviously blackmail."

"Not at all. Mine is protecting Celestine. The guy who
tried to kill her in London was waiting for her in Canterbury when she went to pick up her money. You were the only
person besides the bank officer who knew she'd be in the
city."

"So you think I'm trying to have her killed?"

"The thought crossed my mind."

"Who the hell are you? Because no one I've spoken to at
Tri-C International has ever heard of you!"

"And everyone I've spoken to in Atlantic City and Vegas has heard of you, Sanderson. You've got every reason
to need money. You've got an addiction, and an addict loses
his morals like a bird loses feathers in molting season."

"Who are you?"

"Noah James. The man who's not going to let anything
happen to Celestine St. Gervais. Not ever."

"I wouldn't hurt her. I wouldn't think of it." Whit ran his
fingers through what little hair he had. "I've got a problem. I know I do. But it doesn't have anything to do with
Celestine or her money. I've never touched anything of hers
except to get cash to send her. I haven't touched anything
that belongs to anybody else."

"Then whose money are you spending?"

"Mine. Family money."

Either Sanderson put on a good act, or he was sincere.
But Noah wasn't in the mood to believe him or anyone. Not
when Celestine's life was on the line.

"Here's the deal, Sanderson. Celestine needs her will
drawn up. She wants you to do it just the way the two of you
have talked about."

"Allison Freeman already told me. Where's Celestine?"

"You don't think I'd tell you that, do you?"

"Then how do I know this is her idea?"

"Get it finished. Today. I don't care what you have to drop to do it. I'll send someone by for a copy of it tonight. Then my attorneys are going to look it over carefully. And if everything's just the way it should be, you can meet Celestine tomorrow night and watch her sign it."

"Then what?"

"Then you put your hands together and pray that you're as honest and loyal to Celestine as you say. Because if you're not, and I find out that you've done anything along the way to hurt her, the next time you go to Vegas, you'll be looking for a job shining shoes."

The restaurant that Allison chose was off Wilmington's beaten path, with fishnet decor and nothing steamed or broiled on the menu. Best of all, it was practically empty. Celestine ordered oysters and started on the hush puppies and corn bread before Allison had even made up her mind.

"Do you always eat like that?" Allison asked. "Like you're starving?"

Celestine paused for a heartbeat to consider. "When you're not sure when you're going to eat again, food becomes more than something to fill you up."

"Poor baby. You've had it so rough."

"Maybe it will be over soon."

"I got hold of Whit last night. He asked a lot of questions."

"And you didn't give him lots of answers, I hope?"

"None that I wasn't supposed to." Allison accepted an icy beer mug from their waitress and held it out in toast. "To you and me and the guy at the table in the corner who has his eye on us."

Celestine didn't look, but she knew exactly who Allison was referring to. The guy's name was Hank; he was a former FBI agent, and he had driven her here. "I wouldn't waste a batted eyelash on him."

"Why not?"

"He's with me."

"Then why isn't he over...?" Allison's eyes lit up. "He's protecting you?"

"Sure. Anyone suspicious walks in, he'll fling cole slaw in their eyes, whack 'em over the head with French fries fresh from the deep-fry basket—"

"How did you come up with a hunk like that on such short notice?"

"I didn't. Noah did."

"Noah?"

"Remember the guy I told you about? The one I met in England? Well, he found me. And now he's helping."

Allison gave a low whistle. "You have all the luck."

"Funny, I haven't exactly seen the last four years that way."

"Sure, I know. But imagine what it's going to be like for you when this is over. You were born with a silver spoon in your mouth. Maybe it's gotten a little tarnish on it, but it's going to clean up fine, and you'll be set for life."

Celestine looked up from buttering her second piece of corn bread. "It's funny. I've never given a hoot about everything I'll own when this is over. Sure, Haven House means something to me, but mostly because it belonged to my parents. I would gladly have shared it and everything else with Millie and Roger if they'd just treated me like a human being. Not even a daughter or a niece. Just a human being."

"Noble sentiments."

"Come on, Allie." Celestine touched Allie's hand. "Don't tell me if you'd had to choose between love and money when you were a kid, you would have chosen the dough."

"Surely you jest." Allison watched her over the rim of her mug as she drained nearly half its contents.

"Really?"

Allison wiped her mouth with the back of her hand. "You've lived without money now. Can you really tell me it's not important? I gave up on love a long time ago, but money's the call of the sirens.''

"You didn't give up on love. You still love me. And you're the old softie who's been going out to Haven House to see Grandpa Sutter.''

Allison looked away. "You're the only person in the whole wide world who sees me that way.''

The waitress arrived with their lunches. Halfway through the huge platters they were laughing and chatting easily again, but Celestine was thinking about everything that had been said. After four years of hell, she did have a much better idea of what was really important. Not her inheritance, but the one thing she had truly been denied by her parents' death. The very thing she had begun to find again with Noah James.

Love.

"Celestine, you're looking starry-eyed,'' Allison said.

Celestine pushed her plate away. There was a small mound of fries left and a dab of cole slaw, but even she couldn't eat another bite. "Noah's going to meet us here. I've told him all about you.''

"Oh good. The mystery man. And he's probably rich, isn't he?''

"Comfortable, at least, but I don't know how much money he has, and I don't care.''

"Well, you'll have enough for both of you, in case he's not. Just be sure he's not a fortune hunter.''

"I can be sure of that. The first time he saw me I was serving coffee in a Paris café.'' She looked up in time to see Noah stroll through the door. She saw him exchange glances with Hank, then he came toward their table.

His eyes smiled before his lips followed suit. His tie was loosened, and his white shirt was unbuttoned at the throat. He moved like someone who owned the ground he walked on. She was struck again by how much he had come to mean to her, and how quickly those feelings were communicated to the intimate parts of her body, far away from her heart.

"Celestine..." He nodded at her, then turned to Allison.

"Noah, this is my best friend Allison Freeman. Allison, this is Noah James."

Allison stared at him for a moment without extending her hand. Then she turned back to Celestine and cocked her head. "Are you putting me on?"

Celestine was baffled. She looked up at Noah for clarification. He seemed to sink into himself, to grow more distant as she watched.

"Noah James?" This time Allison's dimples flashed when she looked up at him. "You're talking to a devotee of *People* magazine here. Hell, I read *all* the gossip magazines like some people read the Bible. Noah James my eyeball. You're Noah Colter of Tri-C International, aren't you?" She glanced across the table at Celestine and shook her head. "Jeez, Celestine, it's just like you to fall in love with one of the richest men in America. Your luck knows no bounds."

Chapter 15

Noah watched Celestine's expression. Her drama training surfaced immediately, but he saw the initial flash of disbelief, followed by the stab of betrayal. "You'd better tell Allison the truth," she said, aiming her remark at him but not quite meeting his eyes. "She's nobody's fool."

"I wasn't aware my face was so well-known." He tore his gaze from Celestine to glance at Allison.

Allison was obviously enjoying her discovery. "Maybe not to the rank and file, but I'm obsessed with celebrities."

"I'm not a celebrity. I'm a businessman and that's all."

"Right. A businessman with a past that reads like a bestseller. The media loved you for a while, and so did I. How many men bring their billionaire fathers to their knees, then go on to inherit everything anyway?"

"It wasn't a particularly good time in my life, and I don't like to talk about it."

"He means that," Celestine said. "He doesn't talk about it. Not to anyone."

Allison grimaced. "Well, so much for privacy, huh? I'm

sorry I recognized you, but Celestine would have told me eventually. We're practically family."

"Celie, I think we'd better get back now. There's a storm blowing up outside, and driving's going to be difficult." Noah covered her hand, but she slid it out from under his.

"I've got to run anyway." Allison grabbed the check off the table and stood. "When will I see you again?" she asked Celestine. "Do you want me to come to court with you?"

"I'll call you."

"I want to be there when you get everything you deserve."

"All right." Celestine squeezed Allison's hand.

Noah didn't want to look at Celestine. Not yet. He watched Allison walk to the cash register instead. She was a particularly beautiful young woman, and he expected that if he had met her months ago, he would have found her notable. She was gone from the restaurant before he turned back to Celestine.

"When were you going to tell me?" she asked.

"When you were safe. When you had your life back."

She rose. "I trusted you. Obviously I made a mistake."

Noah rested his hand on her shoulder to keep her from walking away. "I'm Noah James Colter. And I was a consultant with my own business before I took over Tri-C. Nothing I've told you was a lie, just bits and pieces of the truth."

"That's all I was ever worth to you? Bits and pieces?"

"I didn't want to tell you everything at the beginning. When people find out who I am..." He didn't know how to go on.

"What, Noah? What happens? They fall to the ground and worship at your feet?"

"There's nothing about me or my past that hasn't been fodder for the tabloids. They know everything about me. I cease to be real. And I didn't want to go through that again. Your life was in danger, and I didn't know why. My past and everything about me just seemed like an unnecessary complication."

"You want to hear something funny?"

"It would be a welcome relief."

"I don't know *anything* about you. I never even heard of Tri-C International until you told me you consulted for them. And the name Noah Colter means absolutely nothing to me. But then, I've been on the run for four years. There's a lot I missed. Most of the time I was too poor to buy a newspaper." She moved out from under his hand and started toward the door.

"Celestine." He gripped her arm to stop her again. "Will you listen, then? Let me tell you the whole story? I would have, just as soon as it was relevant. I know you feel betrayed—"

"Do you?" She shook off his hand. "Do you really? You have no idea how I feel! Everyone I love is living a lie. This morning you tell me I can't trust any of the people I've counted on to help keep me alive. This afternoon I find out that you're not who you said you were. How can you know what that feels like?" She started toward the door.

"Where are you going?"

"I might as well walk the streets in broad daylight. The people who've been helping me skulk in the shadows are probably the ones who are trying to get me."

"Please. Hear me out. Then, if you want to leave, you can. But for somewhere safe. Please."

She crossed her arms, as if she were physically trying to hold all her feelings inside. He did the same. The posture had once been a natural one for him, but now it felt alien. "Please?" he asked again, softer this time.

She didn't say yes, but she didn't walk away. He gestured for Hank to get his car, and in a few minutes they were heading back toward Atlantic Beach.

The storm he had predicted was beginning to close in. In the distance thunderheads hovered over the horizon, but the storm was moving in their direction. Already a thin haze of rain was glazing the streets.

He had a captive audience and plenty of time to tell his story. But he didn't say anything until they had left the city limits behind and were out on the highway. He glanced in his rearview mirror and saw that Hank was several cars behind them. John, the other Tri-C security officer, was back at the house standing guard.

"First of all, let me set the record straight," he said. "I wasn't keeping the truth from you because I was afraid you were a fortune hunter."

"That's rich. Allie warned *me* about fortune hunters at lunch. Before she knew who you were, of course. Before *I* knew who you were. My inheritance is probably a drop in the bucket compared to what you're worth."

Rain was already falling harder. He was glad he had to stare out the windshield. He didn't want to see her expression. "Try to listen with an open mind. Okay? You told me one lie after the other, and I'm still here. It's your turn to give me the benefit of the doubt, Celie."

"Just tell me, and get this over with."

"My father was James Colter. His grandfather started Tri-C International. It was called something else then. The three Cs represent the three generations of Colters who built it into the giant it is today.

"My father made it clear when I was growing up that there would never be four Cs. He was a hard man, and there was no way I could ever measure up to his expectations. He and my mother were divorced when I was a toddler, and I was lucky after that if I saw him twice a year. I resented his disinterest, of course, and I let him know it. It was a vicious circle. The more obnoxious I was, the less he wanted to see me. Supposedly I lived with my mother, but she was never there. She hadn't wanted a child in the first place, and she'd only had me to satisfy my father's desire for an heir. She divided her time between yachts and ski resorts. I was raised by a progression of servants who quit the moment they realized the biggest paychecks in the world couldn't make up for having to deal with me."

He waited for her to question him, but she remained silent.

"By the time I got out of college, the break with my father was final. I was still a rebel and an indifferent student, and he told me he never wanted to see me again. That was fine, because I'd hardly ever seen him anyway. You can't miss what you've never had. I had a small inheritance from my maternal grandmother, enough to keep me for a while, and I figured that was all I needed to make a start somewhere. I chose south Florida."

He turned and started across a crowded bridge, where the rain had slowed traffic to a crawl. He waited until they were back on land to begin again. Celestine still hadn't said a word.

"I don't know what I would have become if I hadn't met Lynn. She was older than me by a couple of years, and she had a son, Josh. I told you about him."

"Yes."

He took that one word as a good sign. "At first I couldn't imagine myself as a married man. I didn't think highly of my own stability. But Lynn convinced me otherwise. It took me a while, but I finally figured out that she and Josh were the answers to everything I'd been missing in my life." He paused. "I loved her very much. I was happy for the first time in my life."

He changed lanes while he considered how to wrench the rest of the story from the places where he had locked it away.

"I started a business as a consultant. At the beginning Lynn did all the office work. She and Josh would come in every day, and she would answer phones, file, send out letters. I'd majored in engineering, and even though my grades were mediocre, I'd absorbed a lot. I decided to focus on safety. There had been a rash of lawsuits against big corporations because they'd either ignored or missed important safety features in their products. I decided to begin an independent testing and consulting service. The time was right, and I was successful."

He glanced at her. She was staring out her window at the rain, but she was listening. He could tell by the rigid angle of her shoulders. She was tensed, as if waiting.

"Now I realize I wanted to show my father I could make it without him. For the first time in my life I was proud of myself. I made sure he knew what I was doing, but he ignored me. By then it really didn't matter. I had Lynn and Josh. We weren't rich, but we were making it, and little by little I was establishing a reputation in the field and getting more business."

"Why would you keep any of this from me?"

He glanced over and saw that she still wasn't looking at him. He gripped the wheel harder. "Lynn and I were married for two years. Before we married she had told me that she didn't want more children. She adored Josh, but she didn't want to take a chance that her next child would have Down's, too. I respected that, but I asked her not to do anything permanent for a while, just in case she changed her mind. She got pregnant, even though she was on the Pill. It was a tough pregnancy. Josh was always a handful, and she was so worried about the outcome. She refused amniocentesis because she wouldn't terminate the pregnancy whatever the result, but not knowing made her burden harder. After a few months she stopped working and stayed home with Josh.

"I was convinced we would get through it all right. I did what I could to make the waiting easier, but there wasn't much I could do. One morning I got up early to go into work. She and Josh were still sleeping, and I didn't want to wake them. I kissed her goodbye, tucked Josh in tighter and went to the office. I thought she would call when she got up, but by noon I hadn't heard anything, so I called her. There was no answer. I assumed she was out getting groceries. I tried her later, and there was still no answer. There were a hundred places she could have been, but I was beginning to worry. By four, I was worried enough to call it a day and go home early to check on her."

"Noah, you don't have to go on."

He went on anyway. "The house seemed particularly quiet when I drove up. It was winter, and all the windows were closed. But it was getting dark enough that I could see there weren't any lights on inside, either. Lynn's car was in the carport. I parked mine beside it and opened the door into the house. And it was like hitting a brick wall. There was no air. I started to cough."

He was gripping the steering wheel harder now. He had relived this moment for years after Lynn's and Josh's deaths, but it never got any easier. "The house was filled with carbon monoxide. I went outside and yelled for a neighbor. He took one breath and tried to keep me from going in, but by then I was frantic. I covered my mouth and ran inside. I made it to our bedroom and opened the window. Lynn was exactly where I'd left her. I managed to strip off her nightgown and start CPR, but I blacked out. The neighbor was smashing all our windows by then, trying to let the gas out and force air inside. Someone else had called the police. They found me on the floor beside our bed, passed out cold, and got me out in time. Josh was still in his bed, too. He and Lynn never knew a thing."

"Noah..."

"It was the furnace. There was a malfunctioning valve." He slammed his palm against the steering wheel. "And here's the part that made me the man I am today."

His voice was bitter now; he would always be bitter about this. "The valve was made by Tri-C International. And it turns out that they knew some of the valves they'd produced that year were faulty. They'd even considered a recall, but a number cruncher had looked at the cost of replacing the valves or paying off potential lawsuits, weighed the probabilities and recommended that they cover up what they'd found. So they did. They buried it six feet under.

"I had the knowledge and training to find out the truth. I buried my wife and son, then I dug up the facts about the valve one dirty inch at a time. It took me a year working day and night. I was obsessed. When I finally had what I needed, I went up against the corporate attorneys, the billion dollar bulk of Tri-C International, the people who claimed I was just doing it to spite my father, the people who claimed I was just trying to gain something from my own tragedy, and I won a huge judgment.''

"I don't know what to say."

"Don't say anything yet. You haven't heard the real irony. My father died a year after I won the suit. We'd never spoken during this entire ordeal. No call to tell me he was sorry about my wife and son, or his unborn grandchild. No call to tell me he was sorry for the part Tri-C had played in their deaths. He did everything he could to cover up his own culpability. But when he died, he left me everything, and I was suddenly the major shareholder in the corporation that I had tried to bring to its knees.''

"Was that his way of saying he was sorry?"

"No. He made sure I understood that. There was a letter with the will. He told me I had proved beyond all doubt that I was vindictive and single-minded enough to take his place. And he hoped that I enjoyed trying to put back together what I had worked so hard to tear apart.''

"He was wrong. You're not vindictive. You did what was right.''

"I did what was right, but I wanted to punish him, too. I'll never know which was the greater motivation.''

He didn't know what he had expected from her, but not more silence. He had just poured out the story of his life, and she had said very little. He glanced at her and saw that her cheeks were wet with tears, but she was staring at the windshield wipers, not at him.

He stared at them, too. "It was a story the papers loved. Man loses family to corporation. Man sues corporation. Man beats corporation. Man inherits corporation. Somewhere along the way I became a symbol and not a person. I lost everything that mattered, but at the end, all the public could see was that I had triumphed. I was now one of the richest men in America. And very few people cared that inside I was still dying a little more every day.''

"And you didn't want me to see you that way," she said.

"No. I just wanted to be a man again. An ordinary man caught up in an extraordinary situation. I didn't want to burden you with who I was and what had happened to me."

"But you asked me to trust you. You told me I could trust you with my life. And all that time you were lying about who you were. Didn't you trust me enough to believe I could see past the story to the man? That I might just understand what you had gone through?"

"How could I trust you? You wouldn't even tell me who you were!"

"I don't know. I don't know anything. Everything in my life is one big lie." Now the tears were audible in her voice. "I've been so many people in the past four years, I don't know who I am anymore. I don't know who I can trust. Someone I love is probably plotting against me." Her voice rose. "The man I thought I was falling in love with isn't the man I thought he was!"

"I'm exactly who you thought I was. I didn't tell you everything. I should have. I've realized that for a while and regretted it. But I've never lied about wanting to help you, about caring what happens to you. I've done everything I could to keep you safe because I was falling in love with you, too. And that's not a lie."

He heard her sobbing, but there was nothing he could do. They had driven into the heart of the storm, and wind buffeted the car. He wrestled with the wheel and concentrated on the road. He had lost sight of Hank a while ago but trusted that he was still close behind. For the rest of the trip he couldn't do anything except fight the fury of Mother Nature.

By the time he arrived at the beach house and activated the garage door opener, he was exhausted. He didn't know what fury Celestine would unleash now, but it had to be better than the storm and her silence. He parked the car in the garage and turned to her. She was watching him.

"I love you." He bent toward her. She didn't move away. "I don't know when I realized it exactly. Before I knew who you were, I think. But the things I knew about you, your courage, your resourcefulness . . .'' He touched her cheek. "Those were the things that mattered. Not your name.''

"Noah, I—''

He didn't hear her answer. There was a noise behind him. He shifted in his seat, but not quickly enough. The car door flew open and a hand clamped down hard on the back of his neck. Before he could respond, his forehead slammed against the steering wheel. And everything went black.

Chapter 16

Celestine awoke to darkness. A moment passed before she remembered what had happened. Another passed before she realized that she didn't know where she was, that she couldn't see or speak, and that her hands were tied.

She had seen Noah collapse against the steering wheel. And before she could even scream, her door had been flung wide and something had connected with the back of her head. She hadn't seen anyone. Just a hand reaching for Noah. Then darkness.

She was going to die.

For a moment that realization was just a fact, one more piece of the puzzle that was her life. Then she began to tremble. This time she really was going to die. No one would come to her rescue. No one could possibly know where she was. She didn't even know.

And Noah...

She could still hear the sound of his face smashing against the steering wheel. She had been so angry at him. In their last moments together he had told her that he loved her, and she hadn't even answered. She had been too wrapped up in her own pain to understand his. She had listened to Noah recount his tragic past, and she hadn't even told him that she understood his lie and forgave him.

She was going to die, and he was never going to know how she felt.

Or perhaps he was dead already.

She bit back a moan and forced herself to lie still. She didn't know where she was, but until she had more information, it might be best to pretend she was still unconscious. She had to concentrate, to figure out everything she could about her situation. She'd had too many narrow escapes to expect another, but she wanted to stay alive as long as possible. She wanted to know that Noah was still alive. Somehow it would make dying easier.

Noah slapped away the hand of the man whose job it had been to guard the beach house. John was dark-haired, forty-something and, like Hank, a former FBI agent. He was also full of excuses, none of them good ones.

"I don't know who it was! I don't have a clue! I don't know how they got inside. I checked the house, every lousy room of it, just a few minutes before. No one was there. Then I walked into the kitchen—"

"And someone knocked you to the ground. I know, damn it. You told me that!" Noah held his head in his hands. His vision was still blurred, and he heard thunder in his head, although the storm was abating.

"I'm all right, but you've got to get to the emergency room. You've got a concussion."

Noah ignored him. "Where would they take her? Where in the hell would they take her? Why not kill her right here? Leave her in the car, like it was a robbery attempt."

"Maybe not far."

"What do you mean?"

"If it's a professional hit, they'll plug her once and toss her out of the car someplace secluded."

"You don't mince words, do you?"

"You don't pay me to mince words."

"You called the cops?"

"I told you that before. Look, Mr. Colter, you've got to get to the ER. You're in bad shape."

Noah wasn't listening. He willed his head to clear. If Celestine was still alive, she wouldn't be alive for long. All signs led to her aunt and uncle, but they were probably still out of town. They had left Washington late this morning. He knew, because he'd had them under constant surveillance for most of a month.

"They wouldn't kill her themselves," he said out loud.

"What?" John crouched on the floor beside him.

"I said her aunt and uncle wouldn't do it themselves. They would hire someone to make it look like an accident, not a hit."

"Some accident. Whoever it was left you alive to report what happened. No one's going to think it was an accident."

Noah tried to think. His head wasn't spinning as hard now, although it still throbbed unmercifully. "But her aunt and uncle would be the first suspects. This doesn't make sense."

"Then maybe it's not them."

"Celestine was sure they were the ones who've been after her."

"Maybe someone wanted her to *think* it was them."

"Maybe somebody wanted to frame them...." Noah didn't know where that thought had come from. No one else had anything to gain. Millie would inherit the entire estate if Celestine died.

"If that's what they wanted, they'd do it this way," John said. "Kidnap her, kill her. Make it look like the relatives were responsible."

"How would they do that?"

"Plant evidence at the scene, maybe."

Noah willed his head to clear. There was something just out of reach, something that he knew but couldn't remember. Something he hadn't paid enough attention to.

"What about her attorney?" John asked.

Noah tried to concentrate on Whit. He was a man with an addiction, but he had nothing to gain from killing Celestine, unless he was in league with Millie and Roger. And if he was, then he wouldn't be trying to pin this on them.

"I don't think so. The old man, maybe..." But even though Grandpa Sutter might have reason to want revenge against the St. Gervais family, Noah couldn't imagine the old man plotting and paying for murder. He had just gotten out of the hospital, where he had nearly died. Noah shook his head, and stars fell behind his eyelids.

John's voice sounded over the ringing in his ears. "What about the friend she met for lunch today?"

"Allison?" Noah forced himself to consider that. But like Whit, what would Allison gain, unless she was helping Celestine's aunt and uncle? And again, if that was the case, it wouldn't make sense to pin Celestine's murder on them. But perhaps pinning the murder on them wasn't the intention at all. He and John were just guessing about that, too.

The stars cleared, and Noah tried to picture Allison in his mind. She had seemed completely sincere in her loyalty to Celestine. He saw her face, so different from Celestine's but lovely in its own way. He pictured her as she had walked away. He hadn't paid much attention, but he remembered thinking how striking she was.

"Damn it! Her walk!"

Noah's head shot up, and he opened his eyes. The room spun, but he hardly noticed. "Her walk!"

"Mr. Colter, we've got to get you to the hospital...."

Noah grabbed John's jacket. He heard sirens screeching down the main road and growing louder. These were real, not a product of his aching head. "I'm fine. Allison's the one. She walks like Celestine. I just realized it. Damn it, she walks just like her. And she's an even better actress! They're related. I don't know how, and I don't know why Celestine doesn't know, but if I'm right, Allison may have every reason to want Celestine dead!"

* * *

The car stopped. After her initial panic, Celestine had determined she was in a car trunk, gagged and bound, and on her way to a murder scene. Her murder.

She didn't know how long they had traveled, but she thought she had been awake for about ten minutes. The moment she had determined that she was in the trunk, she had attempted to loosen the ropes tying her hands. But whoever had tied her had probably earned a Boy Scout merit badge. She had no hope of getting loose and less hope of getting out of the trunk. She was at the mercy of whoever had put her here.

She heard one door slam, then another. Two people, at least. The odds were getting worse.

She heard scratching above her, then a click. Then air rushed into the trunk. She couldn't see light, since she was blindfolded, but she could feel moisture against her skin. From the muted sounds of thunder, she thought the storm was dying, but a light rain still fell.

"Get her out."

She didn't recognize the man's voice. She lay perfectly still until she felt hands slide under her, then she kicked out and up, contacting something pliant.

"Damn it!" The man dropped her, then slapped her across the face. Despite the pain, she felt a thrill of victory. "Help me, would you?" he screeched.

Someone else grabbed her feet, and the man put his arms around her again.

"Where do you want her?" he asked.

"Over there."

She was shocked to hear a woman's voice this time. Her head rang from the effects of the man's slap, but she was sure it had been a woman's voice. A familiar one. She wondered if the woman was Millie. She hadn't heard her aunt's voice in four years, but even considering that, the voice sounded young. Too young.

Then she knew.

She began to struggle. She couldn't believe her own ears. Surely she was mistaken.

"What's wrong, Celestine? You've been missing your dates with death. Aren't you looking forward to this one?"

Celestine knew she had been right. She tried to speak, but the gag prevented it.

"Untie the handkerchief," Allison said. "I want to hear what she has to say."

The man behind her whined, "I don't think it's a good idea. She'll scream."

Celestine heard Allison's voice in her ear. "Scream, sweetcakes, and you'll be dead that much quicker. One little old shot." Allison made a clicking noise with her tongue. "You understand?"

Celestine nodded.

"Might as well take off the blindfold, too," Allison said.

Celestine gulped air when the gag came off. The blindfold took longer, but she waited to speak until she could see Allison's face. The whiner, whoever he was, was standing behind her with her hands gripped in his. Another man with a gun hovered just at the periphery of her vision.

"I'll bet you're wondering why I've gathered us all together," Allison said, when the blindfold was on the ground.

Celestine knew exactly where they were, although she hadn't suspected they would end up here. They were in the marshlands of Haven House. The house wasn't visible from this spot, but she had played here as a child, much to her mother's dismay and her father's amusement.

"You sold me out." Celestine studied the face of the woman who had been her best friend in the world.

"*Moi?* 'Fraid not."

"What are Millie and Roger going to pay you for this, Allie?"

"Millie and Roger? Not a thing. They aren't in the picture. Never have been. I'm the one who's been trying so hard all these years to do you in. The boys and I even planned to grab you the other night over at Grandpa Sutter's, but you had company by then."

"What do you mean, Millie and Roger—"

"I wouldn't put murder past Roger, only he isn't smart enough to figure out a way that won't implicate him. And he's a coward at heart, our Roger. He's not going to do well in prison at all."

It took Celestine a moment to understand. "You're going to pin my death on Roger?"

"Brilliant, Celestine. But why shouldn't I expect that? Brilliance runs in the St. Gervais genes. You. Daddy. Me."

"What are you talking about?"

"You never even figured it out, did you? Maybe you're not so brilliant after all. It was right in front of you for years, and you never even gave it a thought."

"What was in front of me?"

"God, I'm going to have to spell it out, aren't I? It's so unbelievable to you, you can't even fathom the possibility. You're my sister. Half sister, but close enough."

Celestine stared at her. Nothing was making sense. "We're not sisters."

"Now you just stand there and don't go anywhere, and I'll explain it to you. See, our daddy was a real ripsnorter when he was a young man. He'd had this thing for my mama, and right before he married yours, he got drunk and spent the night with mine. Oh, he was sorry as hell the next morning, but the dirty deed had been done. My mama didn't know she was pregnant until old Daddy was already a married man. By the time she told him about me, your mama was pregnant, too. Imagine that. A good man like Daddy, and not a decent choice to make."

"I don't believe this."

Allison's eyes narrowed into angry slits. "Why not? Don't you think I'm good enough to be a St. Gervais? All those years you were buying little things for me and giving me money from your allowance, you were sure you were better than me, weren't you?"

Celestine knew better than to respond to that. She wanted to live, and the angrier Allison got, the shorter her own life was going to be. "Tell me the rest of it."

"Please, Celestine. Got to say please. Where are your manners?"

"Please, Allie."

Allie lapsed back into her storyteller voice. "Daddy settled money on my mama. Not as much as he should have, you can bet your sweet booties. But some. In exchange, she promised never to tell anybody who her baby's father was or ask him for anything else. And she didn't. Then one day she died. Just like that. I don't know what our dear old daddy was going to do about me. I imagine it was quite a nasty little sore inside him. But he died before he could do anything at all. My mama had made some bad investments, and there wasn't much money left by the time she died. Her relatives took what was left and used it to send me to school so they wouldn't have to put up with me. And nobody was the wiser about who my father was."

"Then how do you know?"

"'Cause old Daddy wasn't quite as brilliant as he'd thought. He wrote my mama a letter after I was born. Just one. At least, that's all I've got. But he asked her to forgive him. And she did, you know. That's the kind of woman she was. She told me once, before she died, that my daddy was a good man. Loyal, but not real bright, my mama."

Celestine's brain was whirling. Allie wasn't looking at her anymore. She was looking at the man behind her, as if to let him know the time had come.

"How are you going to benefit from my death, Allie?" Celestine desperately wanted to keep her talking. Allison so obviously wanted her to know everything before she died.

"Can't you figure it out?"

"No," Celestine lied, although by now it was crystal clear.

"I'm getting worried about you. I thought you were smarter."

"Maybe there's something about being trussed up like a turkey that kills the old brain cells."

"You always had a sense of humor. And loyal? Whew! You could have taught my mama a thing or two, Celestine."

"What are you going to get from killing me?"

"Ev—er—y—thing! See, your uncle will be in jail, and your aunt, too, as his accomplice. I'm glad I couldn't seem to get you killed before, because this time there won't be the slightest question who was responsible. I've got Roger's gun, registered to him all nice and tidy. It even has his prints on it. He shoots birds off the Haven House balconies when he's had too much to drink. Easy as pie to get the gun out of the house and wrap it carefully so the prints didn't smudge."

Her smile widened. "He's due home before long. I've got his duck-hunting hat. What else?" She appeared to think about it. "A letter from somebody your aunt paid to try to find you. They really did hope you were dead. They were looking for proof, but the letter doesn't say that exactly. Just that they were looking. I think I'll snag it on that little branch over there." She pointed to an old log sticking out of the water beyond them. "We'll dump you over there and weight you down, then I'll wait until Roger and Millie show up and have one of the boys here make a call to the sheriff."

"So Roger and Millie will go to jail for my murder. What makes you think that anybody will believe you're a St. Gervais?"

"I've got his letter to mama. And I've got the DNA to prove it. It's a winning combination. Yes sir, we've got a winner here, ladies and gentlemen. See, I'll wait a few months after your death. Then I'll say I found the letter in my mama's old papers. One of my aunts did give me some stuff of hers a couple of months ago, so that part will be easy to believe."

"DNA?"

"I hate to say this, Celestine, but we can dig up old Daddy if we have to. If they can identify Jesse James from his descendants' DNA, my case will be a snap to prove. Then everything will be mine." She looked at the man behind Celestine again, and Celestine's flesh crawled.

"One more question." Celestine tried to take a step forward, but the man behind her twisted her wrists.

"Time's almost up, sweetcakes," Allison said.

"Why did you do it this way? All you ever had to do was come to me, tell me the whole story, show me the letter. I would have shared everything with you. You know I would have. I loved you, and sharing it would have been the right thing to do."

"See if you can come up with a good answer."

"Because you hate me? Because I was his legitimate child and you weren't?"

"You get partial credit. You just forgot one teensy-weensy thing."

Celestine waited silently.

"I don't like to share," Allison said. "I wanted it all."

Celestine felt the man behind her shift. She knew what was coming, and she also knew that there would be a moment when he had to loosen his grip on her. If he was going to use her uncle's gun, he had to take special care not to smudge the prints. She concentrated, pushing down her panic.

"Goodbye, Celestine," Allison said.

Celestine whirled at the exact moment that the gunman loosened his grip and slammed her knee into his groin. Then, as he screeched and the gun fired wildly into the air, she zigzagged toward Allison.

"Don't shoot," Allison screamed at the man on the sidelines.

He shot anyway, and missed.

"Don't!" Allison leaped forward to grab Celestine, but Celestine was ready. Celestine ran at her full tilt, head lowered, and knocked Allison off balance. Then, as one of the men fired again, she ran toward the marsh.

Someone would hear the shots. One gun, probably the one that belonged to her uncle, was barely audible, silenced, perhaps. But the other gun was as loud as a cannon. They'd never intended to use it, she guessed, and were probably regretting it now. Because someone would hear. Maybe Roger and Millie weren't home, but there was a staff, housemaids and groundskeepers. They would assume someone was poaching and call the sheriff.

Celestine knew exactly where she was. The marsh grass beyond her was tall, but not tall enough to hide her for long. Allison and the men would pursue her. They had too much to lose now to let her live.

She dove into the grass as another bullet whizzed by. She didn't even know she'd been hit until her side began to sting. She crouched and slogged through the mud anyway, trying to stay out of sight. But the marsh grasses rippled as she moved. Until she made it to the water beyond, she was an easy target.

Another bullet sped by her head, and the mud sucked relentlessly at her feet. She had fifty yards to go before the water got deep enough to swim, and even then she wasn't sure she could manage to stay afloat with her hands tied.

She was beginning to feel dizzy. She wondered if Noah was alive, and if he would blame himself for her death as he had for his wife's. The next bullet nicked her arm. She felt this one burn all the way to her fingertips, but she didn't stop. She plowed through the grass toward the water.

Then she heard the sirens.

Noah rounded Haven House, calling Celestine's name. John and Hank fanned out, and the sheriff and two deputies followed their lead. If Allison wanted to pin Celestine's murder on Roger and Millie, Haven House was the most likely spot for it to take place.

An old woman wearing a gray uniform stepped out on the front porch. "You here about them shots?"

Noah's heart leaped to his throat. "What shots? Where?"

"Down that way. Down in the bottoms." She pointed well beyond the house.

"Is there a road that goes down there?"

"Little bitty one."

Noah began to run. John and Hank followed, but the sheriff and his men went back for their cars.

"We'll check it out!" John shouted. "Stay back."

Noah ignored them. His head felt as if it were splitting in two, but he ignored that, as well. He was quickly out of breath, but he ran on. He heard the sheriff's siren again and saw movement to his right, but he kept running.

He didn't know how far he ran or how long it took, but when he came out of a small grove of trees he saw the marshland just beyond them.

Thirty yards away two men were running toward an old sedan. As he closed in on them, one of them aimed a gun in his direction. "You get out of the way!" the bigger of the two men shouted. "Just stay out of the way now!" He shot at the ground in front of Noah's feet, as if to make his point. Then he leaped into the car and started the engine. His companion grabbed the door handle just as the car spun its tires in the sand and started forward. He managed to dive in headfirst, but the door flapped as the car sped away.

Noah heard a gunshot and saw John aiming at the tires. One blew on impact, and the car careened back and forth until it reached a narrow dirt road. They might have made it farther except that the sheriff's car came wheeling around a corner and blocked the escape route.

"Celestine!"

Noah started toward the marsh. John started off at one angle and Hank at another. None of them saw Allison until she rose from the edge of the marsh grass just in front of Noah. She stood sideways with a gun poised in her hands. The gun was pointed toward the water.

"Why, Noah Colter. You came to watch me kill her," Allison said. "If I haven't already."

Noah edged closer. "Put down the gun, Allison."

"I don't think so." She waved the gun at him, forcing him to stop.

"They'll put you in prison and throw away the key. They might even execute you."

She swung the gun back toward the water. "They just might. But you know what? If I can't have old Daddy's money, I'd just as soon take out his little sweetheart so she doesn't get it, either." She swung the gun on him. "Or yours."

He stood perfectly still. "There are two men with their guns trained on you, Allie. Give it up."

"Nah. I think I'm gonna kill somebody. You? Her?" She shook her head and dimpled. "I hate decisions."

"We'll get you help. You need help. Just put down the gun."

"Help? Honey, there's no helping me. I already killed a man. Old Stephen Montgomery. Now there was a bright boy. Too bad he was starting to ask the wrong questions. I don't think he'd quite figured out I was Celestine's big sister, but he was chewing on it."

"If you pull that trigger, one of these men is going to shoot you. Is that what you want?"

"Cel-es-tine!" she shouted. "Are you dead yet? 'Cause if you are, I'm going to kill Noah now."

Noah knew exactly what Allison was trying to do, and it worked. Something moved in the water beyond him. He saw the marsh grass part and Celestine straighten until she was swaying dizzily in plain view. She was exchanging her life for his. He didn't think; he didn't hope. He leaped forward as Allison swung the gun toward Celestine. When she realized what he was attempting to do, she swung the gun back toward him and fired.

He heard two more shots, but the first was the only one he felt.

Chapter 17

With Whit at one side and Franklin Billett of Flinders, Billett and Crane at her other, Celestine walked into the judge's chambers. Whit introduced her to the judge, a stern, silver-haired woman with her black robe unzipped to reveal a conservative blue suit. She shook Celestine's hand before she waved her to a seat in front of her desk. Whit tried to assist her by taking her arm, but Celestine shook her head. In the weeks since she had been shot in the hip and forearm, she had recovered most of her energy and all her mobility. She had two new and unremarkable scars, but she didn't need anyone's help.

The judge busied herself with some papers, ignoring them.

Celestine leaned toward Whit and spoke softly. "I thought Millie and Roger would be here already." She wasn't looking forward to seeing her aunt and uncle. Even though she now knew that they had not been behind the attempts on her life, her memories of them were anything but good.

"I imagine they don't see much point in putting on a show. This is a formality and nothing more."

There was a noise behind them. Celestine turned and got her first look at the man and woman who had been entrusted with her care so many years ago.

Millie, dark-haired and petite, was beginning to show her age, although she was obviously struggling hard against it. Not a recently tinted hair was out of place, and her makeup was perfect. Roger was thirty pounds overweight and losing his hair.

The Debhams' attorney introduced them to the judge, who treated them to the same perfunctory handshakes. Then she motioned them to their seats.

The judge lifted the papers she had been studying and tapped them against her blotter to straighten them into a neat stack. "I've studied this matter thoroughly. Miss St. Gervais is obviously very much alive, and there are no grounds whatsoever to find her incompetent. Recent events have made it absolutely clear that she had every reason to fear for her life. She has, in fact, showed the keenest good judgment by running as fast and as far as she could in the years she's been away."

The judge looked up. "Miss St. Gervais is twenty-five. Everything is in order for her to take over the estate that is rightfully hers. Now there's only the matter of the funds that have been drained from it." The judge looked over wire-rim half glasses at Roger and Millie. "Mr. and Mrs. Debham, I have been given a comprehensive list of what is missing and how the theft transpired. Your attorney has the same list. You can choose to fight this allegation in court, of course. But I warn you that if you lose, you may very well go to jail. Your alternative is to repay the estate and ask Miss St. Gervais if that will be sufficient."

Roger and Millie put their heads together with their attorney. Celestine waited calmly with her hands folded.

"Will that be sufficient?" The attorney leaned forward and addressed Celestine. "Or will you prosecute regardless?"

"They can keep the money."

Whit covered her hand to stop her, but Celestine ignored him. "My grandfather had no moral right to disinherit my aunt, and my father wanted her to be taken care of. That's clear from his will. If Mr. and Mrs. Debham will swear in writing that they will never set foot in North Carolina again, I'll allow them to keep what they've stolen from me. But they have to be out of Haven House by tomorrow at noon, and they can't take anything with them except their personal belongings, subject to inspection by my representatives. If they ever break their word or contact me in any way, I reserve the right to reclaim everything and to prosecute them for theft."

There was another buzz beside her. Whit shook his head, but Frank Billett chuckled. "You're a credit to the St. Gervais name, Celestine. Your father knew how to get whatever he wanted, too."

Celestine wondered if she would get what she really wanted. What she wanted most in the world. It was too soon to tell, too hard to predict.

The Debhams' attorney leaned forward. "My clients accept Miss St. Gervais's offer."

Millie and Roger stood; then, surprisingly, Millie turned to face Celestine. Celestine had never noticed Millie's resemblance to Allison before, but she did now. It was there in the eyes and the pert angle of Millie's nose. The evidence had been right in front of her for years, and she had never seen it. Maybe if she had, Allison would still be alive.

Maybe Noah wouldn't have been shot.

"I didn't hate you, Celestine," Millie said. "And I never wished you dead. I just didn't know what to do with you. I've never liked children."

"You made that perfectly clear."

"And for what it's worth, I really believed you were losing your mind."

"For what it's worth, there were times after you came to live with me when I thought so, too."

Millie shook her head. "I'm sorry."

Celestine looked her straight in the eyes. "I appreciate your telling me, Millie. But unfortunately, it doesn't change a thing."

Millie turned away. Celestine watched the three of them file out. She was free of her aunt and uncle. Her new will had already been drawn up. Now there was no reason for anyone to want her dead.

The question was whether someone wanted her alive.

She stood, and the judge stood, too. The older woman extended her hand. "I wish this court could have prevented the hell you've been through, Miss St. Gervais."

"That makes two of us." This time Celestine's smile was genuine. "But it's over. It's finally over."

"Do you have plans for a celebration?"

Grandpa Sutter was waiting back at Rhonda's house for her. Whit had promised to come by, too, for champagne and Rhonda's richest chocolate cake. Only one important person would be missing. "I have plans."

"Good. I wish you the best."

The two attorneys followed Celestine out of the judge's chambers. In moments they were outside. It was a perfect fall day, with golden sunshine and just a nip in the air. Celestine could stand in the sunshine now, without fear. It seemed strange.

She said goodbye to both men and watched them walk away. Whit had told her last week that he had stopped his jaunts to Atlantic City and Vegas, and he was seeing a therapist. She thought he was going to make it.

Her car was parked not far away, but she decided to walk instead. Beaufort was easily mastered on foot, and there had been so many changes in the years she had been away that she still marveled at them.

She strolled slowly through the shady streets, reacquainting herself with the old white frame houses of Bahamian and West Indian construction. She gazed into shop windows filled with antiques and souvenirs, but her mind was somewhere else.

Her walk ended, as she had intended, at the churchyard where Allison had been buried. The headstone hadn't been set in place yet, but the grave already looked old and settled. Neither Hank nor John had fired to kill, but Allison had died instantly. When she had turned to shoot Noah, she had taken one fatal step forward.

Celestine scuffed the sandy soil at the edge of the grave with the toe of her gray pump and tried to remember something real and good about Allison to take away with her.

A familiar voice spoke from behind her. "I'm not sure she could have helped what she became. Somewhere along the way somebody has to love you or you wither inside."

Celestine turned. Noah was standing at the cemetery gate. He was leaning on a cane to steady himself, but his color was good. He didn't look like a man who had been at death's door.

"What are you doing here?" She didn't move toward him.

"Watching you. Something I grew fond of doing in our short time together."

"You're supposed to be at home recuperating."

"Colorado seemed too far away."

She closed her eyes, and she could see him falling to the ground, the dirt turning red around him....

"Celie, it wasn't your fault."

She opened her eyes. "You were almost killed. Whose fault was it?"

"You tried damned hard to get Allison to shoot you instead."

Celestine had only seen Noah once before he was whisked from the local hospital and flown to the nearest medical center for the best care money could buy. He had opened his eyes, but he had been too close to death to know her.

She started toward him. "When they finally let me out of the hospital I tried to come and see you, but no one at Tri-C would tell me where you were. Did you get my messages?"

"Yeah."

"Oh..."

"Allison's bullet lodged very close to my spine. There was some question about whether I was going to walk again."

"And you didn't want me there?"

"I thought I ought to be standing up when we had our reunion."

She wanted to be angry at him. She wanted to be furious. But he was a proud man who had taken a bullet for her. How could she fault him for anything? "Didn't you trust me enough to realize that whether you walked or not wouldn't change my feelings?"

"I didn't want you to come to me out of guilt. And I didn't trust myself enough to say no if you did."

She was right in front of him now. She could open the low metal gate and be in his arms in a heartbeat. "I would come to you anywhere and anytime. I would give up my life for you."

"You already tried that."

"And you very nearly gave up yours for mine."

"Anytime, Celie."

"I love you, Noah."

Something very much like relief passed over his face, and she realized that he hadn't been sure. She threw open the gate and slid her arms around his waist. "I love you. And it doesn't have anything to do with guilt or gratitude or even because I trust you with my life. I just love you. Do you still love me?"

He kissed her hard, and she had her answer. Somewhere nearby sea gulls squawked as they glided on the salt-tinged breeze. She was home again. Really home. In North Carolina and in Noah's arms.

Epilogue

Grandpa Sutter stared out at the sun setting over the mountain peaks that rose above the log house where Celestine and Noah stayed when they were living in Colorado. Haven House was filled with St. Gervais antiques and Noah's art and sculpture collection, but their Colorado home depended entirely on the Rockies for visual adornment.

"Give me the ocean," he said. "Any old time."

"We get the best of both," Celestine told him fondly. "Haven House in the fall and spring. The mountains in the hottest part of summer and the coldest part of winter—"

"I don't like the thought of you skiing down those mountains, baby doll."

"It keeps me in shape. Or at least it did when I still had a shape to keep."

"Your shape is perfect." Noah came up behind her and slipped his arms around her waist. "Especially after you lost all that extra weight."

The extra weight set up a howl three rooms away. Celestine turned in Noah's arms. They had both refused to consider a nanny for the chubby baby boy who was making his desires known so enthusiastically. She didn't care how much money she and Noah had between them. This was one job they wanted to do themselves. "Your turn, Daddy."

"He wants his mommy. He's hungry."

"You can tell?"

"He knows what a good thing he has going here."

She kissed his nose. "Get him, would you?"

She settled herself in the rocking chair until Noah returned with Christopher in a newly changed diaper. He was two months old today, with soft brown hair and his daddy's eyes. Celestine crooned to him as she lifted her blouse. In a moment he was nursing happily.

"That's one big boy," Grandpa Sutter said. He was studying the mountains again, as if he might get used to them if he looked at them long enough.

"He's going to be as big as his daddy." Celestine patted Christopher's bottom. She and Noah had decided Christopher would be their first child, but definitely not their last. They hadn't been fortunate enough to grow up in close-knit families, but they could and would create their own. They were planning to enjoy every minute of the creating part.

"Do you ever miss traveling, Celestine?" Grandpa Sutter paused. "You always wanted to see the whole wide world. Now it's going to be harder, ain't it?"

A smile lit Noah's eyes. She returned it. In the year since she and Noah had been married, she had written letters to many of the people she had met on her long journey. Betty and Marian, among others, had written back, and so had Marshall, who had promised he would come for a visit soon. She even knew from Marshall that Bobby had been picked up for an unrelated crime and was starting a long sentence in prison.

The horrors of a life on the run had subsided, and now she could be grateful for the friends she had made.

"There's no place I want to go where I can't take Christopher," she said. "But I think I'm just going to stay put for a while. I have everything I really want close at hand."

Grandpa Sutter turned, and his craggy old face broke into a thousand happy wrinkles. "I see what you mean."

Noah crouched beside Celestine and brushed her brown hair—on its way to being as long as Marie St. Germaine's—away from her forehead. "What Celie means is that she has me and you and the kid here. What more could she ever want?"

"Had to go all the way across the ocean to find it, didn't you, baby doll? But I'd say you did pretty good."

Celestine thought so, too. She was Celestine St. Gervais Colter now. She had traveled the wide world to proudly call that name her own. And, in the end, every step had been worth it.

*   *   *   *   *

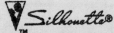

FAST CASH 4031 DRAW RULES
NO PURCHASE OR OBLIGATION NECESSARY

Fifty prizes of $50 each will be awarded in random drawings to be conducted no later than 3/28/97 from amongst all eligible responses to this prize offer received as of 2/14/97. To enter, follow directions, affix 1st-class postage and mail OR write Fast Cash 4031 on a 3" x 5" card along with your name and address and mail that card to: Harlequin's Fast Cash 4031 Draw, P.O. Box 1395, Buffalo, NY 14240-1395 OR P.O. Box 618, Fort Erie, Ontario L2A 5X3. (Limit: one entry per outer envelope; all entries must be sent via 1st-class mail.) Limit: one prize per household. Odds of winning are determined by the number of eligible responses received. Offer is open only to residents of the U.S. (except Puerto Rico) and Canada and is void wherever prohibited by law. All applicable laws and regulations apply. Any litigation within the province of Quebec respecting the conduct and awarding of a prize in this sweepstakes maybe submitted to the Régie des alcools, des courses et des jeux. In order for a Canadian resident to win a prize, that person will be required to correctly answer a time-limited arithmetical skill-testing question to be administered by mail. Names of winners available after 4/28/97 by sending a self-addressed, stamped envelope to: Fast Cash 4031 Draw Winners, P.O. Box 4200, Blair, NE 68009-4200.

OFFICIAL RULES
MILLION DOLLAR SWEEPSTAKES
NO PURCHASE NECESSARY TO ENTER

1. To enter, follow the directions published. Method of entry may vary. For eligibility, entries must be received no later than March 31, 1998. No liability is assumed for printing errors, lost, late, non-delivered or misdirected entries.
    To determine winners, the sweepstakes numbers assigned to submitted entries will be compared against a list of randomly pre-selected prize winning numbers. In the event all prizes are not claimed via the return of prize winning numbers, random drawings will be held from among all other entries received to award unclaimed prizes.

2. Prize winners will be determined no later than June 30, 1998. Selection of winning numbers and random drawings are under the supervision of D. L. Blair, Inc., an independent judging organization whose decisions are final. Limit: one prize to a family or organization. No substitution will be made for any prize, except as offered. Taxes and duties on all prizes are the sole responsibility of winners. Winners will be notified by mail. Odds of winning are determined by the number of eligible entries distributed and received.

3. Sweepstakes open to residents of the U.S. (except Puerto Rico), Canada and Europe who are 18 years of age or older, except employees and immediate family members of Torstar Corp., D. L. Blair, Inc., their affiliates, subsidiaries, and all other agencies, entities, and persons connected with the use, marketing or conduct of this sweepstakes. All applicable laws and regulations apply. Sweepstakes offer void wherever prohibited by law. Any litigation within the province of Quebec respecting the conduct and awarding of a prize in this sweepstakes must be submitted to the Régie des alcools, des courses et des jeux. In order to win a prize, residents of Canada will be required to correctly answer a time-limited arithmetical skill-testing question to be administered by mail.

4. Winners of major prizes (Grand through Fourth) will be obligated to sign and return an Affidavit of Eligibility and Release of Liability within 30 days of notification. In the event of non-compliance within this time period or if a prize is returned as undeliverable, D. L. Blair, Inc. may at its sole discretion award that prize to an alternate winner. By acceptance of their prize, winners consent to use of their names, photographs or other likeness for purposes of advertising, trade and promotion on behalf of Torstar Corp., its affiliates and subsidiaries, without further compensation unless prohibited by law. Torstar Corp. and D. L. Blair, Inc., their affiliates and subsidiaries are not responsible for errors in printing of sweepstakes and prizewinning numbers. In the event a duplication of a prizewinning number occurs, a random drawing will be held from among all entries received with that prizewinning number to award that prize.

5. This sweepstakes is presented by Torstar Corp., its subsidiaries and affiliates in conjunction with book, merchandise and/or product offerings. The number of prizes to be awarded and their value are as follows: Grand Prize — $1,000,000 (payable at $33,333.33 a year for 30 years); First Prize — $50,000; Second Prize — $10,000; Third Prize — $5,000; 3 Fourth Prizes — $1,000 each; 10 Fifth Prizes — $250 each; 1,000 Sixth Prizes — $10 each. Values of all prizes are in U.S. currency. Prizes in each level will be presented in different creative executions, including various currencies, vehicles, merchandise and travel. Any presentation of a prize level in a currency other than U.S. currency represents an approximate equivalent to the U.S. currency prize for that level, at that time. Prize winners will have the opportunity of selecting any prize offered for that level; however, the actual non U.S. currency equivalent prize, if offered and selected, shall be awarded at the exchange rate existing at 3:00 P.M. New York time on March 31, 1998. A travel prize option, if offered and selected by winner, must be completed within 12 months of selection and is subject to: traveling companion(s) completing and returning a Release of Liability prior to travel; and hotel and flight accommodations availability. For a current list of all prize options offered within prize levels, send a self-addressed, stamped envelope (WA residents need not affix postage) to: MILLION DOLLAR SWEEPSTAKES Prize Options, P.O. Box 4456, Blair, NE 68009-4456, USA.

6. For a list of prize winners (available after July 31, 1998) send a separate, stamped, self-addressed envelope to: MILLION DOLLAR SWEEPSTAKES Winners, P.O. Box 4459, Blair, NE 68009-4459, USA.

EXTRA BONUS PRIZE DRAWING
NO PURCHASE OR OBLIGATION NECESSARY TO ENTER

7. The Extra Bonus Prize will be awarded in a random drawing to be conducted no later than 5/30/98 from among all entries received. To qualify, entries must be received by 3/31/98 and comply with published directions. Prize ($50,000) is valued in U.S. currency. Prize will be presented in different creative expressions, including various currencies, vehicles, merchandise and travel. Any presentation in a currency other than U.S. currency represents an approximate equivalent to the U.S. currency value at that time. Prize winner will have the opportunity of selecting any prize offered in any presentation of the Extra Bonus Prize Drawing; however, the actual non U.S. currency equivalent prize, if offered and selected by winner, shall be awarded at the exchange rate existing at 3:00 P.M. New York time on March 31, 1998. For a current list of prize options offered, send a self-addressed, stamped envelope (WA residents need not affix postage) to: Extra Bonus Prize Options, P.O. Box 4462, Blair, NE 68009-4462, USA. All eligibility requirements and restrictions of the MILLION DOLLAR SWEEPSTAKES apply. Odds of winning are dependent upon number of eligible entries received. No substitution for prize except as offered. For the name of winner (available after 7/31/98), send a self-addressed, stamped envelope to: Extra Bonus Prize Winner, P.O. Box 4463, Blair, NE 68009-4463, USA.

SWP-S12ZD2

In February, Silhouette Books is proud
to present the sweeping, sensual new novel
by bestselling author

CAIT LONDON

about her unforgettable family—*The Tallchiefs.*

TALLCHIEF FOR KEEPS

Everyone in Amen Flats, Wyoming, was talking about
Elspeth Tallchief. How she wasn't a thirty-three-year-old
virgin, after all. How she'd been keeping herself warm at
night all these years with a couple of secrets. And now one
of those secrets had walked right into town, sending
everyone into a frenzy. But Elspeth knew he'd come for
the *other* secret....

"Cait London is an irresistible storyteller..."
—*Romantic Times*

Don't miss TALLCHIEF FOR KEEPS by Cait London, available
at your favorite retail outlet in February from

As seen on TV!
Free Gift Offer

With a Free Gift proof-of-purchase from any Silhouette® book,
you can receive a beautiful cubic zirconia pendant.

This gorgeous marquise-shaped stone is a genuine cubic
zirconia—accented by an 18" gold tone necklace.

(Approximate retail value $19.95)

Send for yours today...
compliments of ▼ *Silhouette®*
TM

To receive your free gift, a cubic zirconia pendant, send us one original proof-of-
purchase, photocopies not accepted, from the back of any Silhouette Romance™,
Silhouette Desire®, Silhouette Special Edition®, Silhouette Intimate Moments®
or Silhouette Yours Truly™ title available in August, September, October, November and
December at your favorite retail outlet, together with the Free Gift Certificate, plus a
check or money order for $1.65 U.S./$2.15 CAN. (do not send cash) to cover postage and
handling, payable to Silhouette Free Gift Offer. We will send you the specified gift. Allow
6 to 8 weeks for delivery. Offer good until December 31, 1996 or while quantities last.
Offer valid in the U.S. and Canada only.

Free Gift Certificate

Name: _____

Address: _____

City: _____ State/Province: _____ Zip/Postal Code: _____

Mail this certificate, one proof-of-purchase and a check or money order for postage
and handling to: SILHOUETTE FREE GIFT OFFER 1996. In the U.S.: 3010 Walden
Avenue, P.O. Box 9077, Buffalo NY 14269-9077. In Canada: P.O. Box 613, Fort Erie,
Ontario L2Z 5X3.

FREE GIFT OFFER   084-KMD
ONE PROOF-OF-PURCHASE
To collect your fabulous FREE GIFT, a cubic zirconia pendant, you must include this
original proof-of-purchase for each gift with the properly completed Free Gift Certificate.

084-KMD-R

Your very favorite Silhouette miniseries characters now have a BRAND-NEW story in

CHRISTMAS KISSES

Brought to you by:

LINDA HOWARD

DEBBIE MACOMBER

LINDA TURNER

LINDA HOWARD celebrates the holidays with a **Mackenzie** wedding—once Maris regains her memory, that is....

DEBBIE MACOMBER brings **Those Manning Men** and **The Manning Sisters** home for a mistletoe marriage as a single dad finally says "I do."

LINDA TURNER brings **The Wild West** alive as Priscilla Rawlings ties the knot at the Double R Ranch.

Three BRAND-NEW holiday love stories...by romance fiction's most beloved authors.

Available in November at your favorite retail outlet.

Silhouette®

COMING NEXT MONTH

#721 WILD BLOOD—Naomi Horton
Wild Hearts

Jett Kendrick was untamable, and Kathleen Patterson had the broken heart to prove it. She hadn't even been able to hold on to their baby before tragedy struck. So why, fifteen years later, was Jett looking at her with guilt—and longing—especially when his teenage boy was near?

#722 BORROWED BRIDE—Patricia Coughlin

One minute Gabrielle Flanders was wedding-bound, the next she'd been abducted from the church! Connor DeWolfe claimed she was in grave danger—that he was the only man she could trust. But Gaby didn't think her "honeymoon" was the time to find out...or was it?

#723 THE ONE WHO ALMOST GOT AWAY—Alicia Scott
The Guiness Gang

She always got her man—and Jake Guiness was no exception. The infuriating playboy was Regina O'Doul's only lead in the case of her life, so she got *close*. But somehow pretending to be lovers had led to the real thing—and to very real danger for them both....

#724 UNBROKEN VOWS—Frances Williams

Ex-SEAL David Chandler had nothing left to give—but for Cara Merrill, he would certainly try. The gutsy beauty needed his soldiering skills to locate her ex-fiancé. But amid their dangerous jungle mission, David found himself wanting Cara all for himself....

#725 HERO IN HIDING—Kay David

Mercy Hamilton had one rule about Mr. Right: she had to trust him. Then dark, handsome Rio Barrigan challenged her beliefs. He was all mystery—at times warm and loving, at others almost deadly. And though he broke her cardinal rule, Mercy couldn't help but believe in him—and their love.

#726 THE BABY ASSIGNMENT—Cathryn Clare
Assignment: Romance

Agent Jack Cotter knew about guns, bad guys...but babies? On that subject he knew absolutely nothing. But single-mom-on-the-run Shelby Henderson and her bouncing baby girl taught him all he needed to know about family and fatherhood. Jack only hoped they would all survive to put what he'd learned into practice.

You're About to Become a

Privileged Woman

Reap the rewards of fabulous free gifts and benefits with proofs-of-purchase from Silhouette and Harlequin books

Pages & Privileges™

It's our way of thanking you for buying our books at your favorite retail stores.

PROOF OF PURCHASE

SIM-PP20

Offer expires March 31, 1997

Pages & Privileges ™

Harlequin and Silhouette— the most privileged readers in the world!

For more information about Harlequin and Silhouette's PAGES & PRIVILEGES program call the Pages & Privileges Benefits Desk: 1-503-794-2499

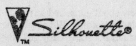

Silhouette®

SIM-PP20